IN OLD NEW YORK . . .

The gang leader reached for his slug thrower and his friends followed suit.

Ray blasted the top of his skull off and shot three more of the gang dead before the leader fell over backwards. Ake was not far behind Ray in taking out his own three. The dog pack circled behind them, growling and snapping.

Pandemonium.

One of the three survivors pulled his slug thrower and fired in one fluid motion; unfortunately, he fired right into the head of the youth in front of him. Ray's energy bolt burned through him. That left one final target for Ake.

The suddenly unleashed dogs did nothing. They stood stock still, quivering in place. It was as Ray suspected: They were untrained at best, brutes at worst. Without direction from their owners, they lacked initiative.

"Don't kill us!" the dog who spoke to them earlier howled.

Beowulf closed his eyes in shame. These were like no scout dogs he knew or could imagine. For the first time, the enormity of what had happened to the dogs of Terra, sold like cattle, sank in fully and completely . . .

"An interesting new approach to the adventure novel."

—SF Chronicle

Ace Books by Kenneth Von Gunden

STARSPAWN

K-9 CORPS
K-9 CORPS: UNDER FIRE
K-9 CORPS: CRY WOLF

KENNETH VON GUNDEN

ACE BOOKS, NEW YORK

This book is an Ace original edition,
and has never been previously published.

K-9 CORPS: CRY WOLF

An Ace Book / published by arrangement with
the author

PRINTING HISTORY
Ace edition / February 1992

ISBN: 0-441-42495-3

Ace Books are published by The Berkley Publishing Group,
200 Madison Avenue, New York, New York 10016.
The name "ACE" and the "A" logo
are trademarks belonging to Charter Communications, Inc.

PRINTED IN THE UNITED STATES OF AMERICA

10 9 8 7 6 5 4 3 2 1

PART ONE

The Spirit of St. Louis

1

"How come they sellin' us the drug runner's ship?" Littlejohn asked.

"Yah," Beowulf added. "How they know we not gonna use it to smuggle drugs?"

"They don't," replied Ake. "As a matter of fact, I'd guess that at least half the private jumpers the government of Alexandria sells to civilian buyers go right back to transporting illegal drugs."

"Sure," agreed Ray. "If you think about it, who else has the money to buy and maintain his or her own starship, even at fire-sale prices?"

"But—"

"Don't worry, Beowulf," Ray said. "You and I can find and remove all the tracers and bugs."

"Can't you do that when we look it over?" asked Ake.

Ray shot him a look of exasperation. "They're going to allow us to closely examine the ship before we buy it," he said. "But they're not going to let us poke into every nook and cranny at our leisure. We'll get the five-credit tour: the control bay, the crew areas, the engines, and so on. That's it until we plunk down hard cash."

"How much do you think they'll ask for?"

"What they can get, I should imagine."

"Even though it's a used ship, they might want ten million," Ake said.

"They might *want* ten million," countered Ray, "but they sure as hell ain't gonna get that much from us even if the ship proves to be in great shape."

"How much, then?"

"Five million, tops. Anything under that and we'll have gotten a bargain."

The ship, a virtually new model, was a Zukovich FTL-1000. In hyperspace, it was no faster than any other jumper. But in normal space, it could move from point A to point B quicker than the latest dirty joke. It was a beauty, too.

"Well, this crate *looks* great," said Ray. "I'll give it that much."

"Aye, laddie," the spaceport's chief engineer agreed. "She's a fine, fine piece of machinery."

"Looks can be deceiving," Ake said mildly, walking along side the ship and running his fingers across its glossy plasteel surface. If the ship had suffered any scratches or pits, they'd been expertly filled in.

"Smooth as a wee baby's bottom, is she not?" asked the chief engineer.

"Hmmphf," muttered Ake noncommittally.

"It seems that you've been awfully enterprising with a ship that merely needed to be given a simple once-over in preparation for a quick sale."

"My people take pride in what they do," the chief engineer said, his chest swelling. "And so do I."

"That's its name?" questioned Ray, pointing at the ship's "bow."

"Aye, laddie. But that's *her* name. A sweet thing like her is neither an it nor a he."

"What does . . . ?" Mama-san stopped to sound out the words silently before continuing. "What does *The Speer-it of St. Loo-is* mean?"

Ake scratched his head. "Gee, I don't know, Mama-san." He threw Ray a glance.

Ray's face displayed his usual knowing smile and he rocked back and forth on his heels, making a great show of humming nonchalantly.

"I assume that means you know what the name stands for, eh, laddie?" the chief engineer said sourly, annoyed that he was going to be denied the opportunity to trumpet the results of his investigation into the ship's name.

Ray pressed his lips together and then said, "Sorry to rain on your parade, but there's not much about twentieth-century culture and history that I'm not familiar with."

"Ray knows *everythin'*," said Tajil proudly.

"Not everything," Ray said, coloring. Then he had an idea. "But why don't you explain to Ake and the dogs where the name *The Spirit of St. Louis* comes from?" he said to the chief engineer.

"That I shall, laddie," the chief engineer said eagerly, delighted that he was going to get a chance to show off his knowledge after all. "*The Spirit of St. Louis* was the name of Charles Augustus Lindbergh's single-engine aircraft. He was the first man to fly solo across Terra's Atlantic Ocean."

"That's all he did?" asked Ake. "Fly across an ocean by himself?"

"It was something special at the time," the chief engineer said. "Lindbergh did what no man had done before."

"I'm impressed," Ray said, surprised that the chief engineer was in possession of such knowledge.

"Don't give me too much credit, lad," the chief said. "We've had this little darlin' a while and I couldn't help but search the databases for the origin of her name."

"We ever gonna go inside?" Mama-san asked impatiently.

"Right you are . . . ah . . . lassie."

As the chief engineer keyed a control and let down a ramp, Beowulf—remembering Ray's twentieth-century tee-vee collection—said to Tajil, "I thought Lassie was a collie."

"Three million two hundred and fifty thousand," Ake said. "This is a great ship, but that's still a lot of money."

Ray shook his head. "*Au contraire, mon ami*. We got a swell deal. Three-mill-plus is peanuts to us. You're forgetting how rich the rubies have made us. We're as rich as Croesus. We're filthy rich. Hell, we're almost as rich as Scrooge McDuck!"

"We rich, huh?" said Gawain.

"Rich enough to buy this flying soapbox and have change enough left over to ransom an emperor."

"Can I have a new collar, Ray?" asked Ozma.

"Hey, you think money grows on trees?"

II

"These pilot cubes were expensive," Ake said, self-consciously touching the place on his skull where he'd loaded the external memory insert that provided him with the ability to fly the ship.

"Yeah," said Ray dryly. "Came to about one-trillionth of our remaining funds." He stared at the top of Ake's skull, his eyes irresistibly drawn to the entry point for the external. "What's it like?" he asked. "What does it *feel* like?"

"It . . . it's hard to explain if you've never experienced it," Ake said after some deliberation. "I'm me, but I'm more than me."

"Can you tell the difference between the external's memory and your own?"

"Yes and no. Yes, if I really concentrate on sorting them out. No, if I'm *using* the additional knowledge; then it's just all me—or so it seems from in here." Ake looked uncomfortable talking about it.

"Gee," said Gawain, who'd been following all this intently. "It must be sumpthin' to have extra brains inside your head."

"Or even any," mocked Tajil.

"Yah, yah," said Gawain good-naturedly. Gawain was not the brightest scout dog ever born, and the other dogs kidded him all the time. Fortunately for them, he was as amiable as he was huge.

"Well, I'm taking you guys back and seeing that everyone is secured safely," said Ray, removing his headset and heaving himself out of his co-pilot's seat. "Between the computer and Captain Brainiac over here, I'm about as needed in the cockpit as teats on a bull."

"Hahahaha," laughed Gawain. "Teats on a bull!"

Trailed by Tajil and Gawain, Ray headed back to the passenger area where the seven dogs waited. The hard-copy printout of the ship's ownership manual called it a lounge, and Ray was hard pressed to disagree. Although *The Spirit of St. Louis* had been constructed with speed in mind, it was also outfitted as a space yacht—and an incredibly luxurious one at that.

The Spirit of St. Louis sported expensively appointed sleeping quarters with Hylof non-image-reversal holo mirrors, and bathrooms complete with tub and sonic shower. There was a lavish food preparation area with every conceivable appliance either built in or cleverly concealed for fast access, all fully automated and set up for food delivery right to the dining area; and all the entertainment facilities one could possibly hope for.

As wonderful as all this was—and it *was* wonderful—it artfully concealed a less savory and less obvious aspect of the ship: It was as heavily armed as military vessels three times its size.

"Hi, guys," Ray said as he ambled into the lounge where the rest of his scout dog team patiently waited for him.

"'Lo, Ray," they chorused, thrusting their wet noses against his palms in greeting.

"We 'bout ready to lift off?" Beowulf questioned.

"Ake and the computer are putting their heads together, so it shouldn't be long now. Once we take off, we have to wait until we get to the edge of the local system before we can safely make the jump to hyperspace."

"Ugh, hyperspace!" Grendel made a face.

"Yah, me too," agreed Frodo.

"I would have thought that you guys would be used to jumping by now," Ray chided them.

"We *never* gonna get used to jumpin'!" Beowulf said emphatically.

"Maria told me it doesn't bother her cats," Ray teased, reminding them of their former comrades, Maria Valdez and her team of telepathic cats.

"I bet it bothers them plenty, but them pussfaces prob'ly too damn stubborn to let on!" Littlejohn said hotly.

Ray laughed. "You may be right about that."

"We gonna use them couches you put in?" asked Sinbad.

"No, dummy, Ray jes' put them in for the heck of it!" snapped Grendel. "'*Course* we gonna use the couches."

"Grendel's right," Ray concurred, aware of how snappish the impending jump was making his team. "When Ake gives me the ten-minute warning, I'll help you guys get strapped in for the jump."

"Can't wait!" Mama-san said sarcastically.

"Jumping's disorienting, sure, but—"

"Ray, get your ass down here on the double!"

Ray turned to Beowulf. "Get everyone into the acceleration couches now; I'll come back and secure you."

"Yes, Ray," Beowulf said—to empty air, since Ray was already halfway down the corridor.

"What's the problem?" Ray asked as he slipped into the co-pilot's chair. Ake just pointed to the communications console.

"*Spirit of St. Louis*, I repeat, this is Alexandria City port control. You are denied permission to proceed with your takeoff procedures. A contingent of Federation soldiers will board you shortly. I have been instructed to reassure you that there will be no problem if you offer no resistance." Wishing to maintain as much privacy as possible, Ake had turned off the video half of the transmission. While this meant that there was no image of the middle-aged female traffic controller for them to inspect, it also insured that there was no returning video to give away any details of their shipboard routine.

The controller's voice lost a bit of its detached, official tone as she added, "Please, for everyone's sake, do as I say and don't try to resist the soldiers. They are heavily armed Cadre regulars. Don't make Alexandria City a battleground."

Ake made sure the "transmit" function was inactive before snapping, "Goddamnit! We were so close to being ready to lift off."

"How close?" Ray asked.

"What do you mean?"

"I mean, can we do it? Can we take off now?"

"I think so," Ake said tentatively.

"You *think* so?"

"Okay—yes, dammit!"

"Attempting to lift off now would be a risky proposition, in my opinion," the ship's computer said, its female voice full of concern. "Her" concern was supposedly simulated—but it was damned convincing, Ake admitted to himself.

"Being flesh and blood and not merely a flow of electronic bits is a risky proposition," Ray told the Computer. He looked at Ake. "Well?"

"Can you operate the weapons systems?"

"Does Popeye like spinach?"

"Then, let's do it."

Ake closed his eyes and began powering up the ship's propulsion, navigational, and defensive systems. Ray dashed back to the area containing the acceleration couches and quickly strapped each dog down securely. "If you need to," Ray told them, "you can just say 'Emergency Cancellation Archimedes' and the computer will release the restraints."

"Okay, Ray," Beowulf said.

"Ray . . ." began Grendel.

"Yeah?"

"We gonna make it?"

"Hey, does Popeye like spinach?" Ray gave her a "thumbs up" signal and hurried off.

"Who's Popeye?" Grendel asked Beowulf.

"Beats me," Beowulf said. "I dunno what 'spinach' is, either."

2

Ray hustled back to the weapons control area and wrestled a battle suit out of a locker. He had never gotten into one on his own before—hell, he'd only ever put one on twice in his life!—and he found the process infuriatingly tedious and slow-going. Finally, he was suited up. So much for the easy part: Now he had to put on the command helmet.

Feeling as though he was in a parody of *Captain Trimble, Space Ranger,* he slipped the unwieldy command helmet over his head. He fastened it to his suit much as a knight of old might secure his heaume to his armor with leather thongs. Certainly, with the heavy command helmet in place, Ray was as weighed down and immobile as any tournament-readied knight of the fourteenth century; his weaponry was a bit more technologically advanced, however.

Moving with all the grace and agility of the Tin Woodman after a rainstorm, Ray opened the hatch to the weapons control bay and eased his bulk down into the freely rotating ball. He touched a control and the small sphere contracted to hold him firmly in place and to put all the controls within reach; it was not for the claustrophobic.

"I'm ready to boogie, computer," Ray said. "Do you read me?"

"They told me things would be different when the new owners took over," the ship's computer wailed.

"Well, have you ever been blown up before? That would certainly qualify as something new and different," Ray said, his eyes scanning the holo displays popping up in front of him as he activated the controls.

"Ah, *Spirit of St. Louis*, this is port control. Our instruments show you at full power. We have been advised to warn you that initiating departure procedures may result in your being fired upon. Do you copy?"

Ake took a deep breath and allowed himself to sense every centimeter of the ship's electro-neurological pathways. With his mind—his very being—linked to every sensor and instrument, he *was* the ship. "Port control?"

"Yes?"

"Is there someone there from the Federation?" Ake asked. He muted his mike and said over the ship's intercom, "Everybody be ready."

"I am Colonel Avram Balkoff," a second, extremely authoritative, voice replied. "What is it you wish to say?"

"Oh, not much," Ake told him. "Just that you can kiss my Scandinavian butt!"

<Now!> Ake projected.

A split second after uncoupling the docking cables that hung from the ship's sides like Lilliputian ropes restraining a sleek, mechanical Gulliver, Ake hit the forward thrusters and the ship shot backwards out of the slot that had held it like a sword being pulled from a scabbard.

<Shields>

The ship surrounded itself with a force-charlie interweave of invisible energy. Ake activated the lower thrusters and the ship executed a flawless VTO. The lift-tube-gentle sensation was suddenly shattered when the ship rocked back and forth as if buffeted by high winds.

"What was—" Ray began.

"Just a little unfriendly fire," Ake told him. "You didn't think they were going to let us just waltz out of here, did you?"

"No, I guess I didn't."

"Everybody strapped in?"

"Yeah."

"Good."

"Jeezz-uzzz!" Ray cursed as *The Spirit of St. Louis*'s after-thrusters kicked in, punching the small, dart-shaped sliver of metal and plastic through the heavy sea-level air. Ake corrected the angle of climb, and the ship shot through the lower atmosphere and into the middle layer of air so fast that ground-based tracking, unused to such speeds over populated areas, almost lost them.

"We gotta go back," Ray said.

"Oh . . . why?" asked Ake, aware that he was being set up.

"We left my stomach behind."

"Well, if we go back now, you'll leave your behind behind."

"Uh-oh," said the computer.

"I'm gonna hate myself for asking, but why did the computer just say 'uh-oh'?" Ray ventured.

"There's a Federation cruiser and five fighters waiting for us in orbit," Ake advised him.

"Uh-oh."

"What the hell's a Federation cruiser doing in this part of the galaxy?" asked an agitated Ray. "There's nothing here!"

"We're here," Ake said simply. "Remember, we're wanted men. The same rubies that made us rich . . ."

"Yeah, but you don't use an atomic cannon on a tsetse fly," Ray retorted. "With so much else going on in the galaxy, I thought we'd be old news by now."

"While you two are having this enlightening conversation," said the ship's computer, "the hostile spacecraft are particle-scanning us and calibrating interception trajectories."

"Can't we jump *now*?" Ray asked.

"That is inadvisable," the computer replied.

"I agree," Ake said. "The gravitation disturbance from Alexandria and the other planets and moons in the system would play hell with our entry into hyperspace. We might come out in another universe or dimension, turned inside out."

"Can I take that as a 'no'?" asked Ray.

"I believe I shall need a complete personality restructuring after being exposed to the highly unusual mental patterns of Citizen Larkin," the computer said. "That is, I might add, in the event that we somehow escape unharmed—despite the thousand-to-one odds against us."

"You can lobotomize the computer later," Ake told Ray. Then he emitted a sharp "Damn! Can you feel that?" he asked Ray.

"That thumping? Yeah, what is it?"

"That's the cruiser testing our shields."

"How're they doing—the shields, I mean?"

"Pretty good, I'd say, since we haven't blown up," Ake replied evenly, turning off the artificial gravity.

"God bless drug smugglers and their defenses."

"But we're gonna be space trash soon if we allow that big guy unlimited opportunities to keep hammering us."

"If you have something planned, now would be an *excellent* time to put it into operation," Ray said with genuine feeling.

"Okay," Ake replied, abruptly killing the rear thrusters and firing the forward ones, dropping speed at an alarming rate.

Even though he was nestled inside the weapons control bay—both he and his battle suit wedged into the confined space—Ray involuntarily gasped as his body insisted on maintaining its forward momentum. Ake's high-gee maneuver caused Ray to be flung against the webbing like an old sinny cartoon character hurled into a steel-mesh net at supersonic speed. Ray's eyes bulged and he felt his face grow hot and fat as his anterior capillaries were flooded.

Several of the dogs, their couches arrayed differently from the others'—head end away from the front of the ship—blacked out for an instant as the rapid braking pulled oxygen-rich blood from their brains.

As the sudden deceleration eased, Beowulf said, "And I thought jumpin' was bad!"

"Hang on," said Frodo. "That prob'ly not the last of it."

"Mommy!" wailed Gawain.

"Now, now, Gawain," Mama-san responded to her son, assuming that he meant his cry literally. "You be okay."

"Son of a bitch!" Ray shouted. "We okay?" he asked Ake.

"We're too busy to talk to you now," said the ship's computer.

"Well, pardon me!" said Ray, feeling an irresistible urge to scratch his hot and itchy skin. Ake paid him no mind as he and the ship's computer activated smaller thrusters to realign the ship's position.

Completely integrated with the ship's nervous system, Ake now reapplied full power to *The Spirit of St. Louis*'s singularity engines and the yacht shot away at right angles to the clumsy cruiser.

"That's one big and powerful piece of machinery," Ake

said, meaning the cruiser, "but she's got too damn much mass and momentum to stop on a decicredit. She'll get turned, but not in time to be much of a threat to us."

"Great!" said Ray.

"Yeah, well—we still got five fighters on our tail."

"*You* fly this hunk of junk, and *I'll* take care of the fighters," Ray told him.

"I'll complete the log and prepare to launch an emergency buoy," the ship's computer said. "It has a better chance of surviving if it's not onboard when we're destroyed."

"I just thought of something, Ake," Ray told him.

"Yeah?"

"You're wired in; can you fly this crate without Miz Confidence?"

"I guess so," Ake said slowly. "It wouldn't be easy, I'd—"

"Then turn her *off*," Ray insisted. "This ship was in custody for a long time. I'll bet you anything that they've analyzed this binary bitch's past programming and defensive tendencies. Let's do this the old-fashioned way—by ourselves."

"Good night, Irene," said Ake, putting the ship's computer's higher reasoning capabilities to "sleep," leaving active only its supervision of routine shipboard functions.

"Thank you," Ray said. "Now give me a minute or two to get ready."

"I don't know if we've got a minute," Ake told him. "What have you been doing back there all this time—playing with yourself?"

"You'd be amazed what this suit can do."

"I'd be more amazed if you told me you were ready."

"Just a minute."

The battle helmet projected the necessary holo displays in front of Ray's face, and slight movements of his eyes were all that were needed to activate most of the functions. He also inserted his hands and forearms into two carefully designed and incredibly responsive waldoes. Merely curling one of his fingers was all it took to activate the "smart" weaponry on board.

"Hello, missiles and torpedoes," he said. "Is everybody in nominal condition?"

Silence.

"Guys . . . ?" Ray said, discombobulated by the lack of response.

"This is missile A-1, commander," one of the missiles replied. "We're Double-AA Class military ordnance. We don't normally speak unless spoken to directly, sir. None of us felt comfortable responding to you on behalf of us all when you asked about our ready status. As for me, I am in a nominal state."

"That's all I need—reticent weapons!" Ray said, remembering not to shake his head from side to side in disgust: that configured the instrumentation for a self-destruct countdown procedure.

"I'll try to remember to ask straightforward, 'individual-directed,' questions," Ray said patiently. "We are in a battle situation, however."

"We are?" said A-1. "Outstanding! We are all prepared to do our duty."

"Wonderful," Ray said dryly. "Now then: Missiles A-2 through A-20, are you all nominal?"

"Yes, sir," they replied in turn. And indeed, now that he knew which readouts to bring up, Ray could see their ready status in the glowing figures dancing before his eyes.

"Good. Torpedoes B-1 through B-20, are you combat ready?"

"Yes, sir," they all replied, save for B-4, whose condition color was red.

"What's your problem, B-4?" Ray asked.

"My gravity-sensors are reading 'not ready.'"

"Did you try back-up circuitry?"

"Affirmative."

"And?"

"Still reading condition red."

"Damn," Ray cursed. B-4 was a primary launch torpedo; that meant a millisecond might be lost in cycling another torpedo into place. The lost time could prove costly in the heat of combat.

"I'm sending a diagnostic/repair crab down to see if it can find and eliminate the problem," Ray said. If he was lucky, between the three of them—the crab, the ship's computer, and the torpedo itself—they could effect a rapid restoration of the weapon's functioning.

Ray took a deep breath. "Okay, laser batteries—what is your status?" They all replied that they were combat ready. "And what about you drop charges?"

The response was an enthusiastic: "A-OK!"

"So what's the story?" Ake interrupted. "Are we ready to take on the whole Federation fleet?"

"Uh, *yeah*," Ray replied. "Actually, we're about as nominal as we're going to get. There is a problem with B-4, however."

"Before what?"

"This is no time to be kidding around, Ake," Ray admonished his confused partner, breaking the connection. Then he giggled and said, "Before."

"Yes, commander?" asked B-4.

"Sorry, B-4, I wasn't speaking to you."

"Oh," said the puzzled weapon. Then: "Sir, the maintenance crab has found the malfunction and repaired it. I am proud to report that I am fully operational and prepared to execute my instructions."

"Attaboy," Ray said. "Let's show 'em what we can do!"

"Affirmative," chorused the weapons, eager to engage the enemy and fulfill their programming.

"Is everything okay back there?" Ake queried.

"Yep—even B-4."

"Before what?!"

"The fighters are closing on us fast," Ake went on. "I think they want to surround us so that we can't make full use of our shields."

"I thought you said this crate was fast," Ray rebuked him.

"It is."

"Then let 'em eat our jets," Ray said. "If they can't catch us, then they can't get past us either."

"You're right," Ake conceded. "But that strategy has its drawbacks, too."

"How so?"

"They may not be fast enough to get in front of us," Ake explained, "but they can keep up with us while they fan out behind us. Then, if we turn right, left, up, or down, we'll be turning into at least one fighter's optimum firing angle. The rear shields can hold off almost anything, but not the front or side fields. A well-placed torpedo or missile could ruin our whole day."

"I'm with you so far, but I still don't see the danger in that if we don't actually make a turn," Ray told him. "Why *should* we turn off in one direction?"

"You're forgetting the cruiser," Ake said, monitoring the big ship's position on his readouts. "While we're playing hare and hound with the fighters, the captain of the cruiser can plot a quick jump that brings it out in front of us. We'll fly right into its cannons."

"How come the cruiser can jump if we can't?" asked Ray, exasperated.

"They've got about ten thousand times our mass; if they jump, they're less likely to be affected by this solar system's gravitational wells."

"Well, paint me blue and call me a turnip!" Ray bitched.

"So, the military strategy's in *your* hands, Genghis," Ake told him pointedly. "Don't let the home side down," he said, as the ship shivered from the shock of another laser blast.

"Thanks . . . I think."

"Five Federation fighters on our tail," Ray noted aloud as he scanned the readouts dancing in front of his eyes. "I gotta pull a few hinky stunts not in the textcubes, fellas," he told the weapons.

"Battlefield initiative, eh?" said A-1.

"Something like that."

Ray ordered one of the mechanical crabs to affix a drop charge to another crab's "back." Then he ordered the bomb-carrying crab to crawl onto torpedo B-2 and secure itself. "I'm to have a passenger, sir?" torpedo B-2 asked.

"Yes," Ray responded, studying the positions of the pursuing fighters. "Now listen up, both of you: here's what I want the two of you to do. . . ."

The sudden burst from *The Spirit of St. Louis*'s rear laser batteries alerted the fighters that the ship they were chasing was preparing to attempt something behind the screen of withering firepower—some sneaky maneuver hidden by the laser batteries' blasts.

Thus primed, they clearly observed the launch of torpedo B-1 and then, seconds later, torpedo B-2. They did, however, fail to note that the second torpedo had a "passenger." Almost disdainfully, the nearest fighter sent out coherent beams of light energy, lancing into the first torpedo and then the second.

In the brief interval between the explosive destruction of B-1 and B-2, the small shape atop the second torpedo disengaged, stilled its forward motion, and ceased all electronic activity.

The victorious fighter's electronic senses did not register the inert drop charge hovering directly in its path until it was too late for any action on the pilot's part except to express a heartfelt "Oh, shit!"

The perfectly circular fireball that blossomed from the wreckage of the destroyed fighter made the unlucky pilot's wing men on either side turn away from the tsunami of hot gases and debris that threatened to envelop them as well.

"We got one!" Ray's gung-ho weapons shouted in celebration.

"Let's go, gyrenes!" shouted Ray as he launched missiles A-1 through A-6 at the momentarily exposed fighters, targeting three missiles apiece at the two wingmen.

The first fighter managed to destroy all three of the onrushing missiles—with a little help from one of his comrades—but the second fighter was not so lucky. Ray heard A-6 say, "Open wide, Mama, this cowboy's home from the range!" Then the missile's "voice" disappeared in a sudden burst of static. The holo showed that A-6 had penetrated the fighter's defenses and impacted the precise spot where the defensive shield dimpled and shimmered around one of its own missile launch tubes.

Taking advantage of the opportunity, Ray directed beam after beam of coherent energy into the blast-exposed opening, and the fighter blew apart like a watermelon with a cherry bomb in it.

"Where were you guys manufactured?" Ray asked one of the remaining missiles as the cheering died down.

"New Dallas, sir," the missile replied proudly.

"That figures," Ray mused, as his fingers twitched and curled, subtly changing coordinates.

The surviving fighters unleashed a furious rain of laser energy and torpedoes at the yacht, only to find that the one-time smuggler's ship's rear shields were sufficiently strong enough to ward off almost any assault from that angle of attack. The "harmless" blasts did shake, rattle, and roll *The Spirit of St. Louis*'s passengers, however.

Ake's voice came over Ray's intercom. "Ray, unless you tell me otherwise, I'm making a course change."

"Which way?"

"It doesn't matter," Ake told him. "The point of changing course *is* to change course. Otherwise, we'll find that cruiser waiting for us like a hungry cat waiting for a canary to fly down its throat."

Ray glanced at the three remaining fighters, jockeying for position around them. "If you're going to change course, go ten o'clock low in fifteen seconds from my mark."

"Say when."

"Mark!"

"You got it. Pack your balls in cotton," Ake said.

"Hang on, guys," Ray warned the dogs. Strapped in their couches, he knew they felt helpless.

"Drop charges C-2 through C-8 prepare for launch in five seconds," Ray ordered the weapons. "Launch at half-second intervals."

"We're ready, willing, and able, sir," replied C-2 as it cycled into position with the other drop charges—each one a cluster mine.

<Now!>

Again Ray felt the wrenching, stomach-twisting sensations of an abrupt maneuver: rapid deceleration followed immediately by sudden acceleration in a new direction. At the instant the ship changed vectors, the drop charges began ejecting behind them: right, left, up, and down.

The pursuing fighters' combat computers instantly analyzed *The Spirit of St. Louis*'s maneuver and calculated the yacht's new direction. The three ships followed as if connected to their pursuee by invisible elastic cords.

Which was what Ray had counted on.

As soon as they left *The Spirit of St. Louis*, the drop charges split open, spewing out over two hundred individual bomblets into the vacuum of space.

Two of the fighters were able to avoid the deadly hailstorm waiting for them.

But not the third.

No single charge—no dozen charges—could have penetrated the fighter's defensive shields. But as the fighter dove into the maelstrom of spinning shards of destruction, the charges began exploding not just on impact but also in response to the explosions of the other bomblets. It was a rapid-fire chain reaction that enveloped the doomed fighter inside an oblong bubble of fire and shrapnel.

"Outstanding!" said one of the remaining smart weapons as the ship's defensive net displayed the fate of the Federation fighter.

"That should do it," an obviously pleased Ray said. "The other two will break off pursuit now that they're on their own."

Watching the fighters doggedly following in their wake, Ake asked pointedly, "And just when do they do that, Dead-eye Dick?"

Ray stared at the images of the two fighters floating in the air in front of him and asked, "What's with those guys? They got a death wish or something?"

"Sir," missile A-10 said.

"Yeah?"

"They're soldiers, sir. They're doing their duty, sir."

Ray couldn't really expect the weapons to "understand." Their raison d'être was to be expended in battle, which made them the perfect "soldiers" since their goal was their own destruction.

Ray sighed. "Our fight is with the Federation—I don't want to kill people just doing their duty, goddamnit!"

"Then how about to save your life?" Ake asked dryly. "If they get a chance, either of them will be more than happy to put a torpedo up our ass and blow all of us into space dust. That includes the dogs," he added after a moment's pause.

"Yeah, yeah," Ray said reluctantly.

"It's them or us," Ake told him.

"I guess it's them, then."

"Yes, sir," said A-10.

"Torpedoes B-3 through B-10, are you ready for launch?"

"On your order, sir."

"Good."

Then Ray asked Ake, "Can you plug me into Sleeping Beauty? I know she's dozed through all this except for her routine ship maintenance functions."

"Done," Ake told him. "What are you going to use the computer for?"

"I want a simple charted analysis of the fighters' pattern of moves during this 3-D chess game we've been playing."

"Oh. Well, tell it that," Ake said.

"Computer: Analysis, please." Ray gave the machine a second or two to produce the requested analysis and then asked for the fighters' probable response to a series of programmed moves.

"Yes, this looks promising," Ray said.

"What're you planning to do?" asked Ake.

"Wait and see," was all Ray would say. Then he asked, "Can you give the computer control of the ship's flight for the next minute or so?"

"Sure."

"Do it," Ray said.

"Done."

Ray activated the program. "Now—execute," he told the computer.

As *The Spirit of St. Louis* responded to Ray's carefully calculated flight pattern, Ray began launching torpedoes. "Launch torpedo B-3," he ordered. After another change of direction, he said, "Launch torpedo B-4." Another change in the ship's flight path was followed by "Launch torpedo B-5," and so forth until all the torpedoes had been fired.

Ray stared at the glowing projections floating in front of him and now began a flow of commands: "Drop charges nine through eleven eject at ten-second intervals commencing . . . NOW." His eyes on a timed readout that marched backwards toward zero, Ray also watched the holo projections and finally ordered: "Fire missiles A-8 and A-9."

The ship made a series of complex maneuvers and headed back into a spider's web of intersecting ordnance.

Seeing what they were going into, Ake muttered, "Sweet Jesus!"

As *The Spirit of St. Louis* and the pursuing fighters zigzagged through space, they began intersecting with the torpedoes and the other weapons fired. Ray smiled, teeth clenched, as torpedo B-5 passed just under the nose of the ship. In a matter of seconds, B-8 hurled over the stern.

"Christ, what the hell are you doing?" Ake demanded.

"Playing a form of chicken."

Studying the projections in front of him, Ake saw that they were flying directly into a labyrinth filled with converging torpedoes, drop charges and missiles. "Ohmygod!"

Ray gulped and crossed his fingers. "You don't *really* want me to detonate right now, do you?" asked one of the drop charges still on board.

"Oops," said Ray, uncrossing his fingers.

He turned back to floating images in front of him. If he had calculated the vectors correctly, then not only would they pass harmlessly through the deadly volume of space, but also the pursuing Federation fighters' defenses would be overwhelmed by the complexity of the weave of weaponry.

Ray slowly became aware of the fact that he was not breathing and gulped down a lungful of air.

"I think we're coming out," said Ake. "But the fighters—"

The web Ray had woven caught both of them at nearly the same instant: A drop charge and a torpedo intersected the path of one of the fighters, and a torpedo and a missile found the other. The first fighter blew apart in a multicolor explosion.

"Way to go, B-9," Ray said an instant before the missile struck the second fighter in a vulnerable location amidships seconds after the force-field-weakening impact of the torpedo.

"Thank you, sir!" exclaimed B-9 before it exploded, proud to have successfully executed its orders. The resulting fireball left no doubt as to the outcome.

"Under the B-9 . . ." Ray paused for dramatic effect, then added: "BINGO!"

3

"How long we gots to be in these couches, Ray?" Beowulf asked as Ray came back to the lounge to be with his dogs.

"Just a little longer, Beowulf," Ray replied, scratching the big dog's head and then the heads of the other members of his team. "We still have a Federation cruiser on our ass."

"Okay," said Beowulf resignedly.

"When can we make the jump to hyperspace?" Ray asked Ake over the ship's intercom.

"Any time now," Ake replied as he continued confirming jump coordinates with the computer.

"Here we go," warned Ake as Ray leapt to strap himself down on one of the couches.

The ship jumped.

Ray gulped as he experienced those old familiar sensations: a wave of nausea and the feeling that every cell in his body had bulged and then contracted.

"This gonna be a long one?" asked Beowulf.

"How about that, Ake?" Ray asked. "Is this going to be a long or a short jump?"

"Fairly short—just a three-minute hop to get us away from the long arms of the Federation." He coughed. "Then we'll calculate and execute a second jump as quickly as possible."

"Oh, why?" asked Ray.

"The cruiser saw us jump, so they can plot along a line our

possible exit points up to thirty light-years—no one jumps longer than that and comes out alive."

"Mr. Reassurance," Ray said dryly, looking at his watch.

Even though Ray, Ake, and the dogs would experience—would *live* the three minutes they would be in hyperspace—*The Spirit of St. Louis*'s clocks would not register the passage of time. Indeed, when they returned to normal space B, it would be at the same instant they had left normal space A. To keep track of the time, however, Ake had the computer flash a backwards-counting readout in front of him: 03:00, 02:59, 02:58, and so on to 00:00.

"I hate jumpin'," stated Ozma.

"Yah," agreed Tajil. "It like runnin' through a nightmare."

"Hey, that's pretty good," Ray said to his big red dog. "I like that—'like running through a nightmare.'"

"What's the count to?" Mama-san asked anxiously. Ake transmitted the readout as it worked its way down to double zeros.

"Two minutes to go."

"Ray, Ake—look!" said Beowulf.

"What is it, Beowulf?" asked Ray.

Then he saw what the big dog was staring at in horror.

The glowing readout read: -00:59, -01:00, -01:01 . . .

"My God!" said Ake. "We've passed the three-minute mark and we're still in hyperspace!"

"We still in hyperspace?" said Beowulf. "What that mean?"

"It means we're in deep shit," Ray said softly. He stared at the steady backwards progression of the elapsed jump-time readout. Each second was taking them farther (deeper?) into hyperspace.

"You know, I just had a terrible thought," Ray said.

"Let's hear it, then," said Ake wearily.

"Yah, what you thinkin'?" asked Beowulf.

"Well, we got such a good price on this little beauty that I'm beginning to wonder it there wasn't a catch."

"A catch?"

"Remember the *Star of India*?"

"The *Star of India*?" Ake asked, frowning.

"It was the first ship to be lost in hyperspace," put in the computer helpfully.

"Oh," said Ake.

"Yeah," Ray said. "That was when they discovered that some kinda weird hypermatter was attaching itself to the hulls of ships transiting hyperspace. And the effect was cumulative: After about eight to ten jumps, there was so much of it that ships lacked the power to break out of hyperspace and reenter normal space." He paused dramatically. "They were trapped in hyperspace—like a sailing ship becalmed in Hell."

"Jesus!" Ake whispered. "I'm going to be sorry for asking this," he said, "but what's this ghost story have to do with us?"

"We bought this baby used—how many jumps had it accumulated before it came into our possession?" he asked. "Better yet: How many jumps since an ESPer's cleaned the hull?"

"I fear Citizen Larkin's—" began the computer.

"Stop calling me that!" Ray snapped. "Just call me Ray."

"Yes, *Ray*," the computer said.

"Well, go on," Ray said.

"Certainly," said the computer, in its irritatingly calm feminine voice. "I fear Ray's theory has a strong chance of being correct. My memories—to the extent that they have not been tampered with by the authorities on Alexandria—indicate that this spacecraft has made nine short jumps without employing an ESPer to sweep the hull clean of hypermatter."

"Jesus H. Nixon!" Ray exclaimed.

"All right," Ake said. "I hear you, Ray, but I'm still not clear about what this hypermatter *is*."

"Nobody is, really," Ray responded. He took a deep breath and stared down at the deck.

Finally he looked up and said. "Okay, here goes: A ship's officer once told me that the best way to understand the hypermatter accumulating on the hull was to try thinking of it as just another form of barnacles."

"Barnacles?" said Ake dubiously.

"A very special form of barnacles, to be sure," Ray said. He frowned. Because of his propensity for telling whoppers in even the most trying times, he was now like the little boy who cried wolf—Ake was resisting the truth because it was coming from him.

"Why don't *you* tell him, Miz Know-it-all?" Ray suggested to the computer.

"Certainly," the computer said. "Normal space reveals nothing; in normal space the hulls of the ships are spotlessly clean. It is only in hyperspace that the hypermatter grows and accumulates like coral deposits, and only in hyperspace where it can affect the course of a ship by exerting a drag on it, and where it can be sensed by those humans with certain psi talents."

"Wow," said Gawain.

"It appears to be strangely, impossibly cumulative," the computer continued. "Each jump adds more, more to somehow *drag* and hold back the ship until the starship lacks the power to burst free of hyperspace and reemerge in the normal universe."

When the computer finished, there was a stunned silence for a long time.

Finally, Beowulf ventured to fill the yawning emptiness by asking, "Ray—you and that machine woman *really* serious 'bout this? You not just pullin' our legs like so many times?"

"I wish we were making it all up, Beowulf, I really do—but we're not."

Ake looked over at the glowing readout: -03:38, -03:39, -03:40 . . .

II

The dogs crowded around Ray, nudging him affectionately. In return, he sought out each one individually, calling him or her by name, and rubbing heads and scratching ears enthusiastically. They acted like puppies although the biggest of them, Beowulf, was one hundred and fifty kilos of mature dog.

"Hey, Beowulf and Mama-san," Ray said, embracing the two and burying his hands in their thick fur. After a few minutes he moved on. "Littlejohn and Ozma," he called. "Get your canine butts over here!" They, too, came in for some serious rubbing and petting.

"You is the bestest man we could have," Ozma said.

"Hey, rusty dog—c'mere." Grinning, Ray put his right arm around Sinbad, thumping the big dog's ribs under his reddish-brown coat.

" 'Member when Ake used to think you was beatin' us when you did that?" Sinbad asked.

"Yeah," said Ray. "He couldn't believe you guys *like* this sort of thing." He gave Sinbad several more solid whacks as if to prove his point. "You're not toy terriers." He grabbed hold of Grendel and rubbed his knuckles over her broad skull.

"Oh, feels good," Grendel said. "My ears, too!" Ray obligingly played with her ears.

Ray saw Tajil, Gawain, and the black-and-white-marked Frodo hanging back, their tails wagging furiously. "And what are you Three Stooges doing over there when I'm over here?" Needing no more encouragement, they bounded toward him with goofy grins on their faces and knocked him off his feet. He landed on his behind and laughed as they swiped his face with their huge tongues. "Ugh—dog slobber!"

Ake stood silently in the hatchway to the lounge, not wishing to intrude but compelled to by the inexorable passage of time—time spent in the nothingness of hyperspace, meaning that they were hurtling deeper and deeper into an unknown future. If they spent as long as two hours in hyperspace, they might emerge in . . . *Goddamnit*, Ake thought. *I don't know where in the hell we might end up! Maybe another time, or another dimension—but nowhere we want to be, that's for sure!*

"Ray . . ." Ake said softly. "It's time."

Ray looked up, his eyes moist. "Yeah, I know, partner. I was just saying goodbye to my mutts."

"You'll be seeing them again in a few minutes," insisted Ake.

"Uh-huh."

With a loud canine sigh, Beowulf padded over with the small leather pouch that contained their remaining rubies. Ray took the pouch, opened it, and spilled a half-dozen or so rubies out onto the floor.

"That's a king's ransom right there," mused Ray, staring at the vermilion-colored gemstones lying on the lounge's plush carpeting. "But money's not much good to a dead man."

Ake pointed at the rubies. "Their worth to us now isn't in how many credits they'll fetch, but in their ability to amplify your crude psi talents."

"True," agreed Ray, touching the trickle of blood flowing from his right nostril. "I can feel their energy already." Then he put a grieved look on his face. "*Crude?*"

"Yah, like the rest of you," teased Mama-san.

"Sure," sniffed Ray. "In the face of death, it all comes out finally."

Ignoring the badinage, Ake walked over to where the rubies lay on the floor, kneeled down, and began selecting likely prospects. "Think these five will be enough?" he asked.

"Probably," Ray said, reaching out and taking the largest and most perfectly formed of the five from Ake's hand. "This one, especially, has the power; this one speaks to me." He smiled and added sheepishly, "Not literally, but I can sense its almost living energy."

Ake and the dogs watched as Ray put the five rubies in a small cloth bag and hung it around his neck. With the rubies so close to him, Ray's ears began to bleed.

"That can't be comfortable," Ake said.

"It hurts so good," said Ray good-naturedly. Then he added, "Get my suit—time's a-wasting."

When Gawain sighed, Ray asked, "What's the matter, Gawain?"

"Huh? Oh, nuthin'," Gawain replied. "Nuthin'."

★ ★ ★

Nothing, Ray thought. *Hyperspace is nothing*. That was not entirely true, he knew, yet it seemed as if it was so. He could not conceive that he was hurtling through nothingness; paradoxically, however, he could not conceive that he was *hurtling* through anything. There was no sense of speed, of movement. There was no *sense* of anything.

Or so Ray thought.

In truth, Ray moved amid a riot of perception for which humankind has no senses: he failed to smell the sounds or hear the colors. Zombielike, he lifted his booted feet one at a time and then put them back down again. A snake held tight to him—he was too big to swallow, too good to let loose. The snake: a cable twisting sinuously in the weightless condition of hyperspace (a product of Mach's Principle concerning the lack of inertial force upon a single particle in a starless universe), more alive, seemingly, than the man it held to warm, breathing life.

Ray was like a bird on the back of a whale, picking here and there to dislodge a parasite that had burrowed deep into the great mammal's back. The light from his helmet reflected off the ship's smooth skin, disappearing into the velvet blackness like rain into thirsty soil, absorbed hungrily.

If I "fell" from the ship, he asked himself, *where would I fall to?* He giggled nervously. *Through the looking glass? To Never Land? Maybe I'd find myself in a white room filled with Louis XVI furniture and a black monolith!* Ray smiled. *Nah. I probably wouldn't go anywhere; I'm in the middle of nowhere, in the middle of nothing.*

Nothing. The ship's skin glowed brightly, awash with luminescent paint, and Ray had only the cyclopean glare of his helmet lamp to illuminate his way.

He felt the tiny hairs on the back of his neck rise as goosebumps marched up his spine. Tensed muscles in his face and neck drew his forehead taut and his mouth white-lipped. He turned slowly, his heart pounding raggedly, but there was nothing inching up from behind him—no slobbering monsters glistening like wet leather, no ravenous but animated heap of gelatin intent upon absorbing him in one slurp of instantaneous osmosis.

"Booga! Booga!" he said, breaking the mood. "You'd think I was eight years old and going down into a pitch-black basement by myself at midnight!"

I must be getting close to the hypermatter, he told himself. *Whatever it is, it's giving me the willies.*

He could feel the small cloth pouch containing the rubies rubbing against his chest, the roseate gemstones blasting him with their power. He sniffed—his nostrils, eyes, and ears continued to trickle blood.

Suddenly, the ship was enveloped by a greasy mist that came out of nowhere. It was as if *The Spirit of St. Louis*, like some ancient Terran freighter plying the seven seas, had sailed into a fog bank. "Christ, I'll know I'm in *real* trouble if we come out of this fog and Skull Island is directly ahead!"

Without quite understanding how he came to that conclusion, Ray slowly realized that the elusive mist was the basis for the hypermatter that formed and attached itself to passing ships.

"Did I say hyperspace was nothing?" Ray asked aloud as the mist encircled and enclosed him, swirling around his legs, nuzzling him like Maria's cats.

"Whatever I do, I must *not* look directly at it," he cautioned himself. "That way lies madness." It was not for nothing, Ray remembered, that the portholes of interstellar jumpers were made opaque to the mind-numbing properties of hyperspace.

His psychic abilities honed to a razor sharpness by the rubies, Ray could readily see the hypermatter. It streamed out from the ship like will-o-the-wisp ribbons of mist, disappearing into the seamless fabric of hyperspace.

Carefully, he reached out a gloved hand and passed it over a ribbon of hypermatter. As if sliced through by a scythe, the translucent ribbons of mist were separated from their point of contact with the hull and fluttered away.

As he cleared away the last of the hypermatter, Ray forgot himself for just a moment and stared into the pulsating maelstrom of fog and mist. Something in the swirling mist of light and color caught his eye . . . faces. Faces heavy with chalky jowls, faces bisected by livid scars, faces tormented from within. They called to him, their soundless voices stabbing into his mind.

And he knew them. . . .

"Join us, Ray," the General pleaded with him.

"Yeah, we could use a guy like you," agreed Waldo Lynch, his disembodied head smiling a terrible smile that made Ray shiver.

"But you're dead."

The others, hovering behind Lynch and the General, spoke up: "That's right, Ray. Won't you join us?" Ray knew them, too.

"It's easy," said the General. "Just open the seal on your helmet. . . ."

Mercifully, Ray's mind did what it could to protect him: He blacked out.

"It bin twelve minutes, Ake," said Beowulf.

"I know, I know." Ake picked at the corner of his mouth, his unease growing. Twelve minutes. What could Ray be doing? Quickly, he came to a decision. "I'm going out after him," he told the dogs.

"Ake—" began the computer.

"I don't want to hear it," Ake said. "Ray's my friend and

partner. He didn't give up on me on Hephaestus and I can't give up on him now. I owe him one; at least one."

Ray kidded Ake that he had no imagination. That wasn't true, of course, but Ake certainly had no psychic powers. For him, hyperspace really was a total vacuum; he saw and heard nothing—neither the hypermatter nor the faces.

Ake kept his eyes to the hull, his gloved hands following Ray's safety line. As he approached his partner, he could see the arms of Ray's suit waving aimlessly in the zero-gee condition of hyperspace.

"Sonofabitch!" Ake swore, quickly closing the gap between them.

"Ray, Ray . . ." Ake stared through the suit's visor. Ray's eyes were closed but he was breathing. With few wasted motions, Ake tied Ray to his line and then began towing him back toward the hatch. As he moved across the surface of the ship, he stared at its luminescent skin, wondering if Ray had gotten all the hypermatter. He could only pray that Ray's current condition had followed his successful exorcising of the weird material.

III

"Ray sleeping?" Ake asked Beowulf when the big leader dog ambled into the cockpit.

"Like baby," Beowulf replied.

"Good," said a distracted Ake, still fiddling with controls. "Sorry I couldn't stay with him—we've been in hyperspace too long as it is—but I knew you guys would watch over him."

"Yah," agreed Beowulf. After a moment's pause, he asked, "We gonna be okay now?"

"I don't know," Ake admitted. "Like I said, I don't know of anyone else being in hyperspace as long as we've been and surviving to tell about it."

"How long it bin?"

Reluctantly—because he didn't want to confront the awful truth of the readout—Ake read off the elapsed time: "One hour and six minutes."

"Golly," said Beowulf.

"At the very least, golly," agreed Ake. Then he said, "You

better go back and get everyone ready, we'll be coming out in a few minutes."

"Okay."

After Beowulf left, Ake rechecked the figures with the computer. "I guess there's nothing left to do but try it," he said.

"I agree," the computer said.

"I'm going to help the dogs get buckled in, and then we spin the wheel and see what comes up," Ake said.

The dogs looked up anxiously as he hurried into the lounge. After giving each of the nine members of the canine scout team a pat on the head or a scratch behind the ears, and an encouraging word or two, Ake helped secure them.

"Good luck, guys," he told them.

"Good luck, Ake," they chorused.

Ake made sure Ray was both resting comfortably and immobilized inside his sleep chamber before he headed back to the pilot's area. "How long now?" he asked the computer.

"Forty-five seconds and counting."

Ake looked down at his hands; there were blotchy red patches all over his palms—the same evidence of nervous tension he used to get before exams.

He crossed his fingers. "Let's do it."

The ship jumped.

★ ★ ★

The dogs watched in concern as Ray sat sipping from the biggest glass of straight bourbon they'd ever seen. "Ray, you be okay?" Beowulf asked, the concern the dog felt evident in his gravelly voice.

"Yeah, how're you doing?" added Ake. "Tell your old doctor what's wrong. What happened out there? It must have been real bad."

"I got rid of the hypermatter," Ray said matter-of-factly.

"And . . . ?"

"And what?" Ray snapped. Recovering his composure, he said softly, "I saw them."

"Saw who?"

"The General. Waldo Lynch." He smiled a terrible smile that made Ake shiver. "Hell, I even saw the pilots of the fighters we destroyed. They're there. All of them. They're there in hyperspace—anyone whose death I had anything to do with." He laughed a mirthless laugh. "That's a pretty impressive mob."

"What did they want?"

"They wanted me to join them."

"But they're dead."

"That's right," said Ray.

"But if'n they dead, then how can you join them?" asked a puzzled Gawain. Ozma leaned over and whispered something into Gawain's ear. "Oh," said Gawain. Then: "OH!"

"Yeah," said Ray, taking another gulp of bourbon. Then he looked around as if he'd just remembered something. "Hey, what happened? Did we make it?"

"Well . . ." began Tajil.

"You see, Ray," explained Ake, "there's good news and there's bad news."

"Oh, no," Ray said, clutching his glass of bourbon.

"Oh, yes," said Beowulf.

"The good news is that, yes, we have returned to the normal space-time continuum after our hiatus in hyperspace," Ake began. "The bad news is that we didn't come back at the same time."

"Ah . . ." Ray searched for words. "We didn't return *before*, did we?"

"No," chimed in the computer. "Time travel, at least in the sense of going back in time, is, in all likelihood, impossible."

"So we went forward in time?" Ray asked.

"All living and sentient entities' travels through time are in the same—and only possible—direction: forward," the computer explained, as if telling a small child why water runs downhill.

"We, ah, just happened to go forward a little farther and a little faster than normal," Ake said.

"Not literally, of course," the computer clarified. "While *The Spirit of St. Louis* was in hyperspace, time passed normally in the known universe. So in that sense we have not really 'traveled in time.' "

Ray looked Ake straight in the eye. "Let's cut the pussy-footing around—how much time passed? Where are we? *When* are we?"

"I don't yet know where we are. It does seem, however, that we came out twelve years into the future, Ray," Ake said.

Ray blinked. "Twelve years?"

Littlejohn said, "Yah. Twelve years . . . we all twelve years older."

"Only in one sense . . ." began the computer.

"Oh, shut up!" Ray said.

"Well, gosh!" said Ake, feigning surprise. "You certainly haven't matured with the passage of time."

"You guys all seem to be taking the news rather well," Ray observed.

"What do you want us to do, gnash our teeth and tear our hair out?" Ake asked rhetorically. "Besides, we've had several hours longer than you to get used to the idea that we're living in the future."

"Twelve years," mused Ray. "Twelve goddamn years . . ."

"Ray?"

"Yes, Gawain?"

"How long that be in dog years?"

IV

"How exactly did you determine that we came out of hyperspace twelve years after we entered?" Ray asked Ake, the two of them sitting in the cockpit nursing drinks with Beowulf and Frodo lying at their feet. Although the dogs appeared to be sleeping, their ears twitched and rotated, following the conversation.

"Well, surprisingly enough," Ake began, "we're not all that far from our part of the galaxy." He sipped his drink. "We're a heck of a lot of light-years away from where we were, and on the other side of the home system, but still remarkably close to being inside Federation space."

" 'A heck of a lot'—oohh, I love it when you talk technical talk! Go on."

Ake shot him a look but continued. "Well, there's a lot of chatter, both tightbeam and subspace, zipping past—personal, business, and governmental. And, in addition to its I.D. and recognition codes, it's carrying the date." He looked at the amber liquid in his glass and then at Ray. "Satisfied?"

Ray shrugged. "Hey, it's not as if I didn't believe you, it's just that I find it hard to *believe* you."

"Yes, I know what you mean."

"So what we do now?" asked Frodo, lifting his head to look at Ray.

"Good question," said Ray.

"Thank you," Frodo replied modestly.

"Well, I'd vote for sitting tight for a few days and allowing the ship's computer to busy herself analyzing the message flow and come to an understanding about what kind of universe we're looking at out there," Ake suggested.

"What do you mean?" Ray asked.

Ake rolled his eyes heavenward. "I mean has the Federation put down the Rebellion? Or has the Rebellion destroyed the Federation? And, more important to us personally, are we still wanted men?"

"Gee," said Frodo. "I wonder if *Captain Trimble, Space Ranger* is still on hol-vee?"

Ray looked at Ake. "Shall I slug him or do you want the honor?"

4

Ray was studying a printout. "Hey," he said to Ake. "You want to know how rich we are?"

"I know how rich we are."

Ray shook his head. "No, you know how rich we *used* to be—twelve years ago."

A spark of understanding was kindled in Ake's eyes. "Oh, right. Okay, Mr. News-of-the-Day, how rich are we?"

Ray showed him the hard-copy printouts of their various investment accounts.

"I think I need a drink," Ake said.

"It's amazing what twelve years of compound interest can do to a mountain of money, isn't it?" Ray commented. "Shall we return to Terra . . . and buy it?"

"We just about could, couldn't we?" Ake said.

"Maybe they're having a 'going-out-of-business sale.' "

"Seriously," Ake said. "I would like to see Terra again. But I wonder what's happened to the Federation since we've been gone."

"Let's visit the nearest colony world and find out," Ray suggested.

"Being executed is right at the top of my least favorite things," Ake replied.

"So, we'll ask the computer to sift through all the messages she's been monitoring and give us the skinny on the current political situation first."

"Yeah," said Ake, brightening.

Ray got up and began to walk away. "Hey, where're you going?" Ake asked.

"I told the dogs I'd run a little with them after I spoke to you," Ray replied. For exercise, he and the dogs had been running up and down the ship's central passageway.

"Well, don't go far and be home in time for supper."

Ake and Ray ran a few names and universal I.D. numbers through the computer's subspace link with the nearest infobank, not really holding out much hope of finding anyone they knew in this quadrant of the galaxy.

"Hot damn!" exclaimed Ray. "I don't believe it!"

"You don't believe what?" Ake asked, peering over his partner's shoulder at the glowing readout. "Shit!" he said. "Now *I* don't believe it!"

"It's Johnny—Johnny Skerchock!"

John Skerchock was one of Ray's oldest friends. It was to Skerchock's team that Mama-san's other puppies had gone when Maximilian challenged Beowulf's status as the leader of the pack. It had been hard seeing them go, but Ray knew that there could be only one alpha dog to a pack, and Max had earned the right to head up his own team.

"Where exactly is he?" Ake asked, studying the coordinates. "Buchanan? Is that a star or a planet?"

"It is a planet," the computer informed them. "Named for a great female warrior-hero of the Erzani uprising of 2209."

"Show off," said Ray. Then: "Just how far is it to this world?"

"Five light-years."

"You mean . . ."

"Yeah—at least one jump," Ake finished for him.

Ray shrugged. "We're good for at least six or seven before the hull needs to be swept again. I say let's go for it."

"You sure?" asked a dubious Ake.

"We need to have someone we can trust fill us two Rip Van Winkles in on the events of the past twelve years," Ray argued. "Who better than Johnny Skerchock?"

"Let's do it, then," acquiesced Ake.

"I'll go tell the dogs."

★ ★ ★

Buchanan proved to be a world of dramatic extremes: flat, sandy desert areas devoid of vegetation; violent, storm-tossed seas dotted with cold, wet, volcanic islands; and frigid poles covered by vast ice sheets steadily creeping toward the icy ocean. Still, both the north and south hemispheres had narrow bands where more temperate weather prevailed. It was in these areas that most of the human colonists had settled.

The dogs were the first to hear the welcome sound of air whistling over the stubby wings as *The Spirit of St. Louis* gradually knifed into and through the atmosphere, following a gradual angle of flight toward the looming mass of the planet below.

Port Hector Air/Space Control tight-beamed landing instructions. Ake scanned them but was content to keep hands off and allow the computer to follow the landing beacon down to the spaceport.

" 'Nother new world," said Beowulf.

"But with old friends," said Ray.

"More than friends," said Mama-san, her tail wagging furiously.

"Mama-san can't wait to see her puppies," Sinbad explained superfluously.

"They're hardly puppies anymore," said Ray. He counted on his fingers.

"Feel free to use the computer if you don't want to take off your boots," Ake chided.

Ray ignored him. "Hey, they're older than you guys!"

"How that possible, Ray?" Littlejohn asked.

"Well, it was all that time in hyperspace, Littlejohn," Ray said.

"Yah . . . but how it *possible*?" Littlejohn persisted.

"You got me," Ray conceded.

"Ahem," began the computer. "It is really just a matter of—"

"Say goodnight, Gracie," Ray said, using the phrase he'd come up with to turn off the computer's bogus human personality. The computer immediately fell silent.

"I *like* doing that," Ray said.

"Heh, heh, heh," chuckled Grendel. "Ray shut up the machine-woman again."

"Yeah," Ray said, patting her head. "Us carbon-based units have to stick together."

"Shall I call you Old King Coal and his loyal subjects?" Ake asked dryly.

Ray's jaw dropped. "Hey . . . Ake made a pun!"

"Well, for chrissakes, Ray, you're not the only one capable of it, you know."

Ray beamed. "I'm proud of you, son."

"We will be landing in approximately four minutes," said the computer's now-dehumanized voice.

"Let's go get everybody strapped in," Ray told Beowulf.

"Okey-doke," the big dog agreed amiably.

Ray laid a hand on Ake's shoulder. "You and the computer can do it, Lance Corporal Smythe-Psmith. You can bring us in safely."

"Oh, get out of here already!"

II

Hardly had the rented hovercraft settled down outside the plascrete building Skerchock and his team called home before Mama-san, Tajil, and Gawain were on the ground and bounding toward the other dogs. Maximilian, heading up the equally enthusiastic welcoming party, led Clementine, Emma, and Telzey to greet their siblings and their mother.

The result was cacophonous. The reunited dogs barked, howled, and whimpered with pleasure. "Jeez, I never heard such a racket in my life," Ray said, climbing out of the hovercraft after the rest of his team.

Ake wasn't fooled; he saw the glint of tears in his partner's eyes. "Hell, don't stand there like a statue, go see Max and the others," he told Ray.

As Ray and the other dogs rushed to join the melee, Ake slowly got out of the hovercraft, stretched his legs, and waved knowingly at a figure standing and watching all the commotion from a respectful distance. "Hi, John," he mouthed. John Skerchock nodded and waved back.

Maximilian whined and licked Mama-san's face like the puppy he once was and not the competent and resourceful team leader he'd become. Telzey, Clementine, and Emma also licked and nipped at their mother and at their littermates, Tajil and Gawain. Ray and the other dogs got their hugs, pats, licks, and head butts in where they could.

Figuring that the greeting was going to go on for a little while longer, Ake skirted the roiling mass of dog fur and confusion and approached Skerchock. "Hi, John." This time he said it audibly. "How've you been?"

John stuck out his hand. "Hi to you, too, Ake. I've been doing pretty good. Better than you, I thought: for twelve years you've been dead . . . or so it seemed when you and Ray dropped out of sight. So to turn it around, how the hell have *you* been?"

"Not too bad." Then Ake laughed like he'd said something amusing.

"What's so funny?"

"Stupid social conventions. 'Not bad' does not *begin* to approach the shit we've been through since Max and his sisters left to join your team. If I only had one arm and leg, I'd probably be standing here saying, 'Yeah, things could be worse.' "

"Now you've got me interested. I can't wait to hear what's happened to you." Skerchock cocked his head then and looked intently at Ake. "It can't have been *all* that bad, though—you look the same."

"So do you," Ake replied.

"Don't bullshit me," said Skerchock. "I mean it—you look the same as you did the last time I saw you. Exactly the same."

"Clean living and exercise."

"Either that or you've got a painting of yourself that is growing older and uglier every day."

" 'The Portrait of Ake Ringgren,' " Ake joked.

"I've got another entry in the things-could-have-been-worse sweepstakes," Skerchock said. "Your ship."

"What about it?"

"Come on, Ake, don't be coy. A friend called me from the spaceport and asked me if I had any idea what had just landed. A Zukovich FTL-1000 goes for at least ten million new—and that's without the disc player."

"We didn't buy it new."

"I can see that—it's at least ten years old. But you did buy it, right?"

"Yes," Ake admitted. "We made a little money in the precious gems trade."

"A little?"

"A lot."

Skerchock pressed his lips together and shook his head in wonder. "And here I never thought Ray would ever have more than two credits to rub together." He looked at the ongoing scene in front of them. "C'mon, let's go break this up before they get *really* embarrassing."

"Okay," Ake said, approaching the yelping mass of fur. "I think that's about enough—"

"Ake!" shouted Maximilian gleefully.

"Oh, no—"

In a flash, Maximilian, Clementine, Telzey, and Emma had surrounded Ake and were licking his face and putting their massive paws on his shoulders. Not surprisingly, Ake lost his balance and tumbled to the ground, disappearing under hundreds of kilos of insistent scout dogs.

While Ake was being inundated, Ray sought out Skerchock. Putting his left hand on his friend's shoulder, he pumped Skerchock's right hand for a moment and then drew him toward him and wrapped him up in a huge bear hug. "Damn, it's good to see your ugly face again, Johnny."

"And yours, shorty."

They pulled back a bit and Ray stared at Skerchock. "You look great."

"*I* look great?" said Skerchock. "You're the one who still looks like a kid." He put his hand on Ray's thick mop of curly brown hair. "Haven't lost any of the thatching over the cottage yet. And if you've got any gray hair up there, I can't see it."

"Ah-h-h," Ray waved dismissively. "So, introduce me to the rest of your team."

"Sure," Skerchock said, making a hand signal. "The, ah, leader and his sisters you know, I believe. The others are Dutch, Yolanda, Fritz, Boris, and Moby."

"Moby?" said Ray incredulously. Then he added, "No offense, Moby." The big white dog nodded his shaggy head—he was used to getting that reaction to his name.

"Well, what kind of name is Beowulf?" asked Skerchock. Quickly, he added, "No offense, Beowulf."

"None taken."

"I've heard more intelligent conversations between amoeba, you two," Ake said as he came over to where they stood, brushing away dog hair and adjusting his disheveled clothing. "I mean, you're debating dog names?"

"Funny, hah?" piped in Gawain.

"Okay, you and Ake are right, Gawain," Ray admitted. He made a "come here" gesture at Moby and the other four and they padded over to him. "Dogs is dogs and scout dogs are the best. I'm very pleased to meet you, Boris, Dutch, Fritz, Yolanda, *and* Moby."

"That goes for me, too," Ake sniffed. "Just because he's the team leader, Ray tends to forget that I exist." He joined in the general ear-scratching and head-rubbing that was going on.

"Now what?" asked Littlejohn.

"How long since you guys have eaten?" Skerchock queried.

"Thought you'd never ask," Beowulf replied.

★ ★ ★

After they'd devoured great bowls brimming with spicy bascane stew, sopping up the flavorful juices with fresh baked bread, and enjoyed some of Skerchock's home-brewed beer, Ray and Ake joined their host around a huge bonfire. Most of the dogs settled in, too, except for Boris, Yolanda, and Dutch, who made their goodbyes and then left to patrol the herds.

Against his better judgment, Ray lit up one of Skerchock's real-tobacco cigars. Ake declined the honor. "Whew," he said. "Do those things taste as bad as they smell?"

"Well, no," Skerchock admitted. "That would probably be impossible. They *do* keep away Buchanan's version of mosquitoes, however."

"So would setting your hair on fire," Ake said. "It wouldn't smell any worse, either."

"You're looking good, Johnny," Ray said, between puffs on his cigar.

"That's baloney and you know it." Skerchock patted his slightly protruding stomach. "I've put a couple of kilos on around my middle and I've got more hair on my shoulders and stickin' out of my ears than I have on top of my head. It's you two who look great. So, what's the story—you vampires or something? You know, the 'Undead.' " He grinned. "Sorry 'bout that. My team loves horror holos."

"Well, we *are* undead."

"We are?" gulped Gawain.

" 'Cept for your brain," said Sinbad. "Ray jes' means we's alive."

"I can explain our appearance, but it could be a long story, John," cautioned Ake.

"I'm not going anywhere."

"That's true," considered Ray. "But we'll give you the condensed version anyway." Then he settled back, a mug of home-brewed beer in his hand, and told Skerchock about their violent and eventful tour of duty on Hephaestus. He also told him how, after they escaped from the planet with the Programmers, they ended up on Alexandria—with more money than most people could imagine.

"That is some story," Skerchock conceded. "But how the holy heck did you come out of all that looking so good? They haven't got a fountain of youth on Alexandria, have they?"

"That's where things get interesting," said Ake. "You see, we were . . . ah . . . advancing negatively from a Federation battle cruiser and five fighters just off Alexandria and—"

"As popular with the authorities as ever," laughed Skerchock.

Ake ignored him and continued: "—And we jumped into hyperspace and didn't come out."

Skerchock frowned. "You didn't come out?"

"Not for over an hour, anyway."

"Jesus!" Skerchock was puffing so hard on his cigar that his head was wreathed in acrid smoke.

"Exactly," Ray said. "When we did manage to pop back into normal space, we discovered that twelve years had passed."

"Ah, come on!" said Skerchock, certain that his leg was being rather severely pulled.

"Star Scout's honor." Ray raised his right hand.

Skerchock studied Ray's face for signs of mockery. "If you're telling the truth, it's no wonder you two look like my sons instead of my friends!"

"Well, let's not get insulting!"

"You can understand why we sought out a friendly face," Ake told him earnestly. "We need to know what's happened during the past decade or so."

"We're not entirely in the dark—our ship's computer's been monitoring communications—but we need to get the word from a real human being," Ray said. "You come darn close to fitting that description, so we chose you."

"You was nearby, too," Beowulf said.

"Damn! I don't know where to begin. Besides," Skerchock added, looking wanly at his cigar, "I think I've just made myself dizzy."

"You were always dizzy," Ray told him. "If you need help getting started, how about: 'Once Upon a Time, twelve years ago . . .'?"

"All right," agreed Skerchock. He took a deep breath of clean, clear night air. "Once upon a time twelve years ago the Terran Federation was in turmoil. The Judge Advocate had been reprogrammed, its restraining functions suborned by a brutish and illegally constituted Triumvirate. Unwilling to exchange freedom for slavery, both the free worlds and the colony planets rose in revolt—a revolt led by the Judge Advocate's displaced Prime Programmers." He paused. "How am I doing so far?"

"Excellent," Ake told him.

"The Triumvirate had the soldiers and the weapons, but the Rebellion had something more valuable: an idea. And the idea was that death was preferable to tyranny. So no matter how many battles the Federation won, the rebels kept fighting. Slowly but surely they began to win some of the battles. Small victories at first; but each hard-won success gave the freedom fighters new resolve."

"Oh, boy!" Tajil said. "Sounds like a happy endin' comin'."

"*Sounds* like it, doesn't it?" said Skerchock tersely.

"Uh-oh," Ray said. "Should I close my ears?"

"Yes and no. The truth is, after about seven years of fighting, everything just kind of fell apart. No one won."

"No one?" asked Ake.

"Okay," said Skerchock. "If you want a winner, I'll give you the Rebellion. The rebels *did* essentially destroy the old Federation."

"But . . . ?"

"But they had nothing to put in its place. With the central government eviscerated, the 'Pax Federation' pretty much went the way of the whales. There's a patchwork of planetary governments out there cooperating to some extent, but most of the Federation worlds are reverting to pre-Federation nationalism, racism, and religious intolerance."

"What about Terra?" asked Ray.

"Especially Terra," Skerchock told him. "With the execution of the members of the Triumvirate, the destruction of the Judge Advocate, and the disbanding of the armed forces, what little law and order there is on Terra is being provided by a motley assortment of feudal warlords." He thought that over. "Delete 'law'—the warlords are imposing order, not law."

"Sounds grim," Ake said.

"Well, I sure as hell don't plan on going back to Terra in the near future," Skerchock said. "It's not a good place to be right now. Shit, even the corporations have abandoned Terra to its fate."

"Things must be bad if Archon Corp., Hammurabi Corp., Sennchak Ltd., Dolan Holdings, Assaad Corp., and all the other big boys have jumped ship," Ake mused.

Skerchock removed his cigar, tapped the ash from it, and put it back into his mouth. Staring at him, Ray said, "It looks to me like you haven't told us the worst yet."

"Damn it, Ray, I never could beat you at poker. Yeah, the bad news just keeps on coming." He sighed. "One of the reasons I don't want to go back to Terra anytime soon is what's happened with the scout dogs." At that, all of the dogs' ears picked up.

"So tell us."

He rubbed the back of his neck and grimaced. "Actually, it's all rumors so far."

"*Tell* us," Ray pressed.

"What I've heard—and I repeat that it's only rumor—is that the genetic laboratories have fallen into the hands of the warlords."

"Why would cheap strongmen want control of genetic labs? They'd be no help in ruling a fiefdom," said Ake.

"Oh, no?" replied Skerchock. "Do you have any idea what the genetic labs have been up to recently?" He thought about that for a second. "No, I guess you haven't. When things started getting desperate for the Federation, it began authorizing desperate measures. The labs moved beyond adapting humans for colony world conditions, beyond enhancing the intelligence and size of scout dogs and cats. They began manipulating the genetic makeup of other terrestrial animals—creatures like grizzly and polar bears, chimpanzees, wolverines, crocodiles—anything and everything."

"That's crazy," said Ake. "That makes no sense."

Skerchock shrugged. "The Federation was doing a lot of things that didn't make any sense." He stared into the fire and continued. "They even began experimenting with xeno-gene manipulation, seeing what kinds of horrors they could produce from the alien lifeforms brought back for study."

"What came out of all this?" Ray asked.

Skerchock shook his head. "I don't know. There's a good chance the Federation collapsed around them before they could produce tangible results. In any event, things fell apart and the flow of information coming from Terra has all but dried up."

"What 'bout the scout dogs?" Beowulf asked.

"Again, I don't know. If they're not all dead, they may be in the hands of the warlords."

"Oh, no!" exclaimed Mama-san.

"Oh, yes," Skerchock said grimly.

Ray's cigar fell to the ground, bounced once, and rolled into the fire—he'd bitten it in half.

III

After Ray, Ake, and Skerchock had gone to bed, the dogs gathered around the embers of the dying fire. Even those members of Skerchock's team supposed to be on guard duty joined the meeting.

"So," said Boris, a large reddish-brown dog. "At last we gets to meet the great Beowulf and his pack."

Ignoring the hint of sarcasm in Boris's voice, Beowulf said, "We meeted before, but you was jes' a whelp. That was twelve of the humans' years ago."

"Yah," said Dutch, "if'n you can believe that Ray guy."

When the fur rose in clumps on Frodo's and Littlejohn's shoulders and back, Maximilian said, "You two stay back, this my team." Then he went over to Dutch and snarled at him. "What with you? You got no manners at all?"

"Sure, stick up for him 'cause he was your master onct, and 'cause your 'mommy' here!"

Maximilian bared his teeth by curling his upper lip back and his lower one down. Maximilian's ears rose and pointed forward, his tail stood straight up, and his legs straightened to make him appear more massive and powerful. Trembling with top-dog anger, Maximilian growled and leapt on Dutch before the black-and-white dog could offer any signs of submission.

The snarling, slashing confrontation was all but over as soon as Maximilian had Dutch on his back. "Yield," growled Maximilian.

Admitting his defeat, Dutch adopted the juvenile position of a puppy, indicating his acceptance of Maximilian's dominance. "I yield to Maximilian."

"Way to go, Max," said Telzey, appreciating her brother/leader's prowess.

"We sorry to cause you trouble," Beowulf said.

"You not cause trouble," Telzey told him. "Dutch jes' a natcherly rambunctious guy. Max a good leader; he not hold a grudge."

As if to prove her point, Maximilian graciously allowed Dutch to nuzzle and lick his face. Having made his peace with his victorious pack leader, Dutch accepted his role in the group—subservient to Maximilian, the alpha dog.

"I wants us all to be friends," Max insisted. "When I was with Ray and Ake, Beowulf was the leader. To me, he will always be the leader." Then he did something as gracious and generous as it was surprising to his own pack—he lowered himself in front of Beowulf and then licked the other dog's muzzle.

"Ah, get up, Max," Beowulf said in a gravelly voice that betrayed how much the gesture had affected him. "You an equal; you not one of my pack."

"No, I not . . . but I *was* onct, and I never forget what I learned from you."

"Come," said Mama-san, ever the keeper of the Ways of the Pack. "Let us say the Law. Beowulf . . . ?"

"No, not me," Beowulf said gruffly. "I think it Maximilian's place to lead us in the saying of the Law. We his guests."

"Thank you, Beowulf."

The dogs formed a large, ragged circle.

"What is the Law?" intoned Maximilian.

"*To place duty above self, honor above life.*"

"What is the Law?"

"*To allow harm to come to no Man, to protect Man and his possessions.*"

"What is the Law."

"*To stand by Man's side—as dogs will always stand. Together, Man and dog.*"

"That is good, very good," Maximilian said.

"Yes, the Law is good," agreed Beowulf, "but I think we will soon be breakin' it—us and our Man."

"Break the Law!" said a shocked Fritz.

"We must help the dogs on my team's birth world," Beowulf explained. "We mebbe gots to kill humans to do that."

"He is right," said Frodo.

"Your Ray will do this?" Moby questioned.

"Yes," Beowulf said without elaboration. Then he raised his muzzle to the sky and emitted a long, soulful howl.

The others took up the cry.

5

With Beowulf and Maximilian by their sides, Ray and John Skerchock reclined on a small hillock, propping themselves up on their elbows and ostensibly keeping an eye on the skittish herds of bascane. Ray's team had temporarily joined Skerchock's, so the well-trained dogs had things well in hand. The outing was really an opportunity for Ray and Skerchock to talk. The two dogs were content to lie close to each other and to their human leaders and friends.

"Damn it, John, this is great. This is the life." Ray sighed and drew on his cigar.

"Yeah, livin' here beats the pants off of livin' just about anyplace else . . . especially some place like Terra."

Ray slowly turned his head to look at Skerchock. "Why'd you say that, John? You thinking of going back to Terra?"

Still staring out over the bascane-covered prairie, Skerchock replied quietly, "No, but *you* are."

"Me?" Ray's voice was convincingly innocent. "*Au contraire, mon frère*."

"The story of your life is that you somehow always manage to put yourself in death-defying situations and then successfully extract yourself and the dogs from them."

"Do I do that?" Ray asked, his face such a study in innocence that Beowulf couldn't help chuckling. "Now stop that!" Ray told the big dog. "You're ruining my act!"

Skerchock grinned. "Beowulf's heard all your bullshit for far too long to be taken in by it."

Evaluating Skerchock's grin, Ray said, "I guess Beowulf's not the only one, huh?" Then he sobered a bit and added, "Yeah, I like to set buildings on fire and then run into them, I must confess."

"Apparently you didn't get enough of that on Chiron and Hephaestus," Skerchock said. "I would have thought that going up against the General and the Cadre and then a pack of homicidal prisoners and the whole damn Federation would have been enough for any man." When Beowulf chuckled at that, Skerchock smiled ruefully and said, "Yeah, I know—now it's me who's shoveling out the cholo manure."

Beowulf glanced over at Ray and then at Skerchock and said, "You both funny. Ray and us dogs likes to do dangerous things—to get into trouble and then get out of it." Beowulf grinned crookedly. "And you knows it, too, John. That why you do the same thing, why you gots a team."

"Looks like Beowulf's got us both pegged, John."

Drawing on his cigar so strongly that he made the ash on the tip glow a deep red, Skerchock exhaled a voluminous plume of smoke and said, "Ah, hell."

"Ah, hell?"

"You *are* going to Terra, you little idiot. Aren't you?"

Ray looked at Beowulf. "Ake and I talked to Beowulf and the rest of our team this morning. They're not happy about what could be happening to the scout dogs back on Terra."

"It not be right to make dogs do bad things," insisted Beowulf.

"No, it not," said Maximilian.

"So you're going?" Skerchock persisted.

"Probably."

"Probably . . . ?"

"Shit, yes!" Ray shouted.

"I knew it," Skerchock said smugly.

★ ★ ★

"Damn," Ray said. "I used to take jumping in stride." He looked at his quivering hands. "I'm shaking like a newlywed."

"For us there will never be a routine jump as long as we live," Ake said. "Once burned—"

"Forever afraid of matches," Ray finished.

"Look on the bright side," suggested the ship's computer. "You could get killed on Terra and never have to make another jump."

"That the bright side?" queried Grendel.

"It is for 'her,' " Ray said. "The iron maiden would like nothing better than to be rid of us both."

"That's not true," the ship's computer objected.

"It's not?"

"No, I would not like to see anything happen to Dr. Ringgren."

"Say good night, Gracie!" Ray snapped.

"Boy," said Beowulf, having listened to this exchange, "the machine-woman good at gettin' Ray's goat."

"Yeah," agreed Ake. "It's wonderful."

"Just set a course for Terra and shut up," Ray said. He pretended to be annoyed with Ake, but his heart wasn't in it.

"Terra it is. That'll do for the next day or so, as we enter the inner system," Ake said. "But then what? Terra's a good-sized world."

"Well, ah . . . NorAm. Boswash, I guess. I think that the gene labs are located near the old Federal City." He thought about that. "Or were."

"So where do we put down? One of the main spaceports?"

Ray shook his head. "I shouldn't think so. I believe the Federation's research complex has its own landing areas—or at least it did. The labs are in a vast triangular area northwest of the Capital. Most of the area was devastated during the Second American Revolution of 2031. There had been a number of medical and research complexes there before the cigarette pack bombs of 'The New Patriots Under God' wiped the maps clean. When they rebuilt, they made an effort to basically duplicate the old configurations."

"Okay, that's where we're landing then, I guess," Ake said.

★ ★ ★

"Shouldn't we have been challenged by the orbiting defensive shield by now?"

Ake glanced at the readouts floating in the air in front of him. "You're right. According to our instrumentation, we are buns-deep into the planetary defensive belt."

"There's no sentry ships, no launch platforms, no anything."

"Well, I wouldn't say that," Ake replied, pointing to the forward-view holo. An object in the center of the picture was growing larger and larger by the second.

"Is that what I think it is?" Ray asked.

"Let's see. Magnify twenty times," Ake commanded the computer. At once the object resolved itself into a jumble of girders, beams, tubes, and spheres.

"Dear Lord!" Ray gasped.

"Yeah. It's Luna Two," Ake said, adding unnecessarily, "the space station."

"It's been gutted," Ray said, staring in awe at the lifeless assemblage of plasteel, slowly turning aimlessly. "John told us what happened to Terra, but somehow it didn't register until now."

The gigantic artificial moon had clearly borne the brunt of a furious attack and a sudden—and catastrophic—loss of atmosphere and gravity. Here and there, corpses floated, some in spacesuits, most not.

"Christ," Ray murmured, "you'd think they'd have had the decency to retrieve all the bodies."

Ake shrugged. "Death is indecent, not what happens to your body afterwards."

"I suppose so."

"I wonder what we'll find down there." Ake pointed at the blue-green planet they'd once called home.

"You want the truth?"

"Certainly."

"A lot more death."

"I changed my mind—lie to me!"

As they approached NorAm, the computer announced that they were receiving a transmission. "Let's have it," Ake said.

A holographic image of a thickly built man with black hair materialized in front of them. "I am Pettis Hagan, aide to General Xian—The Shining Path. Identify your ship and why you are initiating maneuvers which will bring you down in General Xian's territory."

"We are *The Spirit of St. Louis*," Ake told him. "And we wish to visit the genetic labs near the field."

"The genetic labs?" Hagan seemed startled. "There are no

more genetic labs here. This area is under the beneficent control of General Xian, The Shining Path."

"That may be," put in Ray, doing his best not to roll his eyes or otherwise make a face at Hagan's repetition of "The Shining Path." "We still wish permission to land."

The thickset man stared at them for several long seconds; then his wide face broke into a broad smile. "Permission granted. Continue your landing. We are always ready to welcome visitors. The docking fee is fifty thousand credits. Do you have the fee?"

"Yes, we do."

Hagan smiled even more broadly, if such a thing was possible. "Good, then you may proceed."

"Is that all?" Ake asked.

"For now." Hagan's image dissolved into a shower of multicolor specks that quickly disappeared.

"What do you make of that?"

"Wear your armored underwear."

"But what about this 'The Shining Path' business?" Ake asked.

"Probably just the reflection from a mushroom-shaped fireball."

II

As heavily armed and as defensively clad as Cadre shock troopers, Ray and Ake prepared to lower the ship's main loading ramp. Each man wore a flexible moly-weave protective vest under a radiation-resistant jacket and trousers tucked into infantry-issue boots. "I'd feel silly about wearing all this stuff and packing all this weaponry," Ray told Ake, "if Hagan didn't make me think that we will need it."

"The machine-woman ready?" Tajil asked.

"You ready, 'machine-woman'?" Ray inquired of the computer.

"I am always ready, Ray."

Impressed by her bold assertion, Ray said, "Oh, I see you've been talking to the weapons again." Then he frowned. "Don't take them too seriously—their whole purpose for existing is to gloriously sacrifice themselves."

"I have no intention of voluntarily terminating my own existence," the computer reassured him.

"Good."

Frodo, Mama-san, Gawain, and Littlejohn slowly ambled down the lowered ramp, sharp canine ears alert, testing the air with sharp canine noses. "Okay, so far," said Littlejohn. "C'mon down." Ray and Ake, surrounded by the rest of the team, walked down the steep incline, careful not to lose their footing. Ray knew if he slipped and fell he'd bounce and roll all the way to the bottom like a bale of cotton.

They didn't really expect to find much of anyone around, even on crowded Terra, given that the area was a restricted access government reservation for at least twenty-five kilometers in every direction.

"This 'aide' we spoke to," Ake said. "What's his name again?"

"Pettis Hagan."

"That's it. Anyway, he or someone else should be along shortly to collect the 'landing fee.'"

"It's nice to see that the spirit of commerce isn't dead."

"Let's make sure *we* don't end up dead. I expect that we're going to have to buy off local bandit chiefs; I got no problem with that."

"But . . . ?"

"But I don't want us paying our money and then taking a bolt from an energy rifle up the disposal chute."

"Gotcha."

"Speaking of the devil. . . ."

An armored military half-track appeared at the far end of the field and rumbled toward them. The driver was a heavy-set man with a head of flowing black hair. Hagan. Six sullen-looking men, reminiscent of the hard-bitten, hardcore prisoners on Hephaestus, sat clutching energy rifles in the open back. In addition to the other weapons, the half-track sported a laser cannon mounted in the cargo area.

"I didn't think old Hagan would bring six of the General's mercenaries to the party."

"What did you think?" Ray asked. "That he would show up by himself with a carafe of coffee and some pound cake? This is even better than we might have hoped for."

"Is it?"

"Sure, it'll make them even less wary, outnumbering us three to one."

"They don't outnumber us if they count our dogs."

"Mouth breathers like these dildos don't think twice about dogs."

The squat driver and four of the six others climbed out of their carrier. Ray observed that someone had painted a crimson skull's head symbol on the doors. The anthropologist in him laughed. *The "tribe" always feels more powerful if they make a brave show of exhibiting their totems*, he reminded himself.

The group approached *The Sprit of St. Louis*. Two of the men remained seated in the armored carrier, resting the butts of their large energy rifles on their knees. One of them leaned over and said something to the second. In response, the second man put down his energy rifle and manned the laser cannon. When he saw the man's image shimmering, Ray guessed that the troop area of the half-track was protected by a low-energy force field. While such a field was useless against powerful weapons, Ray knew that it was sufficient to turn away small-arms fire.

The heavy-set man stared at the defensively arrayed man/dog team. "I'm Pettis Hagan," he said unnecessarily. Then he added, "Dogs. You didn't tell me you had dogs."

"That's right," Ake said. "We didn't."

"Hmmph." The man folded his arms.

"Nice little troop carrier you got there," Ray said. "Looks like Cadre issue."

"Yeah, we liberated it during the Rebellion."

"I'll bet you did."

Hagan turned around and exchanged looks with one of his six backups. Neither Ray nor Ake could see what sort of expression or signal may have crossed his face.

Turning back to them, Hagan said, "You said you had the money to pay for landing in a territory under the beneficent protection of General Xian." It was a statement, not a question.

"We got it." Ray motioned and Ozma trotted over with the handle of a small satchel clasped between her teeth. Ray nodded and Ozma approached the stocky man and dropped the satchel at his feet.

"Is it all there?"

"All fifty thousand, yes," Ake said.

"I dunno," Hagan said, making no attempt to pick up the satchel. He stared appreciatively at *The Spirit of St. Louis*. "A ship like that, a yacht, costs a lot of credits. I think you two can afford to pay a little more."

"Really?" asked Ake. "How much more?" He took a half step forward. Ray glanced at Ake's back for reassurance.

"Say another fifty thousand."

Ray looked at Ake and then at the heavy-set man waiting for a response. "Ozma." Ozma picked up the satchel and brought it back to Ray.

"The General don't like deadbeats."

"Fuck the General," said Ray, grabbing the slug-throwing handgun he'd taped on Ake's back and shooting Hagan through the forehead.

The thunderous retort from Ray's slug-thrower seemed to paralyze everyone. A fine red mist clouded the air behind the surprised-to-be-dead man, and he wavered a moment before falling forward on his face.

Everyone exploded into motion. Fortunately, Hagan's flunkies had to take a second or so to figure out who to target—Ray and Ake, or the dogs. It was a fatal hesitation: The dogs were on two of them in an instant. The others seemed to be moving as if they were underwater. They were probably ruthless killers; they were not, however, paramilitary professionals in the same league with Ray and Ake.

"Right," shouted Ake as he shouldered his energy rifle and snapped off a succession of short bolts. One would have been enough—the one that burned a hole through the man's torso.

Ray simply moved his still-outstretched arm slightly, targeting the man on the left. He fired two shots, one of which shattered the plaswood stock of the man's energy rifle before continuing on through the man's chest. The unfortunate man's own weapon was knocked off target, and the several bolts struck *The Spirit of St. Louis*. The force field protecting the ship absorbed the energy effortlessly.

<Now!> Ake said.

In response, one of the ship's impressive laser turrets swung around to point at the armored carrier. Several tightly focused beams of energy lanced out, easily piercing the weak force field and striking the two men in the troop area. The laser blasts burned through the two hapless reserves like a white-hot poker thrust through a snowman.

For Ray, it was as if he'd been in the vacuum of an airlock suddenly opened to the atmosphere. He became aware of a rush of sound: the dying screams of the two men the dogs had attacked, and the concussive explosions of the extra energy packs that the men in the carrier had worn slung over their shoulders. After that, there was only silence.

Beowulf, Littlejohn, and Mama-san looked up, their muzzles crimson. "These guys done for," Beowulf said.

Ray stared at him for a second and then went over to the dogs and touched them on their broad heads, reassuring them with his touch. "Beowulf, Littlejohn, and Mama-san—I'm sorry for what I've made you do."

"That okay," Mama-san said reassuringly.

"I'm afraid that this is only the beginning. I must ask you to harm a lot more humans before we're done."

Mama-san nodded. "We prepared to do what it takes to save other dogs."

"Yah," Littlejohn agreed.

"I doan think we can say the Law again 'til this all over," Beowulf said in a heavy voice.

Ray nodded somberly. "Now, let's get this mess cleaned up and get the hell out of here before this General Xian sends more of his goons."

"You think they gonna know who did this?" Tajil asked.

"Thanks for reminding me, Taddy." Ray took a small message cube from a pocket, walked over to Hagan and carefully propped it on the dead man's chest. "When they play that, they will," he said. Then he went white, doubled over, and threw up.

III

Ray took one last look around the interior of *The Spirit of St. Louis* and remarked, "Well, I guess we've thought of everything."

"And then some," the ship's computer told him.

"Ah-h-h, I'm gonna miss you, babe," Ray responded.

"I can use my time alone to excellent advantage."

Ray considered that strangely worded reply. "Hey—you're gonna miss *us*, too, aren't you?"

"I . . . have grown quite fond of Ake . . . and Beowulf and the others have often voiced gratitude for my meal preparation—for which I am grateful."

"And that's all?"

"The time alone will be useful."

"But lonely, too."

"I do not get 'lonely.' That is a human concept. I understand it intellectually, of course. But I will not be lonely and I will not 'miss' you, either."

"Hmmph," Ray grunted. He walked to the exit ramp.

"Ray?" the computer called to him.

"Yeah, what?"

"Be careful, please."

After they had vacated the immediate vicinity of *The Spirit of St. Louis*, it took off, piloted by the computer. Its destination was a geosynchronous parking orbit thousands of kilometers above the North American continent.

"Well, there she goes," sighed Ake. "We're well and truly on our own now."

"Yah," said Beowulf gleefully.

"Now what?" Littlejohn asked.

"Now we locate the gene labs and see what, if anything, we can do. Then we find someplace to stay until General Xian or someone like him contacts us again."

"If that gonna happen," said Tajil, "why'd we do what we done? Why we kill all those mens?"

"That's a fair question," Ray said. "They thought we were victims—prey, not predators. We've shown them otherwise."

"Why you say 'or someone like him'?" Tajil persisted.

Ray tugged at one ear and shrugged. "Because it doesn't matter who decides to hire us for our charming personalities. What does matter—the whole point of this charade—is that *someone* will want us. I don't give a flying donut if it's General Xian or Killer Kane or Luthor."

"Luthor?" Sinbad whispered to Mama-san. "Who that?"

"Marlon Luthor. I think he was the Pope of Germany," she whispered back. It came out as Bope.

"Oh," said Sinbad as if he understood. He had no idea what a bope was.

"What are you two whispering about back there?" Ray asked.

"Jes' talkin' 'bout the Bope of Germany," Sinbad volunteered.

Ray stared at him a long time, then shook his head. "Sometimes I don't understand you guys at all."

"Let's not stand around here all day," Ake said.

"Ake right," agreed Beowulf.

Ray used hand gestures to signal them into position. They moved out smartly, quickly crossing the open space between them and the armored carrier. The dogs stared at the blades of grass which had insinuated themselves through cracks in the weathered pavement.

"Boy, this awful," opined Gawain. "Why this field in such bad shape?"

"I don't know, Gawain," Ake replied. "I guess it's because no one is maintaining essential services any longer."

"Things have really deteriorated," Ray agreed.

It was only after they reached the huge armored vehicle their brief firefight had earned them that its impressive size became apparent. Ake approached the driver's side and said, "I'm driving, right?"

"Absolutely."

"Great." Then he considered something. "Ah, which way should I head?"

"Don't ask me," Ray told him. "You're the driver."

"Yeah, but where are the labs?"

Ray thought for a moment. "Well, let's get off this field first. When we're out on the road, maybe we'll have a better idea which way we should go." He reconsidered that. "Look for anything which says Bethesda."

As Ake clambered up the steps to the cab, Ray and Beowulf did the same from the other side. The rest of the team climbed into the back of the monstrous half-track, into the area meant to hold a squad of troops. "This is really something out of the history books," Ray told Beowulf as Ake found the control that raised and lowered the rear ramp.

"It real old?" Beowulf asked.

"I don't think so. Apparently the Federation started producing them again during the Rebellion. I guess there are times when the tried and true is the way to go."

Ake started up the engine and it roared to life with a deep rumble. "Jeeze!"

"Yeah," said Ray. "*The Spirit of St. Louis* has more power than a thousand of these things, but this monster *sounds* as if it eats hovercraft for breakfast."

Ake pressed down on the accelerator and the half-track moved forward slowly. "Hey, I like this."

Ake awkwardly turned the large wheel and swung the half-track around to retrace Hagan's path. In minutes they'd crossed the broad, flat expanse of the landing field and were out on a crumbling plascrete roadway. Since it was an access road leading to the little-used—or abandoned—landing field, there was no traffic.

"I see something coming up," Ake said.

"That looks like one of the major roads through the complex," Ray said. "Let's take the first side street with buildings that we come to."

"Good idea."

Once they reached an intersection and turned off the access road, they felt less vulnerable to a retaliatory attack from Xian or his lieutenants.

"This is creepy," Ake said as they drove down a plascrete road nearly devoid of traffic. What few hovercraft there were quickly turned down side streets or made U-turns and beat a hasty retreat. "It's not like Terra is deserted. The most recent census said there's still four billion people on the planet. Boswash alone is supposed to have a population of fifty or sixty million."

"The old gray Boswash ain't what it used to be, I'm afraid," Ray said. "Besides, I think the majority of those people are up around Old New York. This may still be the Boston-to-Washington population corridor that began to coalesce in the late twentieth century, but it's started to empty out a bit."

"That's probably true," Ake said. "I remember reading something about Boswash hitting its peak about a century ago, not long after the Second American Revolution, and it's been in decline ever since."

"And if everything we hear about the general lack of central authority is true, I wouldn't expect many people to be out and about." Then he remembered where he was and added, "And I'm sure seeing this baby plowing through the research reservation discourages whatever gawkers might be on the grounds. Everyone still thinks this runaround belongs to the local tough guy."

"Then you don't think these grounds are under *any* sort of official control any longer?" Ake asked.

"Sure doesn't look like it."

"Hey—lookit," Beowulf said, nodding toward the graffiti-covered buildings lining the street. Virtually every building bore vivid markings—the most prominent being the crimson grinning skull that seemed to be Xian's icon.

"Looks like Xian is the big dog around here, but with lots of smaller gangs claiming a piece of the pie." Ray thought about that for a minute. "You know, I don't think this Xian guy carries such a big stick after all; I mean, he shouldn't be just the toughest of the bunch—he should *be* the bunch. The fact that he's got competition doesn't augur well for him."

"Augur? You've been scanning dictionary cubes again." Then Ake looked at the gang-marked buildings again and marveled, "This is out of a hist-holo."

"Things really regressed while we were over the rainbow," Ray told him. He touched Ake's arm. "All this is making me nervous. I'm going to climb in the back and man the laser cannon."

"What about me?" protested Ake. "I don't even know where I'm going."

"Just keep heading in the same general direction," Ray said. "Look for signs directing you to the Terran Federation Institute of Canine Genetics or something similar."

"As easy as that?"

"It should be," Ray said.

"'No Indians around here,' General Custer said. '*Should* be a picnic,'" Ake said pointedly.

"That's right," Ray agreed. "No Indians around here."

Ake slapped his forehead. "I give up!"

PART TWO

Svoboda

6

Ray climbed down into a narrow passageway that bisected the half-track just behind the seats. The passageway connected the cab to the back via a blast-resistant hatch.

As he emerged in the remarkably large cargo/personnel-carrying area in the rear, Ray noted at least three of the dogs up along the sides sticking their heads out into the breeze flowing past. "Ah, guys . . . get down from there, please. I don't think that's such a good idea."

"Why not?" asked Frodo. "The force field is 'round us, ain't it?"

"Yes, it is," Ray agreed. "But it's a weak one that can't stop all that much. The ship's lasers proved that."

"Hey, lookit that!" Grendel shouted roughly.

Ray rushed over and peered over the top of the half-track's sides. "What? I don't see anything."

"There—see?"

Ray did see now. Paralleling the half-track, but a few meters behind, were a half-dozen kids on hoverboards. They ranged in age from around ten or eleven to the late teens. When they saw Ray's face cautiously peering over the top edge of the truck's side, they jeered him and made obscene gestures.

"Well, now we know where all the graffitti comes from," Ray said. Even as he spoke, one of the kids lost control and veered into the side of the half-track.

"Ake, stop!" Ray yelled into the intercom.

As the truck screeched to a halt, Ray said, "Okay, everyone else stay put. I'll be right back."

"What's the matter?" asked Ake, but Ray was already out of the half-track. By the time he got back to where the accident had happened, the youth had picked himself up—apparently none the worse for his tumble—and beat a hasty retreat to where his friends waited for him.

"Hey, you forgot something," Ray called out to no avail. Bending over, he picked up the abandoned hoverboard. Like its departed owner, it too had sustained little damage. Ray shrugged and took it back to the half-track with him.

"What's that?" asked Frodo.

"A hoverboard," Ray explained. "You ride it like a surfboard and . . ." Since they didn't know what a surfboard was, that explanation didn't work. "You just, ah, hover and you . . ." He stopped again. "This is too hard. Take my word for it, it's a hoverboard."

Then Ray became the leader of the pack again. "See, Frodo, those kids could've been armed with heavy weapons, waiting for you to stick your heads out so they could shoot them off."

"Uh-huh," said an unconvinced Frodo. "Then why you jump out of truck altogether? Accident coulda bin trick, too."

Ray knew he'd walked into that one. "Yeah, well . . . ah, yeah." Then he smiled sheepishly. "I'm sorry, Frodo. I just worry about you guys a lot. You and Ake are all I've got."

"Thanks, Ray," Frodo and Ozma said, coming over to lick his hand. "You all we got, too."

"I'm sure that tastes good, but how about some food?"

"Yah!" they all yelled enthusiastically.

"I thought that might be a popular idea." Ray opened one of the packs they'd loaded into the back of the half-track. "Now, let's see . . . yeah, here it is." He got out several flexible vacuum-sealed foodsacs and popped them open.

Gawain strained and shoved and worked his way to the front of the queue. "Hey, you gots *real* food."

"Yeah, I brought along as much fresh ground meat and other perishables as I could. I figured that we'll all be reduced to eating the irradiated and the freeze-dried stuff soon enough." He pulled out nine bowls, filled them with the dogs' provisions, and got out of the way. The dogs' dedication to emptying their bowls as quickly as possible never failed to amuse him. *They have one rule about food*, he thought. *Eat it as fast as you can!*

When the dogs raised their heads, licking their muzzles with large pink tongues, Ray glanced at his watch and pretended to have timed them. "Amazing! You set a new record."

"Now what?" asked Beowulf, his sides heaving as he belched loudly.

"Now I man the laser cannon."

"'Specting trouble?"

"No more than usual, Beowulf," Ray said. "But someone's gonna find the mess we left behind sometime, and when that happens things are bound to get interesting."

"Good," said the big dog.

"Check out this electronic highway sign we're getting," Ake said. After an attention-getting chime had sounded, the message broadcast by the road appeared on the readout.

The display read:

TERRAN FEDERATION
ANIMAL GENETICS RESEARCH
AND DEVELOPMENT
BETHESDA, MARYLAND
AUTHORIZED PERSONNEL ONLY
BEYOND THIS POINT

"Are we 'authorized personnel'?" Ake asked.

Ray tapped his energy rifle. "Yes. And I brought my authorization with me."

"Heh, heh," Beowulf chuckled.

Ake drove the half-track past the sign, turned into the driveway, and roared up an access road. Here and there empty guardposts bore mute testimony to the facility's one-time importance.

The huge armored vehicle ground to a stop. Saying "Why'd I bother coming up front?" Ray climbed back down into the hatchway and followed Beowulf into the rear.

Ake came around to the back of the half-track and lowered the rear ramp, which folded out and down. The dogs scrambled down nimbly while Ray, stiff from the ride, carefully picked his way.

"Don't hurry, old-timer," Ake chided him.

"Just you wait, you young whippersnapper! Someday you'll be an old codger like me, and then you'll be sorry you were fresh with me."

"I'm sorry now."

"Are we there?" asked Mama-san, looking around.

"We're someplace," Ake said. They were in a thirty-by-thirty-meter square, empty except for a motley mixture of surface vehicles and hovercraft. Stripped of anything that could be removed, probably by some of the same kids Ray had seen in the street, none of the vehicles looked operable.

"This is . . . ah, what's the old term for it? A parking lot," Ray said.

Beyond the empty lot was an imposing-looking wall that was at least six meters high. Ake approached the wall and reached out and touched it after a moment's hesitation. His hand skimmed across its surface. "This wall appears to be made from low-friction petropolymers."

"What's that mean?" asked Tajil.

"It's slicker than snot," Ray said. After Ake shot him a disgusted look, he added, "And it's topped by razor-sharp coils of barbed wire. They haven't made it easy to get in."

"Or out," said Beowulf.

"So where *is* the entry point?" Ake wondered.

Frodo trotted a few meters along the perimeter of the wall, stopped, sniffed, and looked at the featureless surface in front of him. "Hey, here." Ray, Ake, and the others followed his summons.

"What is it?" Ake asked.

"Jes' look," Frodo told him.

"There's nothing here. Only another section of wall and . . . Oh!"

"This is definitely cute," Ray said, reaching slowly toward the wall, which was flickering slightly. When his fingertips were only a few centimeters away, he paused. "Yes, I feel it."

"Feel what?" asked Mama-san.

"It's a force field, Mama-san," Ray told her.

"Why's it look like the wall?" Gawain wanted to know.

"'The wall' here is a projection," Ray explained. He

glanced right and then left. "I'd say there's a good-sized force-field gate here." He pointed down at the plascrete surface outside the gate. "If you look closely, you can see the residue of lubricants from vehicles idling outside, waiting permission to enter."

"All right, we found this place, but how do we get in?" Ake wanted to know.

Ray stepped back from the shimmering entryway and began looking around. Finding an empty beer container, he picked it up and threw it underhanded at the section of false wall. When the self-cooling container struck the force field, it disintegrated in a flash of light. "Hmmm. When the door's locked—and this one is—you find another way in."

"Mebbe there be another door," Beowulf said.

"Another door . . ." Ray said, thinking. Then he brightened. "That's it, there's another door just down the wall."

"There is?" said Ake dubiously. "I don't see anything."

"That's because we didn't kick it open yet."

II

"Stay down," Ray commanded Ake and the dogs.

Ray trained the barrel of the laser cannon on a section of wall, aimed, and fired a short series of up-and-down bursts remarkably like someone watering a lawn. The effect was startlingly violent. The polychemical matrix of the wall bubbled and smoked, then gave up its imprisoned energy as heat and light, bursting into flame and exploding.

"Gee, I hope no one heard that," Ray deadpanned.

"Fat chance," said Ake, slowly rising from the floor of the half-track to eyeball the results of Ray's attack. "I think dead people ten years in the grave heard it."

"It couldn't be helped," Ray said.

"We could have tried ringing the doorbell."

Ray slapped his forehead with the palm of his hand. "Ai, Cisco, *now* you tell me!"

"C'mon, Ray, let us out. We wants to see!" Littlejohn implored.

Ray lowered the rear ramp and the dogs scrambled down and out of the half-track. "Hey, don't get too close," he shouted after them. "That rubble will be smoldering for a while yet."

"Yah, yah," Ozma tossed back over her shoulder.

"Boy, lookit that!" exclaimed Frodo.

"Ray sure blasted a hole in that wall," agreed Sinbad.

The dogs edged up closer and closer, until they were almost at the raggedly rectangular opening. Their noses wrinkled in that way peculiar to canines, and their ears stood erect as they peered through the smoke and dust.

"They certainly listen to their lord and master," Ake kidded Ray. Both men knew that the dogs were like unruly teenagers at times, pushing the limits whenever they could. But they obeyed Ray without hesitation when the situation warranted it.

"So, what do you see?" Ray called to them.

"Nuthin'," Beowulf replied.

"Nothing?"

"Well, not much, anyhow."

Ray and Ake joined the dogs at the ruined wall. Ray had to agree with Beowulf—there wasn't much to see. There was nothing immediately inside the wall, and the nearest building appeared to be about fifty to sixty meters away, half hidden behind a stand of evergreens.

"Let's get back in the half-track," Ake suggested. "Not that it's too far to walk to that building—or to one beside or beyond it. But I feel safer wearing the half-track around me."

"Me, too. C'mon, dogs."

"Awww, do we haft to?" said Beowulf.

Ray considered that for a minute. "Okay, go ahead. But keep your eyes and ears open, you hear?"

"We will," promised Littlejohn.

The dogs began picking their way through the rubble of the ruined wall, stopping after every few steps to sniff and stare at the browning blades of grass for evidence of mines or other explosives. It was a routine precaution.

They made their way across the grass and onto the road that ran from the real entrance. Their very presence there meant that Ray and Ake could cross the same expanse of grass safely in the half-track. Ake powered up the huge vehicle and it rumbled through the blast opening like some great prehistoric beast on the prowl.

The dogs both flanked the half-track and ran ahead of it, their keen senses alert to any movement or sign of possible danger. Like the little of Terra they'd seen so far, the compound seemed strangely unpopulated.

"Shouldn't there be *someone* around?" Ake asked, bemused by the eerie emptiness.

"Maybe they were going to welcome us with milk and cookies until they heard what we did to Hagan and his cohorts."

"I'm serious."

Ray made a face. "I'm at least half serious, myself." Then he pointed a finger down at the seat of the half-track. "Don't forget whose car we borrowed and are parading around in like Kings of Kafiristan."

Ake slowed the half-track and then brought it to a complete stop. "Well, here we are—wherever 'here' is."

Ray climbed down his side of the half-track, jumping the last half-meter from the bottom step to the ground. "Next time, I'm asking for longer legs," he told an amused Tajil.

"Now what, Ray?" Beowulf asked as Ake joined them from his side of the vehicle.

"Why, we just go up to the door like this," Ray said as he approached the door. "And we knock—like this." He rapped sharply on the metal door. "And they invite us in." He grinned slyly.

"Please come in, gentlemen," a voice boomed in accented Federation-standard English. "I've been expecting you."

Ray's jaw dropped as the door swung open.

★ ★ ★

"Hello," a voice called to them as first Beowulf and then Ray warily passed through the open door and entered a dimly lighted interior. It was not the same voice that had invited them in.

Ray hung back, letting Beowulf's sharper senses scan the room. "Someone here, but I think it okay," Beowulf told him. Nonetheless, the big dog took up a protective stance.

"Who's there?" Ray said, his vision adjusting to the low light level. "Oh." It was not who, but what.

A small, cylindrical shape appeared from the dimness. It rolled forward, slowly and deliberately as if not wanting to cause alarm. It was a small robot, a domestic servant.

"I am Janos," it said.

"Janos?" he questioned.

"Yes. I am Dr. Svoboda's assistant."

"Well, can we come in or what?" Ake's voice called through the doorway. Though he sounded matter-of-fact, he was not. He was waiting for Ray's response. If Ray had encountered some threat he could not speak openly about, he was to answer Ake by using the word "partner."

"Yes, come in."

"It's about time," Ake said as he entered, trailed by the rest of the dogs. He stopped short at the sight of the robot.

"I am Janos," the little 'bot repeated for Ake's benefit. "And you are . . . ?" it asked politely.

"I . . . ah . . . I'm Ake Ringgren." He pointed toward Ray. "And this is my partner, Ray Larkin."

"I am so very pleased to meet you," the 'bot said, extending one of its many hands, one constructed to look and feel human. "We so seldom have visitors." Ake took its hand awkwardly; it was unusual for a 'bot to offer to shake hands. The hand was warm, and Ake smiled automatically, then grimaced as the 'bot's strong grip squeezed his fingers powerfully.

Dropping Ake's hand, Janos looked at Mama-san and several of the other dogs who'd crowded in with Ake and said, "You are a scout dog team. How wonderful. Dr. Svoboda will be so pleased."

"You say that like he doesn't already know," Ray said to the 'bot. "He told us he was expecting us. That is, if that was Dr. Svoboda who spoke to us."

"It was he. I believe he received word only that there were dogs involved. It was not clear that they were scout dogs."

"Oh."

"We's jes' dogs—no need to know our names," Frodo said pointedly.

"Let me introduce you to my team, Janos," Ray said, conceding Frodo's point. He introduced the whole team and Janos nodded and said "Pleased to meet you" to each one in turn.

"Is you just a robot?" asked Gawain directly. His experience with robots didn't encompass one acting like a person—shaking hands and demanding to be introduced to humans as if it were human too.

"I am indeed," Janos said, exhibiting no dismay over

Gawain's directness. "I have been programmed to speak and act like a normal human being."

"Looks like you two won't be able to communicate," Ake said to Ray.

With the directness of an AI being, Janos asked, "May I take you to see Dr. Svoboda now?"

Ake and Ray looked at each other, and Ake shrugged a "Why not?" shrug. "Sure," he told the 'bot.

"Good."

"Mama-san, Tajil, Ozma, and Sinbad, you four stay here and keep an eye on things," Ray told the dogs.

"Ahhh, jeez," sulked Tajil.

"Don't 'Ah, jeez' me, Taddy," Ray said sharply.

"If you will follow me."

Janos led them down a well-lighted corridor filled with low-volume background music, the sort of ersatz classical music churned out by skilled if soulless computer composers. After they passed several multiarmed beach balls on wheels—other robots, but presumably lacking Janos's specialized programming—they approached a series of lift/drop tubes. A simple "you are here" diagram revealed to Ray and Ake why the building seemed relatively modest from the outside: It apparently went down deep into the earth.

"Five underground levels, eh?" Ray asked.

"Yes," Janos said simply.

A door cycled open and Janos stepped into the drop tube and turned and looked at them expectantly.

"No," said Frodo firmly, shaking his huge shaggy head. Several of the other dogs, including Beowulf and Littlejohn, their tails drooping, also resisted entering the drop tube.

"What is the matter, please?" asked the perplexed little 'bot.

"I'm sorry, Janos, but the dogs really dislike drop tubes."

"You do not like drop tubes?" it asked Beowulf.

"No."

The 'bot wrung its hands. It became agitated and seemed upset. "We must see Dr. Svoboda, he has ordered it, yet . . ."

"Janos," said Ake softly, "is there an elevator that we might use instead?"

"An elevator?" it asked. Then its voice brightened. "An elevator, yes! Yes. An elevator."

Ake looked at Ray and arched his eyebrows. When Janos clapped its hands together delightedly and turned to lead them toward the elevator, Ake put his index finger to the side of his head and tapped it in the universal gesture meaning "out to lunch." After Littlejohn guffawed at Ake's action, Ray ordered him to keep silent with a hand gesture.

The robot led them down a quiet and apparently little-traveled hallway and through an unmarked door. "Here is the old elevator that we use for very heavy, very bulky materials," Janos said. When the doors cycled open, it pointed proudly and said, "The elevator."

"Good," said Beowulf, and they trooped on.

A freight elevator, it easily accommodated them all. A very *old* freight elevator, it abruptly fell for a second or two after Janos said, "Level five," before settling into a constant rate of descent. The initial lurch made Ake gasp and he stared straight ahead with a strange look on his face.

I'll never understand how Ake can pilot a spaceship like he was born to it, Ray mused, *yet still turn white in a shuttle craft or an elevator!*

The freight elevator reached the fifth and bottom level, gently bouncing once before settling down. "We are here," Janos said superfluously.

"You may now kiss the floor, Ake," Ray suggested as they exited into yet another obscure corner of the structure. Clearly, the freight elevator was a little-utilized relic; out of sight and out of mind.

They came out a door that opened into a circular corridor. It seemed an unfortunate design touch to Ray, suggesting nothing so much as the interior of a submarine. The floor of the corridor was surfaced with a nonslip synthetic rubber material, and the walls were institutional green. The off-white curvature of the ceiling gently glowed as a result of a combination of self-contained, fusion-powered lights and colonies of luminescent algae—something similar had been used in the mine shafts of Hephaestus.

At an intersection midway down the hall, Janos turned left down another corridor. Apart from more maintenance and repair robots, they encountered no staff members. Ray wondered where everyone was.

"I know we're going to meet him in just a minute," Ray said

to Janos, "but by any chance is Dr. Svoboda an elderly man?"

"Why, yes," the 'bot said brightly. Then it reconsidered that as if it had misspoken itself. "That is, he is many years of age. He is not really 'elderly.' "

"Uh-huh."

"Please follow me," it said.

Finally, Janos announced, "We are here." It pointed at an anachronistic wooden door that bore, in quaint antique script, the words:

Dr. Stanislas K. Svoboda
Director, Terran Genetic Institute

"Yes, we are," agreed Ray. He took a deep breath and said, "Let's meet the good Doctor."

III

Ray turned the door's knob. *Another anachronism*, he thought. As the door swung open, Ray considered what might be revealed: *A "Bride of Frankenstein" laboratory with huge arcs of electricity crackling and leaping from machine to machine, or maybe a butcher's theater with a neurosurgeon in a bloodstained white operating gown inserting thin wire probes into some poor victim's exposed brain!*

What the open door actually revealed was a rather modest-sized office. The walls were blue-gray and several pieces of artwork were tastefully displayed; Ray knew enough about art to recognize that they were carefully chosen works. At the far end of the room, behind a massive real-wood desk, sat a gnomelike little man smoking a pipe. Blue smoke encircled his balding head like storm clouds shrouding a rocky and snow-capped peak. He gestured at them and said, "Come in, gentlemen. Please come in."

"You're Doctor Svoboda?" Ake asked the wizened old man.

"I'm not the great and powerful Wizard of Oz," cracked the tiny figure.

Ray shot Beowulf a look and said, "I don't think we're in Kansas anymore, Toto."

The old man laughed and pounded the desktop with the flat of his hand. "I like you already, Ray . . . or should I call you Mr. Larkin?"

"Ray will do just fine." Then he did a double take. "Oh, you were spying on us during our introduction to Janos?"

"I was curious to see who had come calling. I had hoped it was the gentlemen who'd left their calling card with Xian's goons."

Svoboda looked quizzically at Ake and asked, "And how about you, Dr. Ringgren?"

"Ake will be fine with me, too."

"Good—and you can call me Dr. Svoboda." Then he burst out laughing as if he'd said something enormously amusing.

"Cheer down," said Ray as the old man wiped tears from his eyes. He liked the old codger, but now guessed that he was nuttier than a fruitcake—or perhaps he simply had not been much in the company of lifeforms he hadn't created.

"You can—heh, heh, heh—call me Stan, of course."

Ray shook his head. "I don't think so. Begging your pardon, but you're more a 'Dr. Svoboda' than a 'Stan.' "

"Quite right," he conceded. "There are few things weirder than calling some old arthritic wreck 'Sean' or 'Bobby,' or calling an old hagged-out bag 'Grandma Tammi.' " He burst into giggles again.

"Oh, there are a few things equally odd," Ray said, nodding his head at his surroundings.

Svoboda sighed. "I should have thought to open the main gate. You've gone and breached my wall and now I must repair it."

"Sorry," Ray said as if he meant it.

"Oh, never mind," waved Svoboda. "It won't take long to fix." He keyed something underneath the desk and a holographic image of the area near the main gate coalesced just above the surface of the desk. A contingent of robots were already clearing away the rubble and moving a replacement section of wall into position.

"Excuse me," Ake said, "but I'd like to know what we're doing here."

Svoboda turned off the holo projector and the tiny images of the works disappeared. He sobered a bit and pointed at Ray. "Your young associate was quick to note my references to that old sinny, *The Wizard of Oz*, Dr. Ringgren . . . ah, Ake. I now have another one from it for you both."

"Yeah?"

"I wish you to bring me the broomstick of the Wicked Witch of the West."

It took Ray a second to decipher Svoboda's request. Then, the enormity of it shocked him. "You want us to *kill* him!" Ray gasped.

"Him?" said Ake. "Him who? Who are you two talking about?"

"Why, General Xian, of course," Svoboda said, blowing a smoke ring.

7

"Why do you wish us to kill General Xian?" Ake asked.

"It's simple, really," Svoboda said. "He's the power in this territory, the top dog." He smiled at Beowulf. "If he is removed as a threat to my work, I can continue my research."

"Won't another General Xian just come forward to take his place?"

"That's true," Svoboda conceded. "But *this* General Xian is special. Before General Xian appeared on the scene, this was the sole territory of a certain General DiCiancia, a man one could do business with. For a reasonable sum of money each week, and other—shall we say 'special'—considerations, he was content to leave me in peace to do my work." He shook his head sadly. "But that all changed once Xian showed up to carve out a piece of the territory. He is not a brilliant man, but he *is* smart and competent—smart enough to know that what I do here is worth much more than I am paying DiCiancia and competent enough to take everything I have achieved away from me."

"What's he waiting for, then?" asked Ray. "I mean, hell, we used *his* armored truck to blow a hole in your wall. If we could do it, why couldn't he?"

"Because I have told him that should he breach my defenses, I would destroy the whole compound and everything in it rather than let it fall into his hands."

"Including yourself."

"Including myself."

"So it's a Mex-a-can standoff," said Beowulf.

Svoboda smiled. "What an intelligent dog."

"Yeah, ain't he," Ray said dryly. "But we were discussing Xian's reasons for holding back."

"Yes, of course," Svoboda said. "So far my threat has been successful. But now I fear the General is losing patience and may decide to call my bluff."

"Your threat to blow yourself up is just a bluff?" Ake asked.

Svoboda paused before replying. "That's it—I don't really know. And I *won't* know until and unless Xian forces my hand. Many people put the gun to their head; few actually pull the trigger."

"So we kill General Xian, and DiCiancia will be content to go back to the way things were before?" said Ray.

"All of the pie is so much more satisfying than one half."

"And why should we do this?" Ake queried.

"Because only then I will tell you where to find the scout dogs that were taken from here."

After Ray went back up and brought down the others, all the dogs found spaces and plopped down. Ray and Ake sat at a table in the small conference room Janos had led them to before leaving them alone. They debated what to do next. "I'm not sure we have a choice, Ray," Ake told his partner. "We have to help this Doctor Svoboda and hope he delivers on his part of the bargain."

"Do we?" Ray wondered. "You know why the 'Wizard' sent Dorothy and the others on their mission to retrieve the Witch's broomstick, don't you?"

"You tell me."

"Because he knew it was a suicide mission. The Witch boils them in oil and they're out of his hair. Or, against all the odds, they actually succeed in killing the Witch. What then? Why, the Wizard wins again—he's rid himself of a powerful foe."

"You think going against Xian is a suicide mission?"

"It ain't Sunday in Luna Park with George, believe me!"

"You're probably right," Ake said. " I didn't want to think about it, I guess." He poured himself a cup of coffee and stirred in cream and sugar—or reasonable facsimiles. "But there's something wrong here, something off center."

"Yeah, I know what you mean, buddy," Ray said. "I sense that Svoboda holding back something about Xian or DiCiancia—or both. I wish I knew what it was."

Beowulf looked up and tossed off, "We could gnaw on him a li'l bit with our teeths—mebbe then he tell us everythin', includin' where them other dogs is."

"That's it," said Ray, an evil grin spreading across his face.

"What's it?" asked Ake. "Torture? I didn't think that was our style."

"Yeah, but the other dogs . . . and . . ." Ray's voice trailed away. He sighed heavily. "You're right, of course," Ray said finally. He slammed the palm of his hand down hard on the table's surface. "Dammit, it's a bitch having to play by the good guys' rules all the time."

"All the time?" chided Ake gently.

"Well, most of the time," Ray conceded. Then he laughed appreciatively. "Dang, Ake, you're good at that—letting a little air out of my big bags of wind when I pump myself up a bit too much."

"Ake good as a wife, that way," said Grendel, swiping a big pink tongue across her muzzle.

<Shit, I hope that doesn't make Ray think of Mary and Taylor!>

"Ah, that's all right, Ake. Thoughts of Mary and Taylor don't bother me all that much anymore."

"Huh? *What* did you say?"

"I said I don't much think about Mary and Taylor anymore," Ray repeated.

"But *why* did you say that?" Ake persisted.

"Well, you started it by saying you hoped that Grendel's comment wouldn't make me think about . . ." He paused. "You know what you said, so what's the big deal?"

"Grendel, did I mention Mary and Taylor?"

"No, Ake."

"That's ridiculous," said Ray. "I heard you and . . ." He stopped as Ake slowly shook his head back and forth.

"Ray, I didn't *say* that, I *thought* it."

"Them rubies again?" asked Beowulf.

Ray's hand involuntarily reached for his throat. "The rubies?

I'm only wearing a single one, and that's on a chain around my neck."

"Maybe that's enough now," Ake said.

"Enough?"

"For your psi talents to be expanded. Maybe one's enough."

Ray scratched his head. "I dunno. The only other time I remember something like this was back on Hephaestus, when there were rubies all around me."

"Your powers are amplified in close proximity to the rubies, especially a number of them," Ake thought out loud. "Yet you were able to pick up my thoughts without being exposed to a quantity of rubies."

"I haven't had close contact with the rubies since that time in hyperspace. I needed them then to walk the ship."

"Hyperspace," said Ake, his eyes narrowing. Then they widened. "Hyperspace! You wore them in hyperspace!"

"Yeah, so?" asked Ray.

"It was only twenty minutes or so . . . but in some strange way of accounting for the time it was really over ten years."

Ray saw what Ake was getting at. "But that was in real space. In hyperspace, it was still only twenty minutes."

"Was it? What we don't know about the paradoxes of hyperspace could fill a black hole."

"Hmmm," Ray mused, beginning to consider the possibility that Ake's thesis could be correct. "You know, you may have a point."

"Sure I do," Ake said. "That experience may have permanently expanded your mind and abilities in special ways."

A look of recognition crossed Ray's face. "Just like Dr. Morbius and the plastic educator!"

"Who . . . What?"

"Never mind," said Ray, waving a hand absentmindedly. "You're right."

"So what am I thinkin'?" asked Littlejohn.

"You'd like something to eat," said Ake quickly.

"That's right!" Littlejohn said. Then his face clouded. "Hey, I thought it was Ray who sigh-kick."

II

"So, Doctor Loveless," Ray began, delving into his bag of twentieth-century popular culture and coming up with the name of a brilliant but homicidal dwarf. "Why are the dogs no longer here?" He looked down at the little man beside him.

"I . . . ah . . ." For once, Svoboda seemed to have lost his glib tongue.

"Spit it out, Doc."

"I sold them to those who had the money to pay. To warlords," Svoboda confessed in a small voice.

"You sold them where?" Ray shouted.

"They . . . ah . . . were developed to work, as you know," Svoboda said, staring earnestly into Ray's skeptical face. "I could not keep them here—penned up inactive."

"A real humanitarian act, eh?" said Ake.

"No, not at all," Svoboda admitted. "I also needed money. First to pay off DiCiancia and then Xian."

"Dr. Svoboda would not do anything bad," said Janos, speaking up for the first time in the conversation.

"Let's have it all," Ray said, ignoring Janos's comment. "Just who did you sell the dogs to?"

"You must understand that most of the breeding and training had ceased during the last year of the Rebellion. There were at most twenty teams in the breeding crèches at the end."

Ray put his hand to his chin. "Hmmphf. It could be worse, I guess, but that's still upwards of two hundred dogs."

"Who'd you sell them to?" Ray repeated.

"As I said, this warlord or that. Mostly men from up north."

"New York?"

"Yes," Svoboda said.

"Yes. And some to buyers offplanet."

"How many?" asked Frodo.

"Less than half."

"So there are maybe ten to thirteen teams in the Old New York area?"

Svoboda nodded. "And two right here."

Ray's eyes narrowed. "Xian and DiCiancia?"

"Just Xian. DiCiancia arrived on the scene too late to get his hands on a scout dog team. Xian has them both."

Behind Svoboda's office was a vast chamber, an immense semicircular excavation carved from the rock and soil by fusion torches. This enormous space was subdivided into numerous rooms and cubicles, rather like a primitive quonset hut built on a grand scale. Ray stood in the middle of the huge, open entry area and, walking around the core, saw corridors radiating out from the center.

"Makes ya feel at home," observed Littlejohn as Svoboda led them down a corridor. "This is jes' like the mine tunnels on Hephaestus."

"Let's hope there are no diggers," Ake said.

"I have a feeling there are worse horrors down here than mere diggers," Ray said knowingly.

"You *are* such a clever lad," Svoboda told him.

"I *like* him," Ray said, clapping an arm around the diminutive scientist in mock bonhomie. "Not only is he perceptive, but when I stand next to him he makes me look like James Arness."

"He wuz Marshal Dillon," Beowulf explained, just in case someone missed the reference. Ray's old black-and-white two-dee television tapes of *Gunsmoke* were among the dogs' favorites, especially the more violent thirty-minute episodes.

"And your dogs are almost as clever as you are."

"What a scene," said Ake sarcastically. "Father and son." Then he asked, "What did you mean that there are worse horrors down here, Ray?"

"Don't you remember what Johnny told us?" Ray asked. "In the last days of the conflict, the Federation had old Doc Svoboda here seeing what would result if he crossed a Tasmanian Devil with a polar bear."

A strange look crossed Svoboda's face. *That's interesting*, Ray thought. *I must have accidentally come close to the truth.*

"Not exactly," Svoboda demurred.

"But close enough for government work, I'd say," persisted Ray, believing Svoboda's expression instead of his words.

"You are so obnoxious!" marveled Svoboda. "I love it." Then he got professorial. "The results of everyday, garden-variety manipulations are known to everyone: intelligent, talking scout dogs and cats. I have gone much farther than that. For the past twenty-five years or so, I have been experimenting with genetic manipulations that go far beyond simply enhancing—or adding to—the normal senses the unaltered lifeform possessed."

"Are you saying the Federation encouraged you to go beyond the basic manipulations?" asked Ake.

"They did not *directly* instruct me to undertake my new studies, but neither did they object to my 'unofficial' research and experimentation efforts. When things began to go badly for the Federation, I was the only one who had been doing this work for years."

"You went far beyond dogs and cats?"

"Yes. It got easier and easier once I learned what I was doing. I had a few missteps, a few mistakes, but not as many as I might have expected."

Svoboda waved a hand dismissively. "After I better understood what I was doing, I discovered that enhancing terrestrial creatures was child's play; no more challenging than dogs or cats. I mean, a bigger, meaner tiger or grizzly bear is just a bigger, meaner tiger or grizzly bear when you get right down to it."

"What was the purpose of all this?" asked Ake. "What did the Federation expect to do with these genetic monstrosities?"

"Ask them."

"They not here," said Beowulf. "Ake askin' you."

"My stars!" Svoboda said, pointing and pretending to be shocked. "That animal spoke!"

"And that animal will rip your throat out if you play games with us," Ray said amiably. He was smiling, but everyone—including Svoboda—knew he meant it.

"You needn't use threats, young man," joked Svoboda, but his eyes weren't smiling. For a moment, Ray thought he glimpsed another Svoboda; a harder, less jovial Svoboda. "As for what the Federation wanted these genetic changes for, you *will* have to ask them—if there is anyone left to ask."

Ake didn't believe Svoboda's protestation of ignorance, but he allowed the matter to drop. "What happened to all these marvels of genetic engineering?" Ake demanded.

"Gone. Sold to the highest bidder."

"Jes' like the dog teams," said Beowulf.

"You have none here?"

"Look around; you will see that I am alone."

"Yeah, we noticed that," Ray said. "Where the hell are all the others—all your lab assistants, all the other scientists?"

"Dead," Svoboda said.

"Dead?"

"Yes. DiCiancia had them all killed."

Ray stared at the diminutive scientist, not sure whether or not to believe him. He reached out with his mind, attempting to use his powers to test Svoboda's word. *Shit, I have to practice this more*, Ray said, probing. Perspiring profusely from the effort, Ray didn't so much "read" Svoboda's mind as get a very clear sense that the little man was being completely honest when he said that DiCiancia had killed all the others working at the genetic labs.

"I guess you're telling the truth," Ray said finally.

Ake said, "He is? Doesn't sound logical to me."

Ray shrugged. "Svoboda's telling the truth. If he *had* been lying to me, this is what I would have used." He pulled his bush knife with its thirty-five-centimer-long blade from his boot.

"You know," said Svoboda, looking at Ray and his team as if evaluating what he saw, "I think you just might do it."

"Count on it," said Ray, still displaying the knife.

"Not *that*," Svoboda said.

"What, then?"

"I think you might be capable of giving me Xian's head on a stick."

"Oh, we can fill that order," Ray said. "But I have one question."

"Yes?"

"You want fries with that?"

III

Janos had left them by the time they reached Dr. Svoboda's inner sanctum, his personal living quarters. Svoboda keyed the lock with his palmprint and the door cycled open.

"There's no one else around but robots!" Ray exclaimed.

"One can't be too careful," Svoboda said prudently.

"Doan it bother you livin' in the ground?" Frodo asked.

"One gets used to it, like anything," Svoboda replied.

Ray whistled. "Yeah, I could get used to this."

As they walked down a hallway covered by a thick, spongy carpet, Svoboda pointed out the various rooms branching off from the central entryway.

"There is the living room. Down there are two bedrooms with full baths. Over there is the kitchen. Down that way is a conference room, a multimedia den, a heated pool, a game room, laundry facilities, and other utility areas."

"This is incredible," said Ake.

"A modest little hideaway, but all mine." Svoboda grinned proudly.

"Stanislas! Is that you, Stanislas?"

Svoboda's grin slowly retreated. "Almost all mine, I regret to say," he told them.

"I thought you said you were alone."

"I forgot to mention Mrs. Svoboda."

"You have a wife?" asked Ake.

"I wouldn't have a mistress who looked like that," Svoboda said *sotto voce* as a tiny, doll-like woman swept into the hallway. "Answer me when I ask you a question, Stanislas!" she demanded.

"Yes, dear," Svoboda said, his small body seemingly further diminished by his tiny wife's scolding voice. For a moment, Ray was reminded of the mayor of Munchkinland and his wife.

"And who are these gentlemen—and these dogs?"

"They are my guests, dear." Svoboda was like a beaten puppy in the presence of his wife. "They are going to help me resolve the General Xian matter."

"Hmmph. Well, see to it that these big dogs don't get on the furniture. Look," she said as she pointed. "I think they're shedding all over the carpet just standing there."

"Doan worry 'bout us," Mama-san assured her. "We won't get up on your furniture, Mrs. Svoboda."

"Aiiee!" she screeched. "More of those talking dogs. I thought they were all dead or sold off." She shook her head sharply. "Well, behave yourselves. Now, I must go see about the cleaning robots." She clicked her tongue disapprovingly. "Dog hair."

"You must forgive my wife," Dr. Svoboda said. "She is unused to receiving company these days."

"Uh-huh," said Ray. "Look," he suggested, "why don't we simply go back to your office or to another area? I don't want to annoy Mrs. Svoboda with our presence in your living quarters. This seems to be her domain."

"Quite so," agreed Svoboda. "That's a good idea." He led them back toward the entrance.

This time it was Ray's turn to lean over and whisper into Ake's ear. "Hell, forget about us. Svoboda should simply sic Mrs. Svoboda on Xian!"

"I don't think Dr. Svoboda wishes to be that cruel," Ake whispered back.

"So," Littlejohn asked Beowulf, "what kinda animal you think *she* mixed with?"

Overhearing the question, Gawain replied in all seriousness, "A wolverine, mebbe!"

★ ★ ★

It all began innocently enough, Ray was to observe later.

Svoboda had found some surprisingly comfortable living and sleeping quarters for them, and they had spent a generally restful first night. Because of the uncertainty over their situation—Was Svoboda to be trusted? Was he friend or foe?—their sleep was not entirely untroubled.

"I want to go up to the surface and get some things from the half-track," Ray told Svoboda in the morning. "I know I'm safe inside the walls of the compound, but I'd like to take a couple of the dogs with me and let them stretch their legs above ground."

"Certainly," Svoboda agreed. "Janos, you will please accompany Ray on his little jaunt?"

"Oh, and why does Janos need to go along? Don't you trust me, Dr. Svoboda?"

Svoboda was the picture of innocence. "Must you think so harshly of your host—the man who has given you food and shelter?" He shook his head. "Tsk, tsk. I mean, I have even allowed you to retain your sidearms, have I not?"

"Let's just say you haven't tried to take them from us," Ray said. "I'm not sure that's the same thing."

"Whatever," shrugged Svoboda. "But you must take Janos along."

"Why not Mrs. Svoboda?" joked Ake. "Ray would have an easier time getting away from a Betelgeuse marrow sucker with its jaws clamped on his leg than from her."

"Mrs. Svoboda rarely leaves the living quarters," Svoboda replied.

"No, she has to be back before it gets dark," chortled Ray. Then he glanced at Svoboda and said, "Sorry, Doc."

"Just be off with you," Svoboda said.

"It doesn't get dark underground, does it?" a puzzled Gawain asked one of the other dogs.

"It was good to breathe fresh air again," Ray told Janos as they reentered the building. In addition to Beowulf and Littlejohn, Frodo, Grendel, and Tajil had come along.

"Yah," said Beowulf. "Livin' in a hole stinks."

"Literally," said Ray.

"Air . . . I don't require it myself," said Janos. Then the robot added, "Beowulf and the others are so . . . smart."

"Hey, we's scout dogs, machine-person!" said feisty Frodo.

They stepped into the freight elevator. "To the bottom, Jeeves," Ray said. The elevator took off without acknowledging his words.

The elevator settled with a slight bump and bounce. "Level six," the elevator announced in a mellifluous voice at odds with its ragged condition.

"Hey, the elevator said, 'Level six,' " Tajil marveled as the doors opened.

"Huh?" said Ray, shifting his gaze from the floor to the opening doors.

The little 'bot immediately realized its error. "No, it is wrong! I made a mistake! Don't get off the elevator, please."

"Too late," Ray said, stepping past the robot. He palmed his needle gun as the dogs scrambled out, ready for any challenge.

Janos hurried after them. "No, no, no," the 'bot pleaded.

Again, the elevator had deposited them in an out-of-the-way location hidden behind a series of doors. Ray patiently made his way out of the obscure exit point and into an open area.

"Who's that?" shouted a voice.

"I dunno, but Janos is with 'em."

Ray saw four men staring in their direction. They were standing, as if engaged in a routine conversation, and their weapons, energy rifles, were slung nonchalantly over their shoulders. One of the men threw down the cigarette he was smoking to reach for his rifle. The dogs growled and bared their teeth.

Please don't, Ray thought.

They did, however.

"Get 'em!" Ray shouted, and the dogs flew toward the surprised men in a blur of motion.

As a tiny part of each doomed man's mind marveled that creatures so large could move so quickly and fluidly, the dogs tore out the men's throats. Ray felt his eyes watering. His tears were not for the men—in his mind they were already dead—but for the dogs, compelled to kill at his command.

"We got 'em, Ray," said Littlejohn, stating the obvious.

"Yeah, we got them," Ray said tonelessly. *They acted on instinct, reaching for their guns that way. They gave me no choice.*

Janos's programming allowed the robot to react in a very human way; the little 'bot stared at the four dead bodies. "My fault, my fault," it said, hugging itself with its many arms and rocking back and forth. "Bad thing."

"Janos, it wasn't your fault," Ray told the 'bot. "I told the elevator to go to the bottom, not the fifth level, not realizing that there was another level." He smiled grimly. "I wasn't supposed to know there was another level, was I?"

"No," it said in a small voice.

"What's down here?" He pointed to the four bodies. "More importantly, are there any more of these guys down here?"

"Bad thing."

"Janos!" he said sharply.

"More? I do not think so."

"Who were those men?"

"I believe they worked for General DiCiancia."

"DiCiancia?" Ray said. "Curiouser and curiouser."

Ray ducked back into the elevator and was about to tell it to stay put when he reconsidered. Svoboda could override a voice command but not a more drastic action, so he pressed the STOP button. Then he told Frodo to keep an eye on Janos.

"Janos, I don't know if you're programmed to accept commands from a dog or not, but I'm ordering you now to obey Frodo. Is that understood?"

"Yes."

"I'm hoping the little guy is telling the truth," Ray said to

Frodo. "If Janos tries to pull something or tries to leave, come tell me immediately."

"Okay, Ray."

Ray relieved one of the dead men of his energy rifle and checked its charge. Satisfied, he said, "Beowulf, Littlejohn, Grendel, and Taddy—let's go."

8

"Right, Ray," Beowulf said. After a second's hesitation, the big dog asked, "Uh, go where?"

Ray made a face. "I think you've got a point, Beowulf."

Like the other floors—or at least the fifth, which was the only one Ray was familiar with—the elevator accessed the level at one end. The drop/lift tubes, however, apparently entered in the center of the floor. At least, that's the way it appeared to Ray. There were two central, bisecting corridors—one north-south, and one east-west. These were augmented by a number of secondary corridors.

"This is Svoboda's real private domain," Ray told the dogs. "He's made the fifth floor so homey that you wouldn't suspect there's yet another level, one that truly represents him."

"Which way?" asked Littlejohn.

Ray pounded the stock of the energy rifle in frustration. "Ah, what the hell," he said. "That way." He turned to Janos. "Stay put," he ordered. The little 'bot beeped nervously in reply.

They moved down an antiseptic-smelling corridor that reminded Ray of every hospital he'd ever been in. Beowulf and Littlejohn moved out ahead to take the point and Tajil and Grendel fell back a few steps to watch the rear.

"How's your new sigh-kick stuff doin', Ray?" Beowulf asked over his shoulder.

"I'm getting the oddest sensations. They're snatches of thought or strange, disconnected images."

"What that mean?" asked Grendel.

"I don't know," admitted Ray. "Well, it probably means there's somebody or some *thing* down here."

Doors on both sides of the short hallway opened into operating rooms stocked with gleaming instruments and complex machines whose functions Ray could not begin to imagine.

"This gives me the creeps," said Tajil.

Ray walked over to a bright and shiny operating table, noting the deactivated robotic surgical "assistants" arrayed along the table's edges. Slowly, he reached out his right hand. His fingertips tentatively brushed the table's slightly dusty top. When nothing happened, he placed the palm of his hand flat against the surface.

"I can sense fear and pain." He withdrew his hand. "This is not a good place."

"Then let's go," said Tajil sensibly.

"Yeah, I think you're right, Taddy."

They went out into the corridor again and Ray debated whether to retrace his steps or to continue his explorations. It was no contest; as usual, his curiosity got the better of him. "Let's see what's down this way and then lose this place."

Ray tried several unmarked doors, but found them all locked. The few unlocked doors opened into nondescript or empty rooms. Several had a few pieces of strange-looking machinery in them, but were otherwise void of anything remarkable or telling.

Behind one door was a short corridor, no more than five meters in length, ending in a massive polycarbon-steel door. "Hey, hey, hey," said Ray. "What have we here?"

Littlejohn peered at a row of lettering just above the door and asked, "What that say, Ray?"

"It says, 'Lions and tigers and bears—oh, my!' "

"Cat poop," muttered Tajil. "That doan make no sense."

"Oh, I'm afraid it does," Ray said. "It makes sense if you know Svoboda's warped mind. He's on some sort of *Wizard of Oz* kick. Maybe I should switch my interest to twenty-first-century pop culture. It's a pisser sharing the same era with a dick like the doc." Ray pressed his palm to the entry patch. As he expected, nothing happened; he wasn't Svoboda.

"Well, we ain't gettin' in there without Swo . . . without that little doctor guy," observed Beowulf.

"What's the 'Wizard of Oz'?" asked Tajil.

"Not now, Taddy," Beowulf growled.

"No, that's okay," Ray said. "It's an old fantasy story about a little girl from Kansas who has many fabulous adventures in a magical land and makes lots of new friends, but who wants only to go home."

"Yeah? She get to go home?"

"Of course, she just . . ." Ray's eyes widened and he clapped a hand to his forehead. "No, it couldn't be—could it?"

"What?"

Ray stepped front and center and said in a loud voice, "There's no place like home."

Nothing.

Beowulf and Littlejohn exchanged concerned looks. "Uh, Ray . . ." Beowulf began.

"That little rat bastid," Ray said. "He's gonna make me do the whole damn routine!" He clicked his heels together three times and again intoned, "There's no place like home."

The door cycled open.

★ ★ ★

Inside was a short flight of steps that led down to another door. "Jeez," said Ray, his brow furrowing. "These damn steps don't make much sense."

"What you mean?" asked Beowulf.

"You can't move heavy equipment or machines up or down steps easily. Steps are so . . . so . . ."

"Twenny-eff century," said Beowulf.

"That's very perceptive," Ray told his leader dog. *Sometimes I forget just how smart Beowulf is*, he admonished himself. "Svoboda doesn't make sense when it comes to his twentieth-century obessions."

"We're almost there," said Littlejohn.

From the bottom step, they could see through a small semicircular opening. Ray double-checked the charge on his energy rifle and stepped through the archway.

"Jesus and Mohammed!" Ray gasped.

"Wow!" said Littlejohn.

"Golly!" said Grendel.

They were in an immense manmade cavern. To the left, straight ahead, and to the right were a number of good-sized dioramas. But it wasn't the dioramas that captured Ray's attention, it was what was inside them.

"What are them things?" asked Littlejohn, indicating the creatures inside each display, as dramatically posed as in any natural history museum on Terra.

"Dr. Svoboda's dirty little secrets," Ray said grimly. "I wish we had more time to check these monstrosities out." He was anxious to get back to the fifth level before they were missed, but loath not to make a laser-fast inspection of the cavern, cataloging Svoboda's experiments, before leaving.

"What's that?" asked Beowulf, tilting his shaggy head toward a white-furred creature that easily reached five meters, standing on its hind legs.

Ray pointed to a small plaque set in the floor in front of the habitat. Crimson script announced, *Thalarctos maritimus Svoboda*. "It says 'Polar Bear Svoboda.' " In his best "What the hay-ell" voice, he added, "Gee, I wonder who created this mutated monster?"

"That little guy, I bet," Tajil said helpfully.

Ray shot him a look. "No, you *are* Taddy; for a minute there I thought you were Gawain."

"Huh?"

"Lookit there," said Beowulf, trotting over to another diorama. It was a swampy environment, with a turgid pool of water in the middle. On the "banks" two massive amphibians lay motionless, their powerful jaws agape.

"Don't dip your toes in the water, boys," Ray said, coming up to read the plaque: "*Crocodylus Horribilis*. Shit, you can't argue with that name."

"That is a . . . a mutated crocodile?" asked Littlejohn.

"It ain't a redwood with teeth, dog breath."

"Boy, it good they all dead and stuffed," said Littlejohn.

"I hate to tell you this, Littlejohn, but I don't think they're dead. They're in stasis."

"Stay-sis? What that mean?"

"They're 'sleeping,' more or less."

"Why does that doctor guy make these things? What *is* they?" asked Grendel.

"Weapons," Ray replied after a moment's hesitation. "They're biological weapons." He thought for a moment more and added, "After the disastrous 'robot wars' of sixty-three years ago"—he paused to add twelve years to the figure—"I mean, of seventy-five years ago, anything more complex than smart weapons was banned. That meant no android soldiers, no robot stormtroopers.

"Their use became such a taboo that I guess even the Federation, in its death throes, was unwilling to violate it. But, as the old saying goes, where there's a will, there's a way. If mechanical warriors are *verboten*, then you just go ahead and develop biological ones."

"But crocodiles, even real big ones," said Beowulf slowly, "they make *good* weapons?"

"In the classic sense, I'd have to guess no," Ray replied. "But as terroristic, last-gasp, piss-in-the-well, fuck'-em-all weapons, they're probably quite effective."

"Oh."

"How many of these cages is there?" asked Beowulf.

"Lots," Tajil said. "But some of 'em is empty. I wonder what happened to what was inside?"

"That's a good question," Ray said. "I would guess that this place is Svoboda's showroom. Come in, shop around, pick the model that best suits your purposes." He shook his head. "Come on, guys. We've been here too long already."

They were leaving when Tajil noticed something in a far corner, covered by a large plastic tarp.

"Hey, over here, Ray. Over here, Beowulf, Littlejohn, and Grendel."

"What is it?" Ray asked. Then he saw the tarp.

"Dunno," admitted Tajil. "But it can't be none o' them cages, 'cause they not covered up like this."

"Well, here goes nothing," Ray said, grabbing one corner of the tarp and yanking it. When it didn't budge, Littlejohn clamped down on one of the other corners. Together, man and dog pulled. The tarp still stubbornly resisted; then it came loose all at once.

The tarp had been protecting upwards of twenty or twenty-five cryogenic hibernation "coffins."

"Lookit!" gasped Tajil.

"Yeah," Ray said, slow to believe his eyes.

"Are they dead?" asked Grendel.

"No, they're in cryogenic suspension," Ray said.

Inside the coffins were maybe twenty scout dogs and a half-dozen human beings.

II

When they reached the fifth floor, they ran into more of Svoboda's contingent of robots in the corridor. They beeped, booped, flashed colored lights, and otherwise acted like common, everyday domestic robots. Only as intelligent as they needed to be, they seemed distracted by the presence of Ray and the dogs. One or two even squeaked, turned around and went in the other direction.

"We gots bad breath or what?" asked Frodo.

"They are not used to people other than Dr. Svoboda," Janos explained. "You are people."

"Coulda fooled me," chortled Frodo. "I thought we wuz dogs."

"I mean Ray is a person."

"You get some argument there, too," kidded Beowulf.

Janos looked at Ray. "Your dogs, they . . . they don't *respect* you."

The dogs bristled at that. "Hey, what you talkin' 'bout?" said Grendel. " 'Course we 'spect Ray!"

"Janos," Ray said patiently, "they're joking. They're my team—they have the right to kid around with me. We've been through a lot together. Just because they give me a hard time about something doesn't mean that they don't respect me. And vice versa."

"I must think about this." Janos looked up to see that they were outside the door to the conference room. "I will leave you now."

"Ah, it's good to see you're back," Svoboda said. "I was beginning to wonder if anything happened to you." Svoboda was at a table having toast and jam. A mug of coffee sat steaming in front of him.

"I can appreciate that," Ray replied. "When I went to the

bathroom and didn't come back for a long time, my old granny would say 'Goodness, Ray, dear, I thought maybe you fell in.' "

"Ha, ha, ha," chortled Mama-san. "Fall in toilet."

"Yes, bathroom humor. Most amusing," said Svoboda. "What happened to Janos?"

"Your 'bot said he had things to do and left me just outside the door. Is that all right with his lord and master?"

Svoboda shot him a funny look but said nothing.

Ake, long used to his partner's unconscious body language, realized that Ray had been up to something. His guess was confirmed when he shot Ray a questioning look and Ray nodded almost imperceptibly.

"Say," Ray asked, "just when did you sell the last of your biological weapons, Dr. Svoboda?"

Ake cringed. *That's Ray—Mr. Subtle. Nothing like showing a sociopath like Svoboda what's on your mind*, he thought.

"I don't remember, exactly," replied Svoboda cryptically. "Why?"

"Oh, just wondering."

Svoboda spread strawberry jam on a slice of toast and took a bite before observing mildly, "I've hired you to kill Xian, not me."

Ake didn't like where this was going. What *had* Ray seen or done while he was gone?

Ray nodded."That's correct. But maybe after we take care of Xian for you, DiCiancia will hire us to take care of you."

"Trust me—that's not even remotely possible."

Ray casually brushed his sleeve. Ake gulped; Ray's needle gun was tucked away there. The gesture's import didn't escape Svoboda either.

Svoboda coolly sipped his coffee. "Mind if I ask my wife to join us?"

The request caught both Ray and Ake off guard. "I . . . ah . . ." Ray wanted to object, but he couldn't find a valid reason to deny Svoboda's request.

"Your wife," he finally said. "Why?" *Someone else, a goon, I could understand*, Ray thought. *But his wife?*

"Yes. I realize you gentlemen don't think much of her—and I can't blame you, after that less than successful first meeting—but she is my valued counselor."

Ray looked at Ake. Ake shrugged. Clearly, he too could think of no good reason to object to Mrs. Svoboda's presence. "Go ahead."

Svoboda keyed the holophone sitting on the small table, taking care to turn off the visual. "She hates to be seen in the morning," he confided to Ray and Ake.

"Yes?"

"Good morning, dear. Would you mind coming over to my offices? I need your assistance."

"My hair's a mess and—"

"Take your time, dear. Say in ten minutes?"

"That's hardly 'taking my time,' Stanislas!" Then she relented. "All right, ten minutes."

"Be especially vigilant," Ray told Beowulf and the rest of the dogs quietly. "I don't know if 'I need your assistance' was a coded message."

"Oh, really," protested Dr. Svoboda. "I am not playing any cheap James Bong tricks on you, for goodness' sake."

"Bond," Ray said. "James Bond."

"Uh, oh . . . yes, right," said Svoboda, embarrassed to have been caught in such a mistake.

As the minutes slowly passed, the dogs grew more and more anxious, sensing the tension building between Ray and Svoboda. They sensed that Ake was also on edge—but it was a tension born of not knowing what was going on.

There was a discreet rap on the door. Svoboda waited until one of the dogs went over and stood there before he said, "Come in, dear."

The knob turned and the door slowly swung open to reveal . . . Mrs. Svoboda. Even though they had all met her once, her tininess still came as a shock.

"Hello, dear," said Svoboda.

"Hello, Stanislas," she said. "Hello, gentlemen and hairy dogs." She stared fiercely at her husband. "I hope you have a good reason for making me miss *All My Clones*."

"You can watch the recording later, dear," Svoboda said patiently. "I just want you to tell our friends here that they have nothing to fear from me. I wish them to understand that they are completely safe here."

"Of course, dear." She turned her little face toward them and smiled disarmingly. Suddenly, Ray felt a bit ashamed for his earlier comments about Mrs. Svoboda. She was clearly a very, very . . . *nice* woman.

"My husband is a wonderful man, don't you agree?"

"Oh, yes," said Ake quickly. *What is wrong with Ray?* he wondered. *How can he doubt that Svoboda's our friend?*

Dr. Svoboda is my friend, Ray thought. *I must trust my friend, mustn't I? I'm ashamed for doubting him. I . . .* Ray felt a twinge of pain in his head. He closed his eyes and rubbed them. When he opened them again, the room swam in his vision.

"You feeling all right?" Ake asked.

"I'm okay. It's just that—" Ray stopped and gaped at Mrs. Svoboda. He swore and raised his arm. His needle gun leapt into his hand.

"No-o-o-o!" shouted Svoboda.

Too late.

Ray fired a ceramic shard directly into Mrs. Svoboda's brain.

"Ohmygod!" Ake exclaimed, horrified by Ray's violent act.

"You killed it!" screamed Svoboda.

"You heard him, Ake," Ray said: "I killed *it*. Take a look."

Ake stared at the tiny body. "What . . . ?"

"Yeah, 'what'?"

"Mrs. Svoboda" was a gray-furred creature about the size of a Terran opossum. She—it—was also clearly dead.

"You didn't have to kill it," Svoboda said accusingly.

"You're probably right," Ray admitted. "But when I realized it was making us think you were the greatest guy since Arne Siggerhaus, I had to do something." He shrugged. "Violent acts are regrettable but just as often effective."

"What this thing be?" asked Grendel, poking the tiny body with her nose.

"A Regalian empath," said Svoboda in a small voice.

"I never heard of it," said Ake dubiously.

"The Federation pretty much exterminated them in a justifiable, if top secret, spasm of self-defense; unchecked, they could have spread across the galaxy like a plague."

"How did you come by this one, then?"

"It was the last one and the Federation wished me to study it before I 'put it to sleep,'" Svoboda said. Then he seemed to reinflate a bit. "I do so love euphemisms," he said, some of his old spark returning.

"And this is how you 'studied' it?"

Svoboda shrugged. "It was not its fault that it posed a threat to the human race. Besides, I did no more than take cellular and DNA samples and store them; I wasn't foolish or stupid enough to actually attempt to manipulate its makeup in any way."

"So you're not a total asshole," Ray said dryly.

"Let's not be vulgar, shall we?"

When the dogs kept nosing at the dead empath, Ray said, "Leave it alone, guys—it was a 'person' once."

"Actually, no," Svoboda said.

"Huh?"

"It has . . . um, *had* . . . very little intelligence or personality of its own. It derived much of its powers from the minds around it. At first, the creature was unable to impersonate being my wife without my active assistance. I had to constantly keep a mental picture of "her" in my mind. Very soon, however, others saw her as I wished her to be seen. You two—and even the dogs—would have unconsciously begun to project the desired image. After all, each time you came in contact with the empath, you would have conditioned yourselves to see 'Mrs. Svoboda.' "

He sighed. "Nonetheless, I still had to provide much of her personality; while unintelligent, the creature could still make contact with and use my mind."

"When you called her, or it, a while ago, you couldn't make us see 'her,' could you?" Ray guessed.

"That's correct. You heard her voice, but the empath was too far away to cloud your perceptions."

"How'd it do the voice, then?"

"Like parrots, or Garthian sloths, Regalian empaths possessed a remarkable talent for mimicry."

"Congratulations on your acting ability, Dr. Svoboda," Ray told him, grudging admiration in his voice. "You two were very convincing as a married couple. And I'll bet you've never been married."

"That is correct."

"Why did you wait so long to attempt to make us your slaves?" Ake asked.

"Free will is so much more effective in the long run, I think. Besides, you would not have been my 'slaves,' as you put it, but you would not have questioned my motives, either."

"Your motives concerning us or your motives concerning all the big, bad beasties tucked away in the basement?"

Recognition showed in Svoboda's eyes. "So *that's* where you were all that time!" He stared at the closed door as if seeing someone there. "Did Janos betray me?"

"No, I found my way down there by accident," Ray told him.

"Found yourself down where?" asked Ake. "What are you talking about?"

"The Doc gotta a whole 'nother level under this one, Ake," explained Beowulf. "It full of monsters and things."

"Yeah, things like scout dogs in stasis," Ray added. He stared at Svoboda. "Xian doesn't have two teams, does he?" Answering his own question, he told Ake, "Mr. Big here has them stashed in the cellar."

Ake looked lost. "Ah, I think I'll just go and take a 'laxer and lie down for a while."

"Don't fret," said Ray, smiling. "It's not that complicated. I'll explain it all to you the first chance I get."

There was a loud pounding at the door. "Yes, who is it?" Svoboda asked, speaking into a small communications device.

"It's Ramsey. Let me in!"

"Ramsey?" said Ake, wonderingly. "I thought everyone else was dead."

"Not everyone," Ray said. *Svoboda said "others" a minute ago when he was talking about the empath. Others!*

Svoboda looked questioningly at Ray. "Okay, let him in but no weapons," he told Svoboda.

"Ramsey, put down any weapon you may have with you. I'll admit you now."

A totally human being, a thuggish mercenary similar to the four the dogs had killed, burst through the opening door. "General DiCiancia, I—" He stopped in mid-sentence when he saw who he was speaking to. Almost immediately, he noticed the empath's tiny body.

"Where is General DiCiancia?" he demanded. Ake shot Ray

a puzzled look that deepened even more when he noticed a smug, know-it-all expression creep across his partner's face.

"Never mind that, Ramsey," Svoboda informed him. "You can tell me what you intended to tell the General."

"It is Xian—he's attacking the compound!"

9

"Looks like your bluff has failed," Ray told Svoboda.

Ignoring Ray for the moment, Svoboda ordered Ramsey to rejoin the rest of the mercenaries. "Tell Captain Spector and the General's other officers to follow the defensive plans DiCiancia drew up and drilled into your heads day after day."

"All right," Ramsey said, "but the General better show his face plenty quick if he expects us to fight for him."

"Aren't you fighting for yourself as well?"

"Hellfire, Doc, it don't matter shit to us who we fight for. If Xian shitcans DiCiancia, he wins us along with everything else. Think it's important who puts credits in our pockets?"

Svoboda looked questioningly at Ray, pleading with his eyes. Ray shrugged and silently mouthed, "Go ahead."

With that, Svoboda pulled an energy pistol from beneath the table and burned Ramsey's face off. "I never liked him anyway," he said. He put the pistol into the pocket of his lab coat as a cloud of malodorous smoke choked everyone and made their eyes burn. The ventilation system quickly purged the offending smoke.

Svoboda picked up the communications device and contacted Spector himself with the message he'd told Ramsey to pass on. Captain Spector, too, was concerned about speaking directly to his General. As the two men argued briefly, Ray stared at the ceiling; he was certain that Spector and the rest of

DiCiancia's mercenaries manned levels one through four, or at least the top level.

"With the empath dead, DiCiancia isn't going to show up, is he, Dr. Svoboda?" Ray asked when the scientist had concluded his conversation with Captain Spector.

"I don't know what you mean," Svoboda blustered.

"Pay no attention . . ." Ray prompted, raising his eyebrows.

"Pay no attention to that man behind the curtain," Svoboda picked up. "I am the great and powerful . . . General DiCiancia."

"No!" gasped Ake.

"When did you figure it out?" Svoboda asked.

"About the time the late and unlamented Ramsey made his appearance. It was the last piece of a puzzle that was slowly fitting together."

"The doctor is the General?" asked Beowulf.

"He was," Ray clarified. "I think he must have really existed at some time, because"—he looked at Svoboda apologetically—"while I have no doubts that the good doctor here is a scientific wonderworker of the first rank, I *do* question whether he could have put together DiCiancia's quasimilitary organization from scratch, even with the empath's help."

"You are correct," Svoboda grudgingly admitted. "The empath read the General's mind each time the three of us got together. Then, later, when the empath and I were alone, it entered my mind and 'fed' me what it had learned from him. Eventually I was able to absorb most of DiCiancia's knowledge about his organization. After that, he was superfluous."

"You killed him?"

"DiCiancia's fate was not unlike poor Ramsey's," Svoboda readily admitted.

"So there is no DiCiancia?" asked Ake.

Both Ray and Svoboda looked at him disdainfully. "You're not paying attention, Ake," Ray told him. "Svoboda is DiCiancia."

"But he said that he killed . . . Oh, never mind."

Sounds of close-in combat penetrated to their level, and Ray, Ake, and the dogs guessed that it was only a matter of time before Xian triumphed. "It sounds like your guys are putting up a good fight," Ray told the diminutive doctor, "but for how long will they continue to fight without their fearless leader showing up to encourage them?" He answered his own question: "Not long, I imagine."

Svoboda looked immeasurably sad. "I am forced to agree with you, Ray." Then he pounded the corridor wall in anger and frustration. "Damn it! I wish you had never showed up here! Things were going so well."

"We only wanted a heart for Ake and a brain for Gawain," said Ray, unable to resist the temptation to twit Svoboda one last time.

Tajil was impressed. "Hey, that rhymes: a brain for Gawain."

Svoboda turned beet red; he looked like an old-time cartoon character. "I never again want to see or hear anything about *The Wizard of Oz* for as long as I live!"

"You started it," admonished Ozma.

"Besides, Doc," said Ray, laying a hand on his arm, "I don't think you have many worries on that final wish. You've probably got the life expectancy of a mayfly."

There was a flash of light and a small explosion far down the corridor, in the direction of the main drop/lift tubes. Someone emerged from the smoke. It was Janos.

"Dr. Svoboda, they're coming. All the mercenaries are surrendering."

"My loyal troops," Svoboda muttered bitterly.

"I told you not paying year-end bonuses was a mistake," Ray said to him.

Svoboda regarded him coldly. "You really hate me, don't you? You've always hated me."

Ray shook his head. "No, only from the moment we met, not a minute sooner."

"Ray, we gots to get out of here," implored Beowulf.

"Beowulf's right," seconded Ake. "You two can insult each other later."

As if to underscore that comment, there was a renewed outburst of energy rifle crackling and snapping from within the smoke at the end of the corridor.

"Are we new at this or what?" shouted Ray. "Let's act like a scout dog team!" He held his energy rifle at hip level and unloosed a volley of bolts into the smoke. Ake followed suit, and they were rewarded with screams and curses.

Svoboda led several of the 'bots into his office and they returned with his desk and other pieces of furniture and began making a barrier in the corridor.

"Attaboy, Doc," Ray said. "Now you're acting like DiCiancia." They hovered behind the barrier and kept up a steady stream of fire down the hall. As long as the robots could not see anyone, their no-harm-to-humans inhibiting circuits permitted them to fire their weapons defensively, without lethal intent.

One of the 'bots was carrying a knapsack. "Let's see what's in the bag," said Ray, rummaging around inside. "What have we here?" He pulled out a round object; it was an MF-40 grenade. "Oh, goody."

A fresh burst of firing came from the other end of the corridor. "Guess they gots their own cover," said Beowulf.

"Heck, let's give them one of our grenades. We can share, we've got plenty," Ray said, pulling the pin. He heaved it down the corridor. It bounced once and disappeared into the smoke and haze.

". . . three, four . . ." The grenade exploded. There was an immediate, and more powerful, secondary blast. "Oh, they *did* have some of their own grenades."

Svoboda tapped one of the robots on its shoulder. "Hold them as long as you can."

"We will," promised the 'bot. "But once they realize that we are not humans and cannot harm them, they will ignore us and come after you."

"We can't just leave these machine-peoples here," protested Ozma.

"No, it is all right," the 'bot said. "You go now."

"Now what, Dr. Svoboda?" asked Ake.

"To the freight elevator. I can't imagine they've found it, yet."

"And then?"

Janos answered that. "We must go down; there is no way up now."

As soon as they exited from the elevator, Ray turned and tossed a grenade through the still open doors. "Let's move it!" he shouted.

The explosion was slightly muffled by the closing doors, but the noise and oily black smoke testified to the grenade's effectiveness in rendering the elevator inoperative.

"Why did you do that?" Svoboda demanded.

"Those aggressive fund-raisers were just getting to be too much of a nuisance, don't you think?"

"You're—you're—nuts!" Svoboda shouted.

Littlejohn grinned at Beowulf and said, "He not so smart if he jes' figgerin' that out now."

II

"So how the hell are we going to get out of here—now that the berserker burned our bridges behind us?" Ake asked.

"The Doc may be a teenie weenie," Ray said, "but I would bet Beowulf's left nut—"

"Hey!" said Beowulf.

"—that he saw to it that there was another egress." Looking at Gawain, he amended that to: "Or even another *exit*."

"Yes, I have an emergency exit down here," Svoboda admitted.

"Is it bigger than a bread box?" Ray asked.

"My escape tunnel is in the rear of the chamber, hidden behind a false front. It is also generously proportioned."

Ray nodded, gesturing to the team to make them gather around. "Okay, guys and gals, here's the plan: We're going to find some way of taking the 'sleeping beauties' with us when we leave. Start looking for some floaters or anything that we can load the coffins on."

"Why we not wake them up?" asked Mama-san.

"Good question. Tell her, Ake."

"It takes humans and dogs up to sixty hours to completely recover from the effects of cryogenic hibernation."

"Oh."

"How come them big animals ain't in little ice boxes?" Ozma asked.

"They're in cellular stasis," Svoboda explained.

"So?"

Although there was really no time for explanations, Svoboda couldn't resist a chance to show off his knowledge. "Cryogenic hibernation is long-term, cellular stasis is short-term. Those who purchase my creatures more often than not make it a condition of the sale that they be fully functional on short notice." He stared at a diorama containing his bizarre version of a Bengal tiger. "For instance, that magnificent specimen over there could be restored to life, so to speak, in a matter of minutes."

"Cats," growled Frodo.

"Can them things have little ones?" Mama-san asked.

"None of Dr. Svoboda's creations are capable of reproduction," said Janos.

"Good," Mama-san said.

"Pretty successful scam you had going here, Doc," Ray told him. "If anyone wants a matched set or even a replacement, he has to come back to you."

"Yes, General Tom Thumb here is not only a brilliant geneticist, but also a first-rate capitalist," growled Ake.

"I agree," concurred Ray. "But, on to other things: The dogs have to find something big enough to transport all those sleep coffins."

"And why, pray tell?" pressed Svoboda.

"Doc, you might not give a mutated rat's ass about those people and dogs, but we sure as hell do. And we're taking them with us, one way or another."

"Yah," agreed Beowulf, baring his teeth and stepping forward toward Svoboda.

"Since you put it that way, be my guest."

"So you want to show us where the tunnel is while the dogs look around?"

"Certainly."

"Taddy, you come along."

Svoboda's emergency escape tunnel was indeed carefully concealed. There was a small forklift parked in front of a dozen or so safety-sealed containers marked, "Radioactive and chemical waste. Handle with extreme caution." Behind them was the bare cavern wall.

"Those fake containers are a nice touch, Doc," Ray told the diminutive scientist.

"Thank you. Though I must caution you that they are quite real."

"You mean . . . ?"

"Yes, we must make every effort not to puncture or overturn any of them."

Ake quickly learned the forklift's controls and before long they had moved the containers a safe distance from the cavern wall. "Whew, I'm glad that's over with," Ake said, climbing out of the little forklift's operator's cage. He looked at Svoboda and Ray, both wiping their shirt sleeves across their sweaty faces. "Okay, let's see this marvel of engineering."

Svoboda scanned the rough, rock surface of the wall until he found a small, perfectly round, white stone in the wall at eye level—his eye level. With that as his starting point, he took three sideways steps to the right and kneeled down. His fingertips searched the base of the wall until he felt a small square protruding a few centimeters from the facade. He sighed in relief and pressed his right thumb firmly in the middle of the square. Stepping back, he watched as the "solid" stone face of the cavern wall split down the middle and the two halves swung inward.

"*Voilà.*"

"Impressive, most impressive," Ray said. "Where does this thing go?"

"To just outside the compound walls; that's roughly half a kilometer."

"How do you get to the surface?" asked Ake.

"We're only sixty meters underground. The tunnel simply rises to ground level."

"Hot diggity damn!" Ray exclaimed. "We're in better shape than I could have hoped for. Now, if only the dogs have come up with something, we're cooking."

"Hey, c'mere, everyone," Sinbad called out after one of Janos's arms pulled back the tarp covering the 'bot's discovery.

"What's up?" asked Littlejohn.

"Lookit these things," said Sinbad proudly.

"What are they?" asked Gawain as they approached what looked to be three large plasteel rectangles, approximately five meters long by four meters wide.

"They are null-gravity freight sleds," Janos said. "They are wonderful for moving heavy cargo around."

"If they work," sniffed Littlejohn. "Gimme old-fashioned wheels anytime, they more dependable."

"Well, let us see, shall we?" said Janos, stepping aboard one of the sleds. There was a meter-high shaft with a control box atop it rising from one of the sled's corners. The 'bot keyed the power switch and the sled's hidden motors began to hum softly yet noticeably. Janos fit his "human" hand into the control waldo, wiggled one of its fingers knowledgeably, and the sled gently rose several centimeters into the air like a flying carpet.

"Climb on, Sinbad," Janos suggested. "With your name, this should be second nature to you."

When Sinbad and the others couldn't figure out Janos's reference, the 'bot explained about the *Arabian Nights* and the stories of Scheherazade . . . about Sinbad the Sailor and flying carpets.

"Heh, heh, does kinda look like one o' them flyin' carpets, if you thinks about it," Beowulf agreed. Then he added, "You know lots of stuff—like Ray."

Janos disagreed with that. "Oh, no. Ray is a real person. He is not like me. I am not worth much."

"That ree-dick-less!" Mama-san scolded Janos. "Why you always sayin' things like that anyhow?"

"Yah," seconded Sinbad. "You found these sleds and they gonna help us get the other dogs out."

Janos looked sharply at Sinbad at that, and then at Beowulf. "I . . . ah . . ."

"What is it, Janos?" Mama-san asked gently.

"I think I will tell you a secret."

"Oh, goody!" exclaimed Frodo, his tail wagging.

"Mama-san only," Janos said firmly.

Mama-san leaned over slightly and Janos began whispering into one of her ears. The other dogs were dying of curiosity, especially when they saw Mama-san's ears lift.

"Now it is time to take these sleds to the others," Janos said.

After the 'bot had gone, steering the first sled toward the place where the sleeping dogs were, with Sinbad riding shotgun, the other dogs crowded around Mama-san. "So, what the machine guy tell you?" they asked.

"I not tell you. It's a *secret*," said Mama-san, refusing to say more.

★ ★ ★

Ray inspected Janos's finds. "Hmmmm, with a little bit of maneuvering and careful stacking, we should be able to load nine hibernation coffins on each of these sleds."

"Your crazy scheme just might work," Svoboda allowed, watching Ray and Ake strongarming the sleds into position.

"It will work," said Janos firmly if almost inaudibly. "Ray and his team will *make* it work."

"Ah, a little bit of allegiance transference, eh, my trusty Indian companion?" Svoboda chided the 'bot.

"You are Dr. Svoboda," Janos said, as if wrestling with some internal conflict. "You have given life. But you are not . . . *good.*"

Svoboda was holding a length of plasteel rod in his hand. "Then it doesn't matter if I do this," he said, smashing the little 'bot with the heavy rod. Even though the 'bot could easily absorb much more punishment than that without harm, and could feel no pain, it stepped back, its hands rising to the point of impact to inspect for damage.

Ray quickly closed the distance between himself and Svoboda. He put his hand on top of Svoboda's balding, slightly damp, head and pushed hard. The little man toppled over backwards, landing with a solid *thump* on his buttocks. Ray pointed his finger at Svoboda and announced, "The Wicked Witch of the East—'General DiCiancia'—is dead; watch your step or maybe someone will drop a house on you, too."

"Sorry. I forgot that things had changed around here," a somewhat repentant Svoboda said.

"Yah," said Beowulf. "Ray is top dog now."

"Come on, let's get these sleds loaded," Ake said. Turning away from Ray and Janos, his back to them, he addressed Svoboda in a soft voice only the doctor could hear. "I would advise you not to do anything else to anger Ray. He will kill you without a second's thought if you press him."

Svoboda just nodded.

"What was that all about?" asked Ray when Ake rejoined him.

"I told him you hadn't changed your underwear in a week—scared the hell out of him, I must say."

"Piss off!" said Ray goodnaturedly.

"I, on the other hand, wash my delicate unmentionables in the sink every night," Ake confided to Grendel.

"Come on, come on," Svoboda said, shifting from one foot to another impatiently.

"We're loading these coffins as quickly as we can," Ray told the scientist.

"Your patience is appreciated, especially since you're not doing any of the work," drawled Ake.

"My bad back," Svoboda said, spreading his hands palms up. "You know how it is."

"Uh-huh."

"I think that's done it," Ray said, stepping back from the third sled.

"How are we going to handle this?" asked Ake.

"Easy. You take the first sled, the homunculus here takes the second, and I bring up the rear with number three." Svoboda shot Ray a sour look but said nothing.

Beowulf turned his head in the direction of the elevator. "Ray, I think I hears somethin' over by the elevator. Mebbe it ain't ruint forever."

"I only blasted the car," Ray agreed. "They could drop some ropes or cables into the shaft and rappel down if they really wanted to."

"Me an' Littlejohn better go take a look."

"Just a look—come back immediately."

"Yah, Ray."

"Maybe we should start," said Svoboda.

"Maybe we should," Ray said. "But we're not going to until Beowulf and Littlejohn return."

Svoboda glanced at the heavily laden null-grav sleds. "I'll never understand your concern for scout dogs. They're bigger and smarter than unaltered dogs, and they can talk . . . but they're still animals."

"For all the gray cells jammed inside your skull, you just don't get it, do you, Svoboda?"

Before the scientist could answer him, Beowulf and Littlejohn came bounding back. "There's voices in the shaft, Ray. I think they is comin', all right."

"Right, let's go."

"Wait a minute," said Svoboda.

"What is it?" Ray asked, exasperated. "You were the one with your pants on fire!"

"I know, but I also just realized that it does us no good if they follow us up the tunnel."

"What do you suggest?"

"Janos, you take my sled."

"And what are you going to do?" asked Ake.
"Turn loose my creations."

★ ★ ★

When the three sleds were positioned in the tunnel, ready to go, Svoboda, Ray, Beowulf, and Tajil hurried across the cavern floor, toward the elevator shaft.

"How're you going to work this, Doc?" Ray asked.

"Simple, really. I'm going to turn off the power to the stasis generators nearest the elevator and farthest away from the tunnel. As we fall back, releasing the animals, they should form a living barrier between Xian's men and our escape route."

"Sounds reasonable," Ray said.

Svoboda stopped at the first diorama, one containing several hybrid rhinoceroses. He opened a control box and began keying coded combinations.

"Boy," said Beowulf. "They really ugly. What planet they from and what they called?"

"They're called rhinoceroses and they're from right here on Terra," Svoboda told the big dog. "They're extinct, like so much Terran fauna, but I had access to the Terran Wildlife Federation's DNA banks. Same thing with these Indian elephant-based creatures in the next cage. They're also extinct, although there were never any elephants this large or with the multiple trunks I gave them."

Ray stared at the four giants Svoboda was talking about. They looked like impossibly huge elephants with a squid's body and tentacles where their heads and trunks should be. Thinking them hideous, he cleared his throat noisily.

"Is that an objection?" Svoboda asked, moving on to the next set of controls.

"Huh?"

"Do you find my wonderful new lifeforms objectionable?"

"No, it's just that . . . well, yes, I guess I do. Most creatures are the result of thousands or even millions of years of evolutionary change and adaptation; when you come in and muck about so completely, I wonder exactly how adequate, how *comfortable*, the creature that results can really be." He frowned. "I know I'm not saying that right, but that's the best I can do."

"What about your dogs?"

Ray saw Svoboda's point but argued against it. "They're just dogs-plus, they're not some strange new combination of dog and monkey or something like that."

Svoboda was about to reply when Beowulf said, "I think they's almost here."

Svoboda looked at the many remaining dioramas. At the same time, the rhinolike creatures began to stir. He quickly made up his mind. "I'm going to override the stasis generators all at once, from this control box. We don't have time to continue cage by cage."

"Then do it!"

Svoboda did it.

"There's one more thing," Svoboda said, pulling his energy pistol from his lab coat pocket. "My lovely carnivores tend to be ravenous when they awaken. They might not allow us to pass unless we distract them with an alternative food supply." He pointed the pistol at Beowulf and Ozma. "A large quantity of fresh, bloody dog meat might just get their attention long enough for us to beat a hasty retreat, Larkin."

"You sonofabitch!" Ray took a step forward.

"Please don't be tiresome about this," Svoboda said wearily. "I haven't time to argue with you over mere mutts. Either accept my proposal or I shall include you on the menu."

Ray glanced behind Svoboda, his eyes widening at what he saw.

"How pathetic and lame," Svoboda said. "I've seen too many of those old twentieth-century private eye sinnys and tee-vee shows for that hoary cliche to fool me."

One of the squid-elephant's trunk-tentacles reached out tentatively and tapped Svoboda on the shoulder. The little man gasped in surprise and whirled, firing his pistol blindly. Burned by a weak energy bolt from the discharged pistol, the massive land behemoth seized Svoboda with its medusalike trunk and smashed him against the plascrete floor once. Then it hurled him into a nearby diorama as if he were a papier-mâché doll.

Seriously injured, but still conscious, Svoboda looked up to stare into the visage of something that was at least partly a Siberian tiger. Whatever its genetic makeup, it found the little man appetizing and immediately closed its jaws on his head and neck. Svoboda shrieked in terror and pain.

"C'mon!" Ray shouted to the shocked Beowulf and Ozma as he picked up Svoboda's pistol. "Let's get out of here before we're next!"

Ignoring the doomed man's screams, which ceased abruptly, they dashed through the cavern. Ray stopped long enough to pick up a ragged sheet of metal and a stone. As they ran, he beat the metal with the stone, hoping to scare off anything that might otherwise be attracted to several fleeing potential food sources.

As they reached the partially concealed tunnel, they heard the hissing and crackling of energy weapons, explosions, and screams and shouts.

"What happened to Svoboda?" Ake asked.

"He disagreed with something that ate him," Ray said, jumping onto his sled and powering it up. "Come on, let's leave this place behind."

10

The team blinked in the bright mid-morning haze. The sun didn't really shine on Terra anymore so much as attempt to burn through the thick and soupy petrochemical smog that blanketed so much of the planet's urban landscapes.

Ray turned off the null-grav sled's Daae-Fujiwara engines and stepped off as it settled heavily to the compacted soil. Walking back to Ake's and Janos's sleds, he announced, "I'd say we're right where the late, unlamented Doctor Svoboda said we'd be when we emerged from the escape tunnel."

"Yah?" said Grendel. "Where that?"

"Just outside the security barrier," volunteered Janos.

"We made it," Ake said without much emotion.

"You didn't say that with a great deal of enthusiasm," Ray noted.

"Sure, we're out, but how are we going to get away from here with our cargo?"

Ray glanced at the heavily laden sleds. "You mean . . . ?"

"Yeah. We got the coffins out, but these sleds are meant for low-speed, short-distance hauling. How long do you think it'll be before Xian and his goons realize we've escaped and come after us? And how far do you think we'd get on these things?"

"Yuck, we in trouble," Frodo said.

"Wait a minute," said Ray, brightening. "The ship! We can

call down *The Spirit of St. Louis,* load everyone on board, lift off, and take our time reviving the sleepers."

"We can do that eventually," said Ake, shaking his head. "But not now. It'll take too long to get the ship here and to load these things. At best, we have fifteen minutes."

"Then what was the point of escaping?" Ray asked testily.

"Did you not come here in a vehicle of some sort?" asked Janos.

"Huh?" said Ray.

Ray, Beowulf, and Sinbad followed the wall until they came to the compound's front gate, blasted open by Xian's people. Inside were a dozen vehicles being guarded by three sentries more concerned about whose turn it was to take a pull on their bottle of joy juice than keeping an eye out for trouble. They proved to be no match for Ray and his dogs.

"Why they not more alert?" Beowulf wondered aloud, his muzzle stained red.

"I dunno," Ray replied. "I guess they think everyone they've got to be worried about around here is inside, not outside, the building."

"This the right one?" asked Sinbad as they approached one of two half-tracks.

Ray looked inside. "Yep. Let's climb on board and get the hell out of here."

"We not blow up the rest?" queried Beowulf.

"That seems the thing to do," Ray said. "On the other hand, with these goons dead, no one knows we're here," he continued. "If we begin destroying the other vehicles, we alert them to our presence. They might be all over us before we can load up the coffins."

"What we do then?" wondered Beowulf.

"Let's sneak out of here as fast as we can and hope that we've made the right decision."

"That didn't take long," said Ake. "We've barely had time to unload the sleds."

"It was a piece of cake," Ray told him.

"Did you get a good price?" joked Ake.

"Initially they wanted too much for it," Ray said as he opened the hatch to the huge storage space under the personnel area. "But we dickered and I finally made them an offer they couldn't refuse."

"All them coffins gonna fit in there?" questioned Mama-san.

"They'll fit," Ray reassured Mama-san. "We're gonna have to leave the moose head behind, though."

"Yes, they will fit," said Janos, scanning the space with his infrared sensors. Then the 'bot looked around. "What moose head?"

"Let's get the hell out of here before we're discovered," Ake said.

"C'mon, Janos," Beowulf said when the little 'bot just stood there. "We gots to go."

"I cannot."

"Sure you can."

"What's the problem, Janos?" Ray asked.

"It is my programming. I am already experiencing strongly disruptive internal directives because I have ventured outside the perimeter of the compound. I can go no farther."

"Janos—" Ray said, taking a step toward the 'bot.

"Please, stay back," the 'bot warned. "I may be programmed to destroy myself if I am compelled to leave the vicinity."

Ray felt a lump in his throat. "Janos, I don't know what to say. Thank you for all you've done."

"Thank you for liking me."

"Ah, gee, Janos," said Beowulf.

"Please. Go. Go now." The little 'bot turned and headed back toward the compound.

★ ★ ★

With Ake driving, Ray elected to man the laser cannon in the half-track's rear. "You see anything on the screens yet?" he asked Ake.

"Not so far. Maybe we're going to get away scot-free."

"Maybe," Ray allowed. "Xian's got his hands on 'DiCiancia's' fiefdom now. Maybe taking ourselves out of his hair means we're one less thing for him to have to worry about."

"And, do you really think that?"

"No. I think he'd like to get his hands on us and cut our hearts out."

Ake sighed. "We also have two scout dog teams. I imagine they're worth a lot."

Over the intercom Ray's voice said, "Maybe he doesn't know about them."

"Oops," said Ake.

That didn't seem like a proper response to his comment, Ray decided. "What's going on?" he asked.

"Look at the road," Ake said. "A kilometer or so back, before I realized it, the cowpath we were on turned into a six-lane highway. Just as suddenly, we got funneled into this strange partitioned roadway. I remember seeing a sign saying something about repairs; of course, that could have been from years ago."

Ray looked. Ake was right: They'd headed down a strip of roadway made into two narrow lanes by tall slabs of plascrete. Apparently, the six lanes Ake had mentioned were now separated from each other by five-meter-high walls. It was like driving in a canyon, a manmade one.

"Well, I guess we can't turn around too easily," Ray said. "Let's hope this doesn't last long."

"Oh, shit!" Ake exclaimed.

Ray put his hand to his face. "I'm afraid to ask, but now what?"

"I think you'd better ready the cannon *now*."

"Why?"

"Look in the 'viewer at what's behind us."

"Jumping Jesus!" exclaimed Ray.

Following them were more than a half-dozen vehicles: four one- and two-man hoverbikes, three armored cars with their own energy cannons, and, bringing up the rear, a half-track the equal of their own. All of the pursuing vehicles bore Xian's crimson skull insignia.

Staring at the armada pursuing them, Ake gulped. "Didn't we just go through this scene off Alexandria?"

"Not recently," said Ray. "That was twelve years ago."

"Picky, picky."

Disdaining the 'viewer, Littlejohn peered cautiously out the back. "Jeez, lookit at that! I guess that General See-on guy really wants us dead."

"Maybe one of us left our wallet behind." When Ozma stared at him, Ray said, "Or maybe not."

Without warning, a bolt of energy from one of the armored cars struck their rear shields. Even with their speed carrying the heated air away from them, they could smell the hot, burned metal odor.

"Now what'll we do?" wailed Ake.

The bolt was all Ray and the dogs needed; their senses vibrated in response to the stimulus, like fire-engine horses to the sound of the bell.

"You make sure no one gets in front of us and we'll do what we can back here," Ray told Ake.

Ake took a deep breath. "Right you are."

Ray grabbed the laser cannon and, after firing a couple of attention-getting blasts at the armored cars, adjusted the setting to emit discrete energy pulses, stellar-hot lightning bolts that would make short work of the hoverbikes, shields or no.

As if reading Ray's thoughts, the hoverbikes quickly closed the distance to the half-track, racing to move to positions close to the lumbering monstrosity so that Ray would be unable to fire at them.

"A couple of those 'bikes are coming up on either side of us, Ake," Ray warned his partner. "Be careful."

"I see them." Ake carefully edged over to the right side of the road, seeming to drift there without purpose. That was what the one-man 'bikers thought.

They were wrong.

Ake glanced at the display showing the left side of the half-track. He smiled. The 'biker on that side had taken the bait and moved up beside the half-track. Ake turned the large wheel like he'd been driving the half-track for years and forced the unfortunate 'biker into the plascrete wall.

The half-track ground driver and 'bike into the wall, sparks flying and plasteel screaming. When Ake could no longer bear the unholy fingernails-across-chalkboard vibration that resulted from his action, he found the center of the road again and the pitiful remains of driver and 'bike, horribly intermingled, slid down the wall and bounced into the path of one of the armored cars—which promptly ran over it.

"Nice job, Ake," Ray congratulated him, slipping down into the half-track's personnel area for a moment's respite.

"Thanks . . . I think."

"Like you told me on the ship: Try not to think of them as people, but as the 'enemy.' They *do* mean us harm."

Ake sighed. "I dislike dehumanizing people the better to kill them, but I'll return the favor if that's the way they're treating me."

"Too much talk," Beowulf said. "Worry 'bout right an' wrong later."

"I agree," said Ray, obliging the big dog by remanning the cannon and directing a steady stream of energy at one of the armored cars, which was more than willing to trade fire with the larger vehicle it was pursuing.

After one especially intense stream of energy had played over the armored car, Ray noticed colored sparks flying from its front shields. "Ake . . . can you put this thing on auto-control for a minute and come help me?"

"Are you crazy?"

"Yes, but that's beside the point. Get your ass back here!"

"Hang on, I'm on my way."

When Ake's head poked out through the hatch, Ray said, "Grab one of those energy rifles and join me in pouring in as much concentrated energy on one spot as we can." He noticed Beowulf's concern: a "I-wish-I-could-do-more-than-just-stand-around-here-like-a-statue" look. "Sorry, Beowulf, you've got everything that counts except hands."

"Yah," agreed Beowulf.

Between the two of them, Ray and Ake overloaded the armored car's front shields, allowing a stream of energy to lance into the suddenly vulnerable vehicle. "Duck," Ray said, just in time.

The armored car's hood, top, and sides were blown out by a powerful explosion, and the other vehicles had to maneuver smartly to avoid the debris. "That's two down and six to go," exulted Ake.

Ray shot him a look. "What are you doing here?" he asked.

"Huh?"

Ray gestured toward the cab. "Get back and drive this thing."

Ake just shook his head and ducked through the hatchway.

The pursuers continued, without observable success, to pepper the back of the half-track with assorted bolts of energy and high-velocity slugs. Nothing got through the shields.

No sooner had Ray said, "Looks like it's a standoff," than a laser beam burned through the air beside his head, so close that his skin tingled.

"Uh-oh," Tajil said.

"I heard that," said Ake from the front. "What happened?"

"I think we just lost our force field. It may have been a piss-poor one," Ray said, "but it *was* a force field."

"You're right. The display up here shows it's gone."

"How could that happen?"

"If our *doppelganger* back there is similarly equipped, it may also be capable of lowering our force field remotely—you know, 'fleet control.' "

"Damn!" Ray swore. "And our shields?"

"I don't think they can touch them."

"Thank heaven for small blessings."

Ake stared into the 'viewer at the picture being displayed of the half-track's flanks. "Hey, something's going on."

"Yeah, what?"

"You aren't going to believe this, but stand by to repel boarders!"

The "boarders" were from the three remaining hoverbikes—the driver of the one-man 'bike and the "shotgun riders" from the two-man 'bikes. Ake's warning was almost too late. An arm appeared over the right side of the personnel bay as the first man attempted to find a secure position from which to fire into the crowded center of the bay.

"Watch the other side!" Ray ordered Beowulf. He leapt down onto the floor of the bay, scrambling to find and pick up the energy rifle Ake had abandoned. In the time it took for him to do that, the boarder—his long blond hair flowing in the airstream—had stabilized his position and stood up to fire at the dogs. He got off one shot. (Later, Ray would recall an indelible image of the man's yellow hair fluttering like a flag and wonder about the ability of the mind to seize and permanently store one striking image in the midst of a *tsunami* of such images. *Why* that *one*? he would ask himself.)

As Ray brought the energy rifle up to his shoulder in a single fluid motion, he heard one of the dogs yelp in pain. Putting that from his mind, he centered the rifle's sights on the intruder and squeezed the firing stud. Ray took such special care—even holding his breath at the right time—that he was flabbergasted when his shot missed.

An energy bolt from over Ray's shoulder caught the man in the Adam's apple and he tumbled from the half-track without a sound. Ray's head whipped around to see a young rifleman on an overpass giving him a thumbs-up signal. "It looks like General Xian and his goons have some detractors among the populace hereabouts," he said.

He rushed to the other side of the personnel area and, ignoring the fire coming from the pursuing vehicles, leaned over and unloosed a bolt at the right boarder, who was about to make the daredevil transfer from his comrade's 'bike. The shot missed the boarder but struck the 'bike, flashing down through the vehicle's power cells. The ball of flame from the 'bike's explosion engulfed the boarder. For several long, agonizing seconds he maintained his grip. Then, his clothes completely aflame, he lost his handhold and slipped beneath the treads of the half-track.

Ray turned to see a boarder from the other side pointing an energy pistol at him. Ray's heart stopped in that instant. But before the man could unleash a fatal bolt, Littlejohn had reached up, seized his arm, and pulled him over the side and into the bay. The pistol discharged harmlessly into the half-track's wall.

The intruder disappeared beneath the dogs, screaming horribly. The screams stopped abruptly and Ray knew the dogs had ripped out his throat. *That's twice someone's walked across my grave,* Ray told himself. *I'd appreciate there not being a third time.*

"Ray, Ozma's hurt," Beowulf told him. It was the first opportunity the big dog had had to report the injury.

"Is it serious?"

"I doan think so. The bolt burnded her side, but it dint really hit her."

"Thank God! That's good to hear," Ray said, his knees suddenly weak.

"Please tell me everything's all right back there," Ake's voice said through the intercom.

"Everything's all right back here," Ray snapped. Then he relented. "We could be a lot worse," he said. He glanced over the right side, saw no one, and then did the same on the left side. The only remaining 'bike had dropped back a bit; not enough to become a target, but far enough to indicate its rider had no intentions of attempting to transfer to the half-track. "It looks like they've given up on trying to join us for tea."

Ray decided that he'd wait until later to tell Ake about his guardian angel.

Making the best of the breathing space, Ray went to the injured Ozma's side. He smelled burnt fur and skin. The wound looked horrible, but Ray realized there was no way of telling the actual extent of the injury without a more thorough examination. There was time enough to do some simple treatment however.

"Taddy, go get Ake's medical bag over in the corner. He's got some first-aid supplies in it."

"Yes, Ray."

"And hurry. I haven't much time to do this." As if to punctuate his words, Ray chanced leaping up to the energy cannon and loosing a few bolts in the direction of their pursuers.

"That accomplished diddly-squat," Ray muttered to no one in particular. "But at least it lets them know we're still here."

After a volley of return fire peppered the half-track's rear shields, Gawain said, "Uh, I think they knows that already."

When Taddy brought over Ake's bag, Ray dug out a disposable syringe. Ake had soon learned that injection guns were useless on the dogs' thick fur and now carried an ample supply of the archaic needles. Ray quickly found a painkiller, filled the syringe, and sought an appropriate spot on Ozma's neck. He plunged the syringe home. "There, that's done. Stay with her, Mama-san."

Ray pointed at one of the half-track's many small equipment lockers. "What's in there?" Ray asked Beowulf. The big dog pressed his nose against the locker Ray had indicated and it popped open, spilling out a dozen grenades.

"Hand bombs!" shouted Beowulf gleefully.

"Don't be so happy," Ray cautioned. "Grenades are about as effective against armored vehicles as ping-pong balls are against a tank."

"Oh." Beowulf deflated a bit.

Ray suddenly thought of something. "Hey, Ake, have those armored cars got force fields?"

"How should I know?" Ake's voice came back. Then he gave more consideration to Ray's question. "You know, now that I think about it, I don't believe they do. They're too small to carry a force-field generator. We've miniaturized a lot of things over the years, but not those types of generators."

"Thanks, Ake. I'll give my idea a shot." Ray crept to the video 'viewer that provided the image of their pursuers. The sole surviving 'bike was out of sight, tucked in close on one side, but their half-track was still being trailed by two armored cars and the enemy half-track. Although one of the armored cars was hugging the wall on the right, the second was almost directly behind them.

Ray pulled the pin on a grenade, held it for a moment, then lobbed it high in the air and over the back of the half-track. He turned his head to the rear-view 'viewer in time to see the grenade land in the road, bounce once, and then veer off to the side of the road and explode harmlessly against the plascrete wall. "Damn."

Ray tried again.

This effort was a bit more accurate, but no more successful: The grenade came down on the hood of the armored car where its blast was deflected by the shields.

Again.

This time the grenade hit the pavement, bounced high in the air, and came down in a perfect arc, dropping directly into the rear of the armored car and exploding almost immediately.

"Yessir!" Ray cheered. "Deadeye Dick scores again!"

Smoke pouring from its interior, the armored car began to weave back and forth across the confined space, finally colliding with the right wall and rebounding out into the path of the half-track trailing behind it. The half-track's momentum smashed the burning car out of the way like it was an empty cardboard box.

The dogs cheered and Ake said, "Way to go, Ray."

"Hey, that's how I used to win top-shelf-choice prizes at the Grange Fair every year."

His elation was short-lived, however. "Jeez, Louise, you'd think these guys would get the message and leave us alone," he complained, observing the doggedly pursuing vehicles in the 'viewer.

Ake knew better. "I'd guess that General Xian and his 'shining path' comrades have no room for quitters and . . . oh, shit!"

"What?"

"The 'reader just displayed a sign informing us that this partitioned-lane business ends in eight kilometers. If these guys get us in the open, they've got the edge on us, even if there's only three of them left."

As another futile blast rocked the half-track, Ray slumped slightly and muttered to himself, " 'Go get 'em, Ray, you can do it, Ray. Attaboy, Ray.' "

"Ray?" said Littlejohn.

"Yeah?"

"You *can* do it—you our Man."

Ray sighed. He was touched by Littlejohn's confidence. The only problem was living up to it.

"How many of those grenades we got left?" Ray asked. If they were going to stubbornly persist in this notion that he was a hero, then he was just going to have to act like one.

Beowulf pushed them around with his nose. " 'Bout eight or nine."

Ray picked up three and told Ake, "Be ready to act the moment I tell you to."

"You're the boss."

Ray pulled the pin on one grenade and tossed it over the right side of the half-track. Hardly had the first one left his hand than he tossed a second, and then a third.

"It didn't work," Ake told him, having seen the results of the explosions on his right-side 'viewer. "The 'bike just dropped back and fell in behind us, I think."

"Then it worked," said Ray.

"Huh?"

"Hit the brakes when I tell you."

"But—"

"Now!"

Ake hit the brakes.

Staring at the 'viewer, Ray saw the unfortunate 'biker, unable to dump his forward momentum in time, smash into the rear of the half-track. Rider and 'bike might have recovered if the remaining armored car, also unable to slow down in time, had not sandwiched the 'bike between its front and the rear of the half-track.

"Jesus!" exclaimed Ake, averting his eyes.

"That's a little trick I learned from you on *The Spirit of St. Louis*. Now floor it!" Ray said, climbing up to man the cannon once again.

As the mangled remains of the 'bike and armored car came into view, Ray unleashed a flurry of bolts into the middle of the smoking mass. The resulting explosion left them with only one antagonist now—their sister half-track.

"Just four kilometers to go," Ake informed everyone.

"Yeah, yeah . . ." said Ray.

"And more good news: If anything, this lane is narrowing."

"It is? Hmmm."

That "hmmm" sounds promising, Ake thought. *But what can Ray possibly have left in his bag of tricks?*

Ray opened more lockers: food, battle gear, drugs, glue packets, plasteel rope, and assorted nudie holozines. "Mom!" he exclaimed when the image of one especially well-endowed young woman leapt off the cover at him.

"That really Ray's mom?" asked Gawain, staring at the strawberry-blonde young woman. "She not look like him."

Frodo just shook his head. "Gawain, you is truly amazing."

"Thanks."

One locker—the very last possible locker, as a matter of fact—yielded up a treasure. "Ah-ha, what have we here?" Ray brought out a plain, plasteel container. Inside was an impressive-looking piece of machinery. Ray stroked it languorously, the way a lover might stroke his partner's silky smooth inner thigh. "Hello, beautiful."

Beowulf's eyes widened in recognition. "Is that another one o' them smart bombs?"

"It ain't a giant vibrator," Ray said, carefully removing it from its shock-resistant container. Then he pressed a color-coded blister on the bomb's side. When the weapon powered up and came to life, he said matter-of-factly, "Good, that activated it. I figured I had a fifty-fifty chance of either activating it or setting it off. Seems I guessed right."

"Heh, heh," said Frodo nervously. "He guessed right."

11

"Well, hello, bomb."

"Hello, sir. Since I have been activated, I presume there is a mission for me?"

"A very important mission," Ray told the weapon.

"Outstanding!"

"One question: Do you have a remote communications device?"

"Here you are, sir." The bomb raised a pen-sized microphone from its casing.

"Clever," said Ray, removing the tiny 'phone and staring at it with interest. Then: "Okay, bomb, stand by."

He picked up the abandoned hoverboard and activated it. "Yes, a standard hoverboard. They haven't changed all that much since I was a kid." He dropped it and it floated—*hovered*—several centimeters off the floor of the bay. "Perfect."

"One kilometer to go," announced Ake.

"And what's the time and temperature, Mr. Information?" Ray asked absently. Ake didn't get it but the dogs chuckled.

Ray opened a glue packet, spread it liberally on top of the hoverboard, and then gently laid the smart bomb on top of the viscous layer. It bonded to the board immediately. Next, Ray glued the plasteel rope to the front of the hoverboard and loosely coiled it. "Okay, let's go," he said, picking up the bomb-laden hoverboard.

Ray climbed back down into the hatchway and set the bomb down. It bobbed gently atop the hoverboard. "Let's hope the gyros are working well."

He opened the bottom escape hatch and carefully lowered the hoverboard toward the road's surface. It bucked and jerked slightly, but no more than he had anticipated. "Okay," Ray told the bomb. "When I give the order, bomb, you are to detonate."

"Yes, SIR!" beamed the bomb.

"I admire someone who likes his job," Ray said as he played out the plasteel rope. "Beowulf, Ake—either or both of you tell me when this thing is under the half-track on our ass."

"A littler farther," said Ake, staring intently into the rear 'viewer.

"Yah, you gots more to go," agreed Beowulf.

"It just went under the half-track," Ake told him.

"Good. I'll feed out another two meters."

"That's great right there."

"Bomb?"

"Yes, sir?"

"Do your thing."

"Thank you, sir."

Ray averted his face from the escape hatch just in time. An enormous explosion rocked their half-track and a wave of hot gases radiated out from the destroyed vehicle and under their own. Ray dropped the rope and slammed the hatch closed. "God!"

"Yah, stink," agreed Sinbad.

"I take it we eliminated our last pursuer?" Ray asked Ake.

"What pursuer?"

"I get your meaning." Ray sighed. Now he could attend to Ozma.

Ray cleaned Ozma's wound and carefully applied some antiseptic salve to her burn-reddened skin. "That hurt?" he asked.

"Nah, feels good. Nice an' cool."

He finished slathering on the salve and stopped to stare at his handiwork. "That'll have to do for now," he said, reaching for a roll of sterile gauze to wrap around Ozma's chest. It took a lot of bandaging to encircle Ozma's rib cage several times. "Hey, do you know how much this stuff costs by the yard?" Ray asked, using the old British/American unit of measurement. "Nobody else get hurt. We can't afford this."

The dogs laughed at Ray's carping about money. They knew his good-humored complaining meant that Ozma's wounds weren't serious. "Well, if that's all the respect I get, I'm going up front with Ake. *He* knows the value of a credit."

"I go with you," said Beowulf.

"Okay."

"How's Ozma?" Ake asked as Ray ducked through the hatch and climbed up into his seat.

"It's nothing serious. You can take a look at her when we pull over to contact the ship's computer."

"Okay." Ake glanced at his watch. "Give me another hour or so to put more distance between us and anyone else from Xian's gang who may wish to thank us for all our good deeds."

"I think we've left that behind us," Ray said.

"Is that just a hunch, or do you have an actual reason for feeling that way?"

Ray gestured at the highway. "Look how much the traffic's picked up in the last few klicks. We're away from those damn semiautonomous government areas and back in the real world again."

"Yeah. This is more like the Boswash I was expecting to find when we landed," Ake said, observing the ever-increasing number of vehicles crowding the highway.

"I guess not everybody had the money to go to the colony worlds and start a new life when the Federation fell apart."

"Judging from the condition of their floaters and cars and trucks, they haven't the money for repairs and body work, either."

Ray couldn't fault Ake's observation. "Yeah. Nothing looks new, not even the vehicles I don't recognize—the ones that must have been produced in the last twelve years."

"Can you punch up a map showing us how to get to New York?" Ake asked.

"I'll try." Ray fumbled with the dashboard computer. "Ah, here we go: Once we hit 695, we head east until we find 295.

Then we follow that north. It'll take us all the way to New York."

Ake rubbed the side of his mouth. "Hmmm. Can you find a good place for the ship to rendezvous with us for the transfer of the coffins?"

"Just a minute." Ray punched in coordinates and then pored over the display. "How about the old Baltimore-Washington airport?"

"The airport?"

"Yeah, it was destroyed by heavy fighting during the Second American Revolution. Someone on one side or the other took it out with a really dirty nuke. Seems the radiation residue meant the whole area had to be pretty much abandoned."

"Is it still hot?"

"A little, not much," Ray said. "If we get in fast, transfer our cargo, and get out as quickly as we got in, there won't be a problem."

"The ship should have no trouble finding those coordinates. Okay, let's do it," Ake agreed. "Go ahead and call the computer now."

As the half-track plowed on toward its rendezvous with the ship, Ray dozed. It was a fitful sleep, punctuated by snorts and half-formed words. Ake gazed over at his partner and supposed that any sleep was better than no sleep at all.

Ray's head lolled to one side, waking him, this time for good. "Sorry," he said through a yawn. "I guess I must have dropped off for a while. Everything okay?" Ray picked at some gummy sleep residue in the corner of his right eye, glanced disinterestedly at it, and wiped his finger surreptitiously on his shirt.

"Yep," Ake replied. "Just don't get alarmed when you look in the rear 'viewer."

"Huh?" Ray looked. He saw a number of vehicles trailing them at a respectful distance. "Yeah, so what? It's a busy highway."

"They've been back there for about thirty klicks or so, content to keep their distance. See how they're spaced across the lanes to keep anyone from passing them and getting closer to us?"

"Now I do. What do you think—are they more of Xian's men?"

Ake shook his head. "I don't think so."

"Then who are they?"

"Locals is my guess."

"I wonder what they want?"

"Probably this half-track."

"As far as I'm concerned, they deserve to have it." He told Ake about the youth on the overpass who'd saved his life during the fight.

"That's good enough for me," Ake said. "Once we get back to the ship, this monster's theirs."

The Spirit of St. Louis was waiting for them when they arrived at the site of the long-abandoned airport. "There she is," Ake said, the first to spot the ship as it sat on a crumbling plascrete runway.

"I'm sure glad to see the old pile of nuts and bolts," Ray admitted.

"I wonder why no one's making a play for the ship?"

"The area's hot, but I think a more immediate reason is that no one wants to commit suicide." Ray pointed: The computer was sweeping the laser cannons in broad arcs, ready to lay down a terrible enfilade should anyone attempt an attack. "I'm glad we told the Iron Maiden what we'd be driving."

"Let's get moving," Ake said, stopping the half-track beside the ship. "The faster we can unload the coffins and get them into the ship, the less time we expose ourselves to the residual radiation."

"Aye, aye, Cap'n Bligh," Ray said, saluting, opening the door, and climbing down from the half-track's cab as Ake lowered the rear gate and freed the dogs.

"Let's get moving," Ray said as Ake joined them. "I may or may not want kids, but I definitely don't want to roast my chestnuts."

"Welcome back, gentlemen," the computer said via a small speaker on *The Spirit of St. Louis*. "It is good to see that no harm has come to you."

"Even to me?" pressed Ray.

"Even to you," the computer said agreeably.

"I think I'm in love," Ray told Beowulf.

"With the machine-woman? Good, then you don't need no 'chestnuts,' " Beowulf said. The other dogs chuckled.

"Remind me to get a new team," Ray told Ake.

II

Aboard ship, the seconds, minutes, and hours passed slowly, allowing Ray and Ake ample time to think things over and to put the events of the past few days into perspective.

"The dogs are kidding me about 'the machine-woman,' but it's the 'machine-man' whom I really miss," Ray confessed to Ake as they sat in the lounge, the pack forming a semicircle around their chairs.

"Yeah," Ake agreed. "I miss that little 'bot, too."

Bemoaning lost opportunities, Ray said, "If we'd had time to question him, he might have given us some answers about where to find the rest of the scout dog teams."

"Uh, Ray," said Mama-san, lifting her massive head from paws and looking him in the face.

"Yeah?" said Ray absently, annoyed at himself for having lost both Svoboda and Janos.

"I know where the other teams are."

"What?" Ray straightened up.

"How can you possibly know that?" asked Ake.

"Janos tole me," Mama-san confided shyly. "He tole me it was an important secret. That awful doctor guy tole him not to tell another human being." She grinned a crooked canine grin. "So he dint—he tole me."

Ray shook his head in admiration. "That little guy had more soul than Svoboda could ever have hoped for."

Beowulf sighed. "I jes' hope he's all right."

It took the full sixty hours for the twenty dogs and seven humans to "thaw out."

"The first thing we have to do, unless these freezer babies have some special knowledge," said Ray, "is to get them to a place of safety."

Ake nodded. "Sure. But that's easier said than done."

Ray took a sip of his Beefeater martini. "Ake, do you or the computer have any ideas? Where we can take these guys, I mean?"

"I can offer several immediate suggestions," the computer said. "But I must have more input before my advice has any real value."

"What would you like to know?"

"Are these fully trained, fully educated teams?" the computer asked.

"What you mean?" queried Beowulf.

Ray pulled an olive on a toothpick out of his drink and stared at it; he plunked it back into the alcohol to allow it to soak up more flavor. "I confessed my doubts about the readiness of the teams to the computer, Beowulf," Ray told his leader. "Very few of the dogs seems to be full-grown adults."

"Are you sure about that?" Ake asked him.

"I don't *know* it, but I sense it; I sense their immaturity." Ray looked at his watch. "Besides, we'll know for sure in less than forty-eight hours."

"What the big deal 'bout that, anyway?" questioned Gawain.

"Qualified trainers educated your mother and your uncles and aunts, Gawain. Later, when you and the other puppies were born, I educated you and your siblings. Untrained scout dogs are worse than useless—they're dangerous."

"Oh."

"Let's assume, for argument's sake, that they will have to undergo more training," Ake said. "How does that color our thinking?"

"Then they will need a complete and professional training facility," the computer said.

Ray shook his head in irritation. "And maybe Santa will bring us all toys and chocolates, too. We have to face facts: 'Complete and professional training facilities' don't exist any longer. They're gone with the wind—as extinct as dodo birds and humpback whales."

"Ray's right," Ake said. "Even if we should succeed in finding and rescuing any of the dogs Svoboda sold off to the warlords, their personalities will be so warped that they'll need to be put through an exhaustive program of psychological rehabilitation."

"Sounds complicated," Sinbad said. "Sounds 'spensive, too."

Ray snapped his fingers. "I've got a whole jar of coins in the closet in my room, hidden behind my *Captain Trimble* action figures."

"You gots some *Captain Trimble* dolls!" exclaimed Gawain excitedly. "Can I see them?"

"Later," Ray said. He shot Ake an intense look.

"Don't give me that stare," Ake laughed. "Spend the damn money; that's what it's for, isn't it? What are you gonna do, buy a whole planet with it?"

"There's an idea." Ray popped an olive into his mouth.

★ ★ ★

Ake looked up when Ray entered the communications room. "How are the 'sleeping beauties' coming along?" he asked.

"Everything seems fine," Ray told him. "Maybe another twenty-four hours."

"Good." Ake turned back to what he was doing.

"Ah, is all this necessary?" Ray asked. "Having to stand by and watch as you disconnect the engines from the power cores and bring another five cores on line is a bit disconcerting. Why do we need all that brute power?"

"That's what it takes to blast a signal through subspace to Skerchock. Buchanan's light-years away, not around the corner."

"I guess it's necessary, then."

"Uh-huh," Ake said, his fingers dancing across the complicated communications console. Row after row of readouts began to light up and a low, powerful hum began to resonate as all the power of the ship was focused on creating a wave of energy capable of piercing the fabric of space.

"Here we go," said Ake. He touched a glowing red cube which slowly sank into the top of the console. A clear yet unobtrusive chiming announced that a connection had been made. "We have contact with Buchanan. It'll take a few moments for the relay station there to route us to Skerchock."

Within sixty seconds, a second, deeper, chiming sound proclaimed someone on the other end.

A figure coalesced in the center of the holo projection area, electronically painted in the air. It was John Skerchock.

"This better be important," Skerchock said, stifling a yawn. "It's the middle of the goddamn night, for Pete's sake!"

"It's important," Ray told him.

"Ray! You're still breathing, you old sonofabitch!" He saw Ake now, as well. "And Ake. Ray hasn't gotten you killed yet, either, eh?"

Ake looked down at himself. "I seem to be still alive."

Skerchock's look of amusement turned serious. "Hey, where are you guys and what's up?"

"We're just off Terra," Ray told him. "Well, out a ways, a bit past the belt and Jupiter—you know, the wide-open spaces where a man can stretch his legs."

"Uh-huh. So, did you just call to pass the time of day?"

"We've got some dogs on board who are going to need a place to grow and develop. They've got some humans attached to them, too, but we don't know who or what they are. They might be trainers, leaders, or even be completely unrelated to the dogs."

"I think it's unlikely they'd have no connection to the dogs since they're with them," Ake said with authority.

Skerchock shook his head. "You guys do lead interesting lives. I've got to get out more myself."

"Well, that's why we're calling you, squarehead," Ray told him.

Skerchock sighed in resignation. It wasn't very convincing. Even across the vast emptiness separating them, Ray could sense that his friend was eager to help.

"What's the story? It won't hurt to listen to your pitch, I suppose."

"We need you."

"You *need* me?" He reconsidered that before adding, "Let me rephrase that: You need *me*?"

"We want to hire you," Ake informed him. "Can you get out of your current contract?"

"Sure. But the buyout clause mandates a fifteen-thousand-credit payment for me to say bye-bye with two weeks' notice."

"Two weeks is too long. How about immediately?"

Skerchock whistled. "I could wiggle off the hook for twenty-five thousand."

"Wiggle off; the check's in the mail," Ray said.

"Then what?"

"Hie yourself over to Gandhi and wait for us there."

"Gandhi?" Skerchock's image look puzzled. "Isn't that the world originally colonized by pacifists?"

"That's it," confirmed Ake.

"What about the colonists? Won't they be less than thrilled to welcome a bunch of semimilitary types like us and our scout dog teams?"

"Normally, yes," Ray replied. "But we've checked up on it. And things have changed. Several dissident groups established their own sects and went their own way. And, since they were no more immune to basic stone-age human nature and foibles than anyone else, they quickly became holier than thou."

"That sounds typical," Skerchock interjected.

Ray nodded. "The hostility between the various factions got so bad that a civil war broke out over the best way to embody the ideals of Gandhi and nonviolence. Some dickhead introduced atomics into the equation and almost everyone bought the farm in the two hours of tit-for-tat exchanges that followed." To preempt the obvious question, Ray added, "Clean bombs—they killed the humans but did little damage otherwise."

"No shit."

"So we're buying the planet from the survivors, and at fire-sale prices," Ake said. "Well, for several hundred million credits."

"Several hundred million . . . I got to sit down," Skerchock gulped.

"Here, you need this," Ray said, holding out his glass as if offering it to his friend. Skerchock actually began to reach for it before he caught himself in time.

"Very funny," he growled. A dog padded into the projection, joining him.

"Hi, Max," Ray said.

"Hi, Ray, hi, Ake," Maximilian said in return. "Everyone else there? Everyone okay?"

"Yepper."

"You comin' back here?"

"We'd like to—I miss John's cheap cigars," Ray told the big dog. "But that's up to your boss. He hasn't officially accepted our offer yet."

"I accept, I accept," Skerchock said, waving his hand. "Hell, I always wanted to work for someone who owned his own planet."

"I think we got a good deal," Ray deadpanned. "It needs

work, but the location is great—there's a nearby sun to provide heat and light—and the back yard is big enough for a pool and a vegetable patch. Ah, the flavor of fresh rutabagas."

"When do you want me to leave?"

"Why are you still there talking to us?"

"I get the point."

"We've advanced you some money," Ake said. "You'll find there's been one hundred thousand credits deposited to your account."

"You just assumed I'd say yes, eh?"

"Of course." Ray reached for the switch to terminate the signal. "Any other questions?"

"Give me some time and I'll think of some."

"Time is what you ain't got," Ray said, breaking the connection. Skerchock's image wavered, then dissolved into a thousand glowing specks of light that fell away into nothingness.

"It'll be good to see Johnny again," Ray said.

"Yeah," agreed Ake dryly. "What's it been—a week?"

★ ★ ★

It was the humans, not the dogs, who began to stir first; probably because they had less body mass, even though the canines weren't fully grown.

The awakenings followed a predictable pattern: First, the sleeper would sigh and open his or her eyes; second, he or she would ask, "Where am I?"; and, finally, the revived person would be helped to a sitting-up position in his coffin, still too feeble to do more than follow Ray, Ake, and the dogs with his or her eyes.

The four men and three women didn't seem especially surprised to find themselves aboard a private spacecraft. Then again, they seemed not to be surprised by anything except for the fact of their continued existence.

"Why are you folks so startled at being alive?" Ray asked one of them, a burly bearded man called William Kelly. Ray already knew that Kelly had been unfortunate enough to have been touring the compound when Svoboda decided to keep the last generation of scout dogs for himself. The man had just completed his training, but had never actually worked with his team.

Sitting up ramrod straight, Kelly considered the question gravely for a moment—he considered everything gravely, it seemed—and then said, "Because of Dr. Svoboda. He told us he was going to put us into cryogenic suspension, but nobody believed him. We thought he was humoring us. We believed he was really putting us to death, painlessly and efficiently."

"Yeah," agreed one of the other newly awakened sleepers, a pinch-faced young man with a shock of thick, wavy brown hair and a light dusting of brown freckles. "Svoboda had no use for Bill and me, no use at all except for the fact that we'd both worked our asses off the learn to run a dog team. I believed him when it came to keeping the dogs alive, but I thought the rest of us were dead meat."

"I wonder why he *did* keep you alive, then," Ray said, staring thoughtfully at the tight-faced young man. His name was Kyle Sterling. *Kyle Sterling—that sounds like the name of someone in a romance holo,* Ray mused. *'Course, he doesn't* look *like someone in a romance holo.*

"I guess it didn't cost Svoboda anything to freeze us," Kelly said. "Then, if he ever needed team leaders, we were at hand. Anytime he wanted to, he had the option of pulling the plug on our life support systems."

"Hmmm. Like HAL," Ray said. His reference drew puzzled stares.

The other two men and the three women proved to be trainers, validating Ake's reasoned guess. As trainers, they were responsible for taking brash young whelps and turning them into nearly grown dogs prepared to meet their leaders and complete the process that would fuse man and dogs into a cohesive team.

"I guess it's the same with you five," Ake told them.

"Yes," said Ahmad al-Robayan. "That we're alive is a pleasant surprise."

The others nodded—or, rather, tried to. They were still too weak to do much except move their eyes. The fourth male was Kenneth Kamala, a Kenyan. ("Yes," he said with a smile, "Kenneth Kamala from Kenya.") The three women were Sinead McGarry, tiny and blonde; Monique Vanel, full-figured and raven-haired; and Ludmilla Cherkassov, a brooding, brown-haired Russian.

"May we now ask some questions?" queried Cherkassov.

"Certainly," Ake said. They wanted to know where they were and how they had come to be there. Then they wanted to know the date.

When Ake told them, Kamala said, "Then we have been asleep for five years. We are no older, yet we have misplaced five years." He looked at Ray, his eyes widening. "Can you imagine such a thing?"

"Yeah, I think I can."

"How are the dogs?" asked McGarry. "Are they all right?"

"They seem to be," Ray told her. "They're still asleep, which means they'll have an easy time of it when we jump in an hour."

"We're jumping?" al-Robayan said. "To where?"

"To . . ." Ray paused, then closed his mouth. "I don't know."

"You don't even know our destination's name?" said Cherkassov incredulously.

"It *was* called Gandhi, but we haven't give it a new name yet."

"Gandhi," said Monique Vanel. "Isn't that the peace planet?"

Ray nodded. "It's extremely peaceful now."

"Where is this Gandhi?" persisted Cherkassov. "You do know where it is, don't you?"

"Sure," said Ray, throwing Ake a look. "It's out past Sirius."

"Sirius?"

"You know—the Dog Star."

When the hissing died down, Kelley said, "I think we were better off as ice cubes."

PART THREE

Old New York

12

Their final jump took *The Spirit of St. Louis* to within a few million kilometers of Gandhi. Like all colonized worlds, Gandhi was within Terran norms. Some planets had a higher or lower percentage of their surface covered by water, some were hotter or colder, dryer or wetter, heavy-metal richer or poorer, had higher or lower gravity. It didn't really matter; humans were an adaptable species. It so happened that in addition to being deficient in desirable metals, Gandhi was also not in an efficient jump-line for commercial freighters; two of the reasons for its low selling price.

While it was no Cousteau, Gandhi's ocean-to-land ratio was about sixty-five percent to thirty-five percent. The areas where the continents collided had produced tall, young mountains guarding vast plains and steppes. Occasional low mountain ranges, extremely old systems worn down by millions of years of weathering, provided relief from the flat sameness of the central basins.

"This is your planet?" Sinead McGarry asked, staring into the holoviewer as the ship approached.

"Ours and the bank's," Ray joked.

"It looks wonderful."

"It's your new home."

"And we have no say in the matter?" she asked.

"You can get off the ship now, if you'd like," Ray said

hotly, tilting his head in the general direction of one of the airlocks. Then he blew some air through his lips and added, more levelly, "We took you out of Svoboda's hands, defrosted you, and . . ." When she tried to interrupt, he said, "No, let me finish. We revived you and now we're giving you the opportunity to stay and finish training the two teams we found with you. We're giving you a chance to pick up your lives again. But that's up to you." *Stop me!* Ray thought. *How'd I get myself into this pompous mode?* "You don't 'owe' us anything, and Ake and I aren't going to attempt to use moral blackmail to get to do what we think is right. You must choose for yourselves. *Now* you get to talk."

She stepped up to Ray and kissed him hard and long, her tongue teasing the outer curve of his lips. Then she drew back and said, "Thank you for saving us. I didn't mean to imply you were acting like a taller, handsomer Svoboda."

"That's the first time someone ever called me taller than anyone else," Ray marveled.

"Am I interrupting anything?" Ake asked, approaching the two of them.

"Ah, no," Ray said, feeling slightly flushed.

"Good. The dogs are waking up."

After Ray and Ake had introduced everyone to John Skerchock and vice versa, Skerchock said, "Am I glad to see you! It's strange having a whole planet to yourself and your team." He reconsidered that for a moment. "Well, mostly to yourself: There are a few dozen families on the far side of Gandhi who haven't left the planet yet."

"Hey," said Beowulf loudly. When Ray and Skerchock looked at him in surprise, the big dog added, "Oops, sorry. Dint mean to shout, but can we go with Max and the others while you guys talk?"

"Yah!" said Maximilian.

When Ray offered no objection, Skerchock also agreed, saying, "Go ahead, but don't go too far away."

After the dogs had left, barking and making happy *whuffing* sounds in their throats, Ray looked around. "You've picked a good place for the new facilities."

"I like to think so. Gandhi's not the most hospitable planet in the galaxy, but it has its advantages." He raised his right arm and swept it in an arc that took in the rolling prairie and, in the distance, hills building to mountains. "This is one of the nicer areas. We're not only on the edge of the great continental grasslands, we're also within spitting distance of an impressive mountain range."

"How then were you able to buy this planet?" wondered Kenneth Kamala. "I would think such a 'paradise' would not come cheaply."

Skerchock cocked his head, a smile on his face. He'd heard the quotation marks around paradise. "You'd think so, wouldn't you?" He nodded at Ray. "Mighty Mite over there and I are both anthropologists. Most primitive tribes"—he considered that for a moment—"hell, just plain most *people*, back on Old Earth considered themselves unique. So their name for themselves was often simply 'The People.' "

"What does this have to do with the price of this planet?" Ludmilla Cherkassov asked impatiently.

"Hold on, I'm getting there. Old Earthers *also* thought it was entirely possible that Earth was the only such planet in the entire universe." He paused to allow that absurd notion to sink in. "Notice, I said in the entire universe, not the galaxy. The idea that there might be dozens, hundreds, thousands, even millions of planets capable of sustaining Terran lifeforms was beyond their imaginings."

"And your point is?" Cherkassov pressed.

"My point is that there *are* many such planets. If Gandhi isn't the norm, neither is it extraordinary. With hyperspace allowing us to jump from one point in space to another in the blink of an eye, our little oxygen-sucking race can find habitable planets at will.

"Sure, there are hundreds of thousands of planets where conditions *aren't* right for humans to live and work, just as the naysayers predicted, but there are also just as many where they are."

"There's another reason buying Gandhi wasn't beyond our means," Ake added. "Its siblings aren't equally hospitable to oxygen-breathers or to terraforming. The economics of a one-planet system, especially one so far off the starway, sours many investors."

"So just like that you bought this planet?" asked Sinead McGarry.

"Just like that," Ray confirmed. "And imagine how many green stamps you get with a purchase this big."

"Green stamps?" several puzzled voices said. Ray smiled, happy to have flummoxed everyone again with his arcane twentieth-century pop culture trivia.

"Ah, maybe this is a good time to present you with this," Skerchock said as he handed Ray a small sheet of plaspaper.

"What is it?" asked Ake. Ray passed the sheet over. "Jumping Jesus!" Ake exclaimed.

"Yeah, I know you advanced me a hundred thousand," Skerchock said. "But you also wanted this camp built as quickly as possible, so I ordered more material than I could cover with that amount. That's the rest of the bill."

"What are we using to build this facility?" Ray asked. "Platinum?"

"The first hundred thousand credits covered the building materials," Skerchock told him. "The rest of the money went for six all-purpose construction 'bots. Them little fellers don't come cheap."

"Construction 'bots?" asked Ray, thinking of Janos.

"Yeah, construction 'bots—you know, little metal-and-plastic guys that work all day and all night without complaint. You never heard of them before?"

Ray looked away. "He's heard of them before," Ake said softly.

★ ★ ★

The new dogs were allowed to join Ray's and Skerchock's teams when they went roaming for fun and exercise. Before they ran off, however, Skerchock put some limitations on both teams and the still-unproven whelps from Terra. "You can chase other animals, especially those rabbitlike things," he told them, laying down the ground rules, "but no killing. The new guys haven't learned all the conventions yet."

"Okay," agreed Maximilian and Beowulf, happy to be free to run and play.

Now, as the sun beat down with midday might, they paused by a small, fast running brook. Some of the dogs lapped up the cool, refreshing water while others lolled about in the shade provided against Gandhi's +4.90 (Sol-standard) magnitude sun by a few stubby, but leafy, trees.

"You new guys," Maximilian said. "Why doan you introduce yourselves all at onct? We knows some of your names, but let's do it right."

"Yeah," agreed Beowulf. "Who are you all?"

The new dogs looked shyly around. Finally, one brown-and-tan dog, bolder than his compatriots, stepped forward. "I am Bunter." He then approached Maximilian and submissively licked his face, doing the same for Beowulf.

The other dogs followed suit: "I am Nell . . . Jack . . . Sasha . . . Tim . . . Genghis . . . Susie . . . Bluto . . . Zazu . . . Topper . . . Otis . . . Kong . . . Conan . . . Morgana . . . Cosmo . . . Hercules . . . Agamemnon . . . Cromwell . . . Ivan." The last dog introduced himself as "Napoleon."

"Twenny dogs," mused Beowulf. "That prob'ly too many for two teams."

"Yeah, even if theys both as big as ours," seconded Maximilian, staring at them.

"Why they too big?" wondered Gawain.

"Teams is usually odd number," Littlejohn explained. "Nine, like us, or seven, or few as five. Some teams gots as many as eleven, but that a lot."

"Well, eleven and nine is twenny," Gawain said. A stunned look appeared on his face as he realized he'd gotten the arithmetic correct for a change.

"Jeez, Gawain is right," said an awed Sinbad.

"Yah, he right," Beowulf said, "but them is still two really big teams."

Mama-san noticed the new dogs standing around, tails lowered, silently observing the team's animated conversation. "What's the matter?" she asked. "Why you dogs so shy?"

Several of the young dogs exchanged glances. "You is like a *family*," Nell said softly.

"Yah," agreed Bunter. "We is twenny dogs, all individuals, but you all is a team. You acts together."

"Ah, it ain't so hard," said Sinbad. "You just needs to train and train and train. And when you knows the rules and how to act in any situashun, you gets to 'dopt a Man and vicey versy."

Beowulf was pleased by Nell's and Bunter's observations. Their words meant they had normal dog I.Q.s. From the negative way Ray and Skerchock had spoken of the newer dogs, he had expected them to be somehow less than they should be. It wasn't true; the new dogs had the potential to be complete and functioning scout dogs, to become part of a real team. More than ever, then, it meant that they had to rescue as many of the lost teams on Terra as they could.

"Doan you whelps worry," Mama-san told them. "You work hard with the trainers and you be just as good as anyone."

At that moment, several furry little hoppers bounded over a rise, stopped short at the sight of the mass of dogs, and beat a hasty retreat.

"Hey!" said Mama-san, getting to her feet and tearing off after them. She was quickly followed by the rest of the dogs, and the chase was on.

Getting the new facility ready to house the twenty untrained dogs took a week. Amazed at the capability with which the 'bots worked, Skerchock thought, *I can't believe that all this took just seven days*. Ray, anxious to get back to Terra, thought, *I can't believe this took a whole seven days!*

Completing all the structures and preparing to receive upwards of another two hundred dogs would take much longer, of course, so Ray and Ake decided not to delay their return to Terra until the work was done. As Ake told Skerchock at one point, "Who knows how long it's going to take us to locate and rescue the few Terran teams we know about? You and the others can continue finishing up here while we're doing what we have to do."

II

Emerging from hyperspace, *The Spirit of St. Louis* was still many hundreds of thousands of kilometers from Terra. "The slow part of the journey," Ray complained to no one in particular. "Slogging through the belt to Terra."

"You'd have made a great pioneer," Ake admonished him.

" 'Fifteen miles on the Erie Canal,' " Ray sang as low as he could drop his voice.

"Ray?" said Ozma.

"Yeah?"

"Doan sing."

"No one appreciates good music anymore," Ray complained.

"Sure we do," Ake said. "That's why we don't want you to sing."

"Yah," piped in Frodo. "Sounds like death cry of a—"

"Okay, okay! I get the message." He sighed. "I don't know why I even started all that."

"You wuz sayin' somethin' 'bout a long trip," Beowulf said helpfully.

"Thanks, Beowulf. That's it: I just hate crossing parsecs of space only to spend hours or even days completing the one-millionth of the journey that's left."

"Since we will not reach Terra for two days, you could use the time to study maps of the Old New York area," the computer's feminine voice suggested.

"I will, I will," Ray insisted.

"He not really upset about the trip," Beowulf explained to the computer. "Ray jes' like to complain. It makes him feel better."

Ray looked at Ake and said, "I feel the way a small child must when adults talk about him as if he isn't in the room."

"An apt simile," the computer said. "In many ways, you are much like a small child, Ray Larkin."

Ray knew the computer was waiting for him to respond, so he decided not to give it the satisfaction. "Ake's going to load up one of his externals with tons of map coordinates and other such information, so it's hard for me to concentrate on learning things I probably won't need to know."

"I see," said the computer. "And of course nothing could ever happen to Dr. Ringgren. No, you needn't study the maps."

Ray knew the computer had him on that point. "I hate it when you're right."

"What would be at least as valuable would be if we went over the information Mama-san received from Janos," Ake suggested.

"Good idea," agreed Ray. "Hey, Mama-san—c'mere and let's hear the run-down on the dogs' locations again." He brought up a holo of the New York area as Mama-san hunkered down beside him.

"Okay, let's see if I remember all this correctly," Ray said, staring intently at the holomap of the city and its environs. "You tell me if I make a mistake, Mama-san."

"Sure."

Ray pointed at Brooklyn. "There are . . . ah, two warlords in Queens, each with several teams." He looked expectantly at Mama-san.

"Yep," she said.

"This is easy. Then there is a warlord in Manhattan—he's the hog. He's accumulated five or six teams."

"That's not two hundred dogs, is it?" Ake asked.

"No, it isn't," agreed Ray. "Some aren't in teams, some were resold or probably died on the job—protecting drug deals is a high-risk occupation." He looked at Mama-san. "But I've pinpointed the ones Janos told you about, haven't I?"

"Yah, you got 'em all now, Ray."

"Brains *in addition* to beauty," Ray crowed. "It's not fair being so blessed, but I have the humility to handle it."

★ ★ ★

"Hey, aren't we coming in a little too fast?" Ray asked Ake as *The Spirit of St. Louis* plunged toward Terra's northern hemisphere.

"Fast, yes. Too fast, no," Ake replied, watching the flashing of the readouts. He glanced over at his friend. "Don't worry, the computer is landing us. My reflexes are pretty good, but not that good."

"We gonna land in the old Fed'ral City, agin?" Beowulf asked.

Ray answered that one. "No, we've seen the last of Svoboda's domain." He pointed at the land mass rapidly rushing toward them. "The computer's going to put us down right there, on the lower edge of the city at JFK Spaceport."

"Ray, go strap the dogs in, please," Ake said. "We're going to be landing shortly."

"Let's go, guys."

The computer landed the ship and then docilely allowed the robotic ground crews to tow it to a temporary parking pad. At the first sign of a hostile act, the computer would have fought back with the ship's weapons.

"You had no problems with the spaceport authorities?" Ray asked.

"No," Ake replied. "They were content to allow us permission to land in return for their rather stiff landing fees." He shrugged. "And why not? I see no reason they should treat us any differently from any other private jumper flying under an Alexandria registry."

"I wish I shared your confidence."

"Well, Mr. Ruby Man—your psi powers aren't picking up hostile intentions, are they?"

"No, they're not," Ray admitted.

"So relax."

When the port authorities did communicate with them, they readily agreed to rent them a high-security parking space for *The Spirit of St. Louis*. With that arranged, they were free to disembark—which they did under the watchful eyes of several heavily armed spaceport security guards.

"Hi, there," Ray said to the stony-faced guards. "Nice day, isn't it?" He smiled, getting only silence and uncomfortable glares in return. "Welcome to New York," Ray said *sotto voce* to Ake.

"Your weapons," said one of the security people, a young woman who appeared to be overweight until one looked closely enough to see what could be mistaken for fat was muscle.

"Huh?"

"You'll have to unload them while you're on JFK grounds."

With the guards watching them closely, Ray and Ake slowly and carefully pulled the charge packs from their energy rifles and pistols, unloaded their slug throwers, and deactivated their needle guns. It was probably a standard security measure, but it made both Ray and Ake aware of just how much firepower they normally packed.

"That's it—I left the surface-to-air missiles on the ship," Ray joked. Nobody smiled.

"Boy," said Frodo as they walked away. "I wonder what stink so bad. Gandhi not smell like this."

"Oh, give Gandhi a chance," Ray said. "It took thousands of years of civilization to royally screw up Terra's air."

"It a screwy place," agreed Gawain seriously.

Wrinkling his own nose—he was much more aware of the

malodorous air now that Frodo had called attention to it—Ray said, "At one time, they'd really done a lot to improve air quality standards. But the recent wars, especially the Rebellion, have put them back to square one. I doubt there *are* standards any longer. Terra these days is pretty wide open. Anything goes."

"Anything?" Ozma asked.

Ray just shrugged and slung his now-unloaded energy rifle over his shoulder. "Beowulf, Littlejohn—get everyone into formation and let's move out."

"Where we goin'?" asked Beowulf.

"We need to rent or buy a hover van," Ray told his leader dog. "We need transportation and I want something where we can keep you guys out of sight as much as possible."

As they took their time finding a walkway to carry them to the terminal building, the glistening thousand-meter-tall spires of Manhattan beckoned them in the distance. *Even from this far away*, Ray thought sadly, *I can see that there are a few gaps where there didn't used to be*. The fighting had claimed many famous skyscrapers. Even the legendary Nakatoma Tower was gone.

"What's all them tall buildings?" Tajil asked, seeing where Ray was looking.

"That's it—that's Manhattan. That's what most people in NorAm mean when they talk about 'the City'. It's the one and only."

"Hunh," snorted Tajil derisively. "Cities is cities; theys all litter boxes." The big red dog's nose wrinkled in disgust.

"Being a country boy myself," Ray said, "I would usually have to agree with you, but the Big Apple is special."

"The big apple?"

"An old and forgotten term for 'Noo Yawk,'" Ray said. "Once the greatest city in the world."

"Doan look so great no more," snorted Tajil.

"No, it doesn't," Ray said softly. "It sure doesn't."

III

An anthill of activity, the terminal was jammed with little shops selling schlocky tourist items. Fast-food restaurants competed with pushcart vendors hawking hot and cold comestibles of dubious digestibility. A wizened old Japanese man smiled a gap-toothed smile at them and asked, "Sushi?" Ake glanced at the old man's wares and shook his head.

"Hey, Ake," Ray said. "See those 'Coney Island hots' that guy over there is selling?"

"Yeah?"

"They say an urban anthropologist took a core sample of an old landfill and—"

"What's a landfill?"

Ray frowned at this interruption. "It was a place where they used to bury garbage, back in the days when there was land enough to do something that weird. But forget about that," he said, waving a hand. "To continue, when the core sample was examined, there was a section of a 'hot dog' in it and it hadn't decomposed one iota in over a hundred years!"

"You mean it was still edible?"

"Depends on how you define 'still' and 'edible,' doesn't it?"

Tajil hooted at that. "Don't give me that," Ray told him. "You dogs would eat stuff maggots would turn their noses up at."

"Maggots got noses?" wondered Sinbad.

"The belts are coming up," Ake announced. "Everyone be careful getting on." The dogs weren't thrilled with the belts, the people-movers that took the "walk" out of sidewalk, but they tolerated them. With four legs, they usually had less trouble getting on than did Ray and Ake.

Ray noticed that the throngs of travelers on the moving belts did more than give them ample room for passage; they seemed almost to flinch away. Many went so far as to risk ill-advised hops across several of the moving walkways rather than be carried in near proximity past the team.

Not everyone ignored them, however.

"Heathens! Usurpers of God's plan for Man," shouted a young man in a business suit. *His tie's soiled*, Ray observed. *That's interesting*. "Animals were put upon this earth to serve Man, not to become as Man—to talk and to think. Such blasphemous creatures are an abomination in the eyes of God!"

"Keep it to yourself, St. Francis," muttered Ray as the belts carried the outraged man to and then past them. He continued to rant and rave and to point after them as they left him in their wake.

Other passersby moved quickly and uncomplainingly past them, except for an occasional hostile glance.

"We's sure pop'lar, ain't we?" muttered Tajil.

"What's going on?" wondered Ake. "Why are we the objects of such scorn and fear?"

"We can thank our little buddy Svoboda for that, I'll wager," Ray said, returning a little old lady's scowl. "Damn, I wish the little bastard was still alive so I could kill him!"

"Oh," said Ake, understanding Ray's point. "The only scout dogs these people have probably seen in the past decade have been untrained teams run by warlords and gangs."

"Worse than untrained," Ray said. "Trained. Trained to be vicious. Trained to be killers." Patting Tajil on the rump, Ray said, "Taddy, get mean." Tajil snarled, his lips curling back to reveal his impressive set of teeth.

"See—that's what the locals think of when they think 'scout dog.'" Ray made a hand signal and Tajil's mask of savagery was replaced by his normal placid expression. "If I tried that with one of Svoboda's graduates, he'd probably tear my hand off."

"Great!" exclaimed Ake. "We've got everybody against us."

Ray's shoulders hunched as he turned his hands palms up. "So what do you do when someone breaks all your eggs?"

"Huh?"

"You make an omelette." Shaking his head at Ake's blank expression, Ray said, "If it's a given that everyone thinks ours is also a team of vicious killer dogs, then we should use that fact to our advantage."

Ake brightened. "Hey, that's right." He patted Ray on the back and said, "You know, you're not as dumb as you look."

"My friend and partner—Ake Ringgren," Ray said to Tajil. "He sees to it that I don't have to be insulted by complete strangers but by someone close to me."

"Come on," said Ake. "We have a hover van to buy."

13

The agent at the rental place said he had no authority to sell the franchise's vehicles, so Ake just shrugged and signed the contract. "What the hell," he said to Ray later when they were in the hover van they picked out. "If we can return this crate in one piece, all the better. If not, well, then I guess we've bought it after all." Ray just grinned at that.

The streets outside the spaceport were choked with vehicles of all sorts—from null-grav floaters which appeared brand-new to one-person autos which looked to be held together by prayers and molecular glue. The street-level walkways also pulsed with humanity.

"Johnny Skerchock told me that New York took the brunt of the fighting during the recent unpleasantness, even more so than the Old Federal City," Ray said. "So don't take one of the expressways—I want to see what this part of the city looks like and the only way we can assess the damage to the city and its population is if we travel the streets. It shouldn't take long to get an idea how extensive the devastation is. I mean, if lower Queens is a mess, then Manhattan is probably in really bad shape."

"The worser it is, the more some peoples prob'ly wants a top scout dog team," piped in Beowulf, sticking his head into the front of the van.

"It's probably a sellers' market," agreed Ray.

What they saw wasn't encouraging, but neither were things as bad as they might have been, considering that the city had been a fiercely contested battleground during the Rebellion.

"The thing is," Ray said, watching four Half-Heads, dressed in black leather and ostrich feathers, cross in front of them at an intersection, "anyone with any prospects for a better life has taken off for the colony worlds. Those left behind haven't the money, the skills, or the sense to leave."

"That's a bit harsh, don't you think?" Ake asked, staring at a lavishly garbed Skinnerite, apparently none the worse for having to contribute one-tenth of his gross earnings to the Prophet of the One.

Ray shrugged. "Harsh? No. Actually, it's more of an exaggeration than anything else. But not much of one." He stared out the polyglas windshield. "Hey, where we headed?"

"An area called Rego Park. It's just five or six centimeters from the tunnels and skyways into Manhattan."

"Five or six *centimeters*?"

"On the map, dummy. On the map." He tapped the side of his head.

"Oh, yeah, I nearly forgot," Ray said sarcastically. "You're not just Ake, you're 'Ake-plus.'"

"Hmmm. Do I detect a little bit of envy over my external? Don't forget: You're 'Ray-plus' with the powers the rubies gave you."

"Yeah, yeah." Ray hated admitting Ake was right.

Seeing a huge floating holo announcing nearby C. Everett Koop Hospital, Ake said, "I've got an idea. How'd you like to have a new hole in your head?"

"Ouch," Ray said, his hand reaching involuntarily toward the bandage.

"Oh, come on," said Ake. "You couldn't have felt that. That part of your head's numb."

Tapping the ruby around his neck, Ray said, "Don't forget, as you yourself just pointed out, I have powers far above and beyond those of mortal men."

"Uh-huh," Ake said, giving the bandage one final pat. "Tell me, Ray, what's it like to have only a part of your head numb instead of the whole thing?"

"Very funny," Ray said, slipping off the white-sheet-covered operating table. He looked at his watch. "Shouldn't we be out of here soon?"

Checking his own watch, Ake said, "We did rather well—we have five minutes to spare." He depowered the robotic arms and the other surgical instruments.

Looking around at the surgical facility they'd rented for an hour, Ray said, "You know, I thought you were kidding when you told me you could walk into a city hospital and rent an operating room by the hour."

"I was scanning through the Yellow Pages," Ake said. "The ad jumped out at me."

"And the price was right, too."

"They charge more for normal-sized brains, so we got a bargain," Ake chided him.

"Uh-huh," Ray said sourly. Then, as they took a drop tube down to street level from the forty-seventh floor, he added, "I don't know why we didn't think of doing this sooner."

"One reason was because it didn't occur to me that, in addition to medical and other technical information, you could insert a communications device." When Ray gave him a look, he added, "Well, it didn't."

Ray considered that. "I understand, but now we can communicate."

"Not yet," Ake said. "First, we have to stop by a Hol-vee Shack to buy miniature transmitter/receivers tuned to our own private frequency."

"Let's hope it's private—I don't want to be picking up cop calls or pizza orders!"

A strange rumbling sound came from the rear of the van, followed by deep-throated canine laughter. "Hey, Ray," Littlejohn called.

"Yeah?"

"I think we better get some food real soon—Beowulf's stomach is growling." Both the sound and the laughter were repeated.

"I could do with a sandwich myself," Ake said.

"Well, we just passed some sort of bar." Ray told him. "Let's find a place to park and check it out."

They found a lot protected by razor wire and lasers. "This looks about as secure as they come," Ray said. He understood why when he saw the rates: ten credits for the first half-hour and five for each portion of a half-hour.

"Car theft must be pretty damn rampant, huh?" asked Ake as he pulled into the lot.

Ray opened the back and the dogs scrambled out. As they ambled down the street—no moving sidewalks here—Ray said, "Ake, you better check to see that you reloaded your weapons."

"Why?" Then he saw the street gang that prompted Ray's words coming toward them. "Hell!"

The dogs assumed a semidefensive, semioffensive stance around their two humans. Ray and Ake held their energy rifles loosely, almost lackadaisically, but in such a way that they could bring them to bear on a target in the blink of an eye.

"In the doorway," Littlejohn said to Beowulf.

"Yah, I know," replied Beowulf. Ray didn't have time to wonder what they were talking about.

The eight or nine young toughs looked like characters out of a bad holodrama. Each was dressed in what could only be described as post-apocalyptic chic: plasteel forearm and leg protectors, open-faced skull protectors, and enough spikes, studs, imitation leather, jingling chains and fighting spurs to announce their coming from a dozen meters away. Since they also sported ostrich feathers, Ray could only surmise that such avian finery represented the latest in Terran fashion among the riffraff.

But more important than any of that was what else they had. Each of them had a snarling scout dog on a choke chain.

Ray decided it was the better part of valor not to laugh out loud at the garish spectacle the solidly built thugs presented.

He wasted no time. "Golly, has school been dismissed already?" Getting no reply, he asked, "You guys *do* speak Fed-stan?"

The thugs stared dumbly at the team. "Huh?" said the young man at the front of the group, who Ray assumed was their leader. "'Course we speak Fed-stan 'glish." He sneered.

"What about your dogs?"

"Yah," replied the leader's dog. "We's scout dogs. We talk, too."

Ray shook his head and the dog that spoke cocked its head at this unexpected response. "No," Ray said. "You *were* scout dogs. I don't know what you are now, but you're no longer scout dogs."

"Just who the hell are you?" asked the gang's leader.

<A better question might be just what the hell do you think you're doing?> Ake said. It was their new transmitters' maiden usage.

<Trust me,> Ray told Ake. *<But be ready to act.>*

<Shit!>

"Why, I'm the man who wants to buy your dogs," Ray said to the young man. "If the price is right; are they for sale?"

The young man grinned uneasily, revealing teeth studded with various gemstones, and scratched his head. Ray noticed that one side of the kid's head sported much shorter hair than the other. Ray guessed that the young thug had been a Half-Head not all that long ago.

Ray considered that. It probably meant that one product of the constant street warfare in the city was a certain amount of side-changing as relative strength flowed back and forth between the various contenders for ultimate supremacy.

"You got money?"

"Enough to buy your dogs."

"Hear that, guys? They got enough money to buy our dogs."

"Yeah," one of them said, resting his hand on the slug thrower he wore in a holster slung cowboy-style from his belt.

Ray felt a familiar tingle. *<Get ready,>* he warned Ake.

<Sonofabitch!>

<Hey, I offered to buy the dogs, didn't I?>

"Then if you got money to buy our dogs, you got money to—" The gang leader reached for his slug thrower and his friends followed suit.

Ray blasted the top of his skull off and shot three more of the gang dead before the leader fell over backwards. Ake was not far behind Ray in taking out his own three.

Pandemonium.

One of the three survivors pulled his slug thrower and fired in one fluid motion; unfortunately, he fired right into the head of the youth in front of him. Ray's energy bolt burned through him. That left one final target for Ake.

The suddenly unleashed dogs did nothing. They stood stock still, quivering in place. It was as Ray suspected: They were untrained at best, brutes at worst. Without direction from their owners, they lacked initiative.

"Don't kill us!" the dog who spoke to them earlier howled.

Beowulf closed his eyes in shame. These were like no scout dogs he knew or could imagine. For the first time, the enormity of what had happened to Svoboda's dogs sank in fully and completely.

"We're not going to kill you," Ray said softly. "But until we can figure out what to do with you . . ." He set his energy pistol to its lowest setting and fired it at each of the dogs, one by one. The dogs crumpled to the sidewalk, stunned into unconsciousness.

Ray heard a noise behind him and whirled, his lethally set rifle ready to fire, but Beowulf was way ahead of him.

"Don't let him bite me and don't shoot!" begged a pale young man stepping out of a doorway. Littlejohn and Beowulf's cryptic exchange suddenly made sense to Ray.

"Who are you?" asked Ake suspiciously.

"Nobody," the youth said, nervously. "Boy, you sure handled those bunnies like pros."

"Bunnies?" asked a confused Ake.

Rolling his eyes at Ake's denseness, the youth pointed to his teeth. "They got lots of carets in their mouths, understand?"

"Oh."

"Yeah, I never seen anything like . . . uh-oh." The boy's eyes widened and he turned and began walking away.

"What got into him?" wondered Ake.

"There's a cop floater comin' this way," said Sinbad.

"About time, don't you think?" Ray said. "I was beginning to wonder where the police were."

"I got the impression from John that there weren't any police, that the Rebellion pretty much decimated their ranks," Ake told him.

"There's *always* a police force. The question is, who do they work for?"

The floater approached the curb and kicked up whirlpools of dust as it gently settled to the ground. It disgorged its two passengers.

"Hello, officers," Ray said when the two policemen warily approached, hands resting lightly on the butts of their energy pistols.

<This must look really good through their eyes, don't you think?> Ray transmitted.

"I don't recall seeing you people around here before," one of the blue-jacketed policemen said. "And what can you tell me about this?" he asked, indicating the carnage on the street. His eyes were shielded by a pair of mirrored rad-repel wrap-arounds.

<I hate those,> Ray told Ake. *<I like to see a man's eyes.>*

<Not mine, you wouldn't.>

"This?" asked Ray. "Why, these gentlemen tried to rob us."

"Tried to rob you?" said the second policeman, also wearing rad-repels. "What the hell does that mean?"

Ray bit his lip. "It means when we offered to buy their dogs, they realized we had money and they tried to have it all—our money and their dogs."

The dogs had begun moving back toward Ray and Ake, tightening the circle around the four men. The policemen suddenly noticed what was happening.

"Hey," said the first cop. "Make your animals stop right there."

"Animals, stop right there," Ray said. Then he casually took out a wad of bills and peeled off a few thousand credits. "I feel we made a legitimate offer to buy their dogs. What say we still take the dogs and pay you two the money we were going to pay them? You can see that it gets to their survivors."

<I don't believe you!> Ake said.

The policemen exchanged careful glances. With their rad-repels on, Ray wondered how they "read" each other.

"That sounds fair to me," the first cop said. "What do you think, Juan?"

"It sounds fair to me, too. I know these boys. They thought they ran this neighborhood. I'd say they picked on the wrong people today."

The first cop said, "Let's call the meat wagon and let them clean up this mess." Then he held out his hand. Ray smiled and pressed the money into it.

"You boys working for anyone?" the second cop asked.

Ah, thought Ray. *Here it comes*. "Can't say that we are. Besides ourselves, that is."

"The city doesn't take kindly to free-lancers," cop number one told him. "We got all the trouble we can handle now."

"Yeah," said the second cop. "Find yourselves an employer real soon or keep moving. Canada's supposed to be nice and warm these days."

"You got any suggestions?"

"As a matter of fact . . ." The first cop reached inside his jacket.

Beowulf and Littlejohn both produced a deep, gravelly growl from the back of their throats and stepped forward a few steps, their lips curling menacingly. The policemen seemed to realize for the first time how vulnerable their situation was.

"I'm just getting this out," the officer said, slowly withdrawing his hand. In it was a small address cube. The policeman's fingers tapped across the cube's surface and it disgorged a plaspaper printout the size of a business card. "Here," he said, holding it out.

"What's that?" Ake asked.

"A name. And an address."

Ake took the proffered piece of plaspaper. "Who's Poppa Dalvi?"

Again the policemen exchanged glances. "You *are* new to the area, aren't you?" The cop sighed. "He's someone who's always looking for a few good men . . . and dogs. There's others, of course, but Poppa Dalvi is fair to his people."

"And he sells only the best," the second cop said, mimicking sticking an injector against his neck and activating it.

"I think I'm going to cry at our good fortune," said Ray.

"Good luck," the second cop told Ake as the two officers began backing slowly toward their floater. He pointed at Ray and added, "You'll need it with that crazy fucker on your side."

Ake and Ray watched the laser-scarred floater power up, leap into the sky, and peel off back down the street, rising higher and higher.

"G'bye," said Gawain loudly.

"Whew," said Ake. "For a minute there I thought we might be in for it."

"From two lousy donut-dunkers?" said Ray incredulously. "We'd have had them for lunch if they'd tried anything. We outnumbered them eleven to two. They were never a threat."

"Maybe you're right."

"C'mon. Let's get these dogs loaded into the van."

"And then what?"

Beowulf's stomach rumbled, this time louder than ever.

"Oh, right."

II

"What kinda place is this?" Tajil wondered.

"It's a barandgrill," said Gawain.

Tajil rolled his eyes. "I knows that. But this not look like a reg'lar bar looks."

"You're right, Taddy," Ray said, glancing around. "This place has all the earmarks of having been something like a warehouse before the Rebellion."

Eying the tall, cylindrical plasteel beams that held up the high ceiling, Ake was compelled to agree. "Yeah, there's too much space in this joint for a normal bar."

"Well, I kinda like it," declared Beowulf. He swept a practiced eye around the smoky interior. "You doan feel so closed in an' it's easier to see what everyone else is doin'."

"Defensively, it has a lot going for it," Ray agreed. The dogs had already eaten their sandwiches—they ate everything in two or three bites—and Ray knew he'd have to order more soon.

Ake sipped his bottled beer. The servibot had just stared blankly at him when he asked if they had white wine, so he ordered a Rhinegold. "I always like to sample the local brew if I'm forced to drink beer," he told Ray.

"Uh-huh." Ray wasn't keen on beer. He knew the dogs liked it, especially Beowulf, but he preferred harder stuff. For a while, back when he was married to Mary and Taylor, he'd actually given up drinking. That didn't last long once he had discovered that killing people, even in self-defense, wasn't the sort of thing he could live with without resorting to a stiff jolt now and then to make him forget the pain and guilt. And, he confessed to himself, he enjoyed drinking; it was his only vice.

"'Cept for killing people," he said softly.

"Hunh?" asked Littlejohn, the only one to have heard him.

"I said killing people makes you thirsty." Ray sipped his bourbon and water.

"'Fore you get too 'laxed," said Beowulf, raising his shaggy head from his bowl of beer, "you oughta check out Ozma."

"Christ!" Ray said, covering his eyes with one hand. "I'm a good one: suckin' down Kickapoo joy juice when I should be taking care of my dogs."

"Take it easy," Ake told him. "Don't be so hard on yourself all the time. Besides," he said, going over to and digging into one of the packs, "I can put the ointment on and bandage Ozma as well as or better than you can. Sit back and watch a pro at work."

"Oooooh," said several of the dogs.

"Ahh, I'm in a good mood—I'll let him live," Ray told them. Then he shook his head and said, "Listen to me: 'let him live.' I sure got bloodthirsty all of a sudden."

"It's the atmosphere," Ake replied, slathering cool healing salve on Ozma's rapidly healing burns. "Violence is in the air."

"Or in the streets, at least."

"Well, at least we've made a great start to finding the missing dogs."

"Yah," said Mama-san. "Boppa Doll-vee gots dogs."

As the little servibot that had been their waiter approached their table, it vibrated severely, said, "A gin and tonic?" and then jerked to a halt. A piercing whine and small cloud of acrid blue smoke came from its poorly maintained chassis.

"Hey," said Tajił. "The little robot guy burned out."

"Damn!" said Ray. "I was going to order a refill."

"Me too," said Beowulf.

"Me three," added Frodo.

"Well, none of you look crippled to me," Ake told them. "You could mosey on up to the bar and actually place an order yourselves."

"Mosey?" asked Mama-san.

"They bin watchin' westerns with Beowulf agin," Ozma explained.

"Oh, all right. I'll go." Ray stood up and patted his clothes for money. "Beowulf never counts the change anyway."

"Here." Ake pushed a wad of five-credit notes across the table.

Ray pushed the bills back, reaching into his pocket and pulling out the same wad he'd extracted the money from to pay the cops. "I have money," he said.

His money clasped in his hand, Ray bellied up to the bar. "Hey, barkeep." Ray did feel like he was in an old western sinny. All he needed was a ten-liter hat to add to the illusion that he was Johnny Mack Brown, Lash LaRue, or Bob Steele.

"Yeah?" The bartender was human, something unheard of anywhere offplanet except for the Belt. She was also a bare-breasted woman. Ray noticed that she wore rouge on her nipples to highlight them. *It works*, he thought.

"I'll have 'nother bourbon and water, and three beers." After a moment's consideration, he added, "Oh, and throw in some more sandwiches if you got 'em."

"Sandwiches?"

"Yeah, another two dozen. Ham, chicken, whatever. It doesn't much matter."

"Comin' up."

The hair on the back of Ray's neck rose. He sensed trouble on the way.

Ray felt a tug on his shoulder. He turned to face the ugliest man he'd ever seen. He had droopy bulldog jowls, a mottled red complexion, and "Ice boils"—the dermatological nightmare caused by heavy Ice use. Ray's revulsion must have shown in his expression. Either that or the man had already made up his mind to start something.

"Hey, shorty, who said you could come into my favorite joint and march right up to the bar like you owned it?"

"No one," Ray replied mildly. "I thought this was a public place." *Please don't start anything*, he silently wished. *I don't want to hurt anyone else today. Besides, I'm getting too old for this shit.*

"Maybe you thought wrong."

"Maybe I did. I'm sorry if my presence offends you." Ray bit his lip, determined to do everything in his power to avoid a fight.

"You'll be more than sorry if you don't watch out, shorty. I'm dangerous! Look at this." The man rolled up his sleeve to show a tattoo of a dragon head on his forearm. "That's from Camp Easton, the toughest penal colony in the system. I've killed men. I'm wanted for murder by the Blue Coats from here to the Belt!" Spittle flew from his mouth.

"I can see that you're a very dangerous man."

The tough had a companion. He wasn't as repulsive as his

buddy, but if there had been an "Ugliest Man" contest he would have placed in the money anywhere in the galaxy. "Ah, quit blabbing. Let's just open this little fucker up and see what he's got for guts."

In his mind's eye, Ray "saw" ugly number two pulling a slug thrower from his belt. That prescient flash made him contract a muscle in his left forearm and his quiver blade leapt into his hand. He brought his arm across his body in a slashing motion. As the quiver blade flashed across the man's throat, Ray pulled his bush knife out of his boot with his right hand; it was one continuous motion, fluid and effortless.

As the startled ugly who first confronted Ray raised his arm, ready to shove it and the energy pistol he held in his hand against Ray's chest, Ray chopped downward with his bush knife. The weapon discharged harmlessly into the floor, and the man shrieked and backed away, blood spurting from the end of his severed arm. A woman at a nearby table gasped, "Ohmygod!" and pushed back from the table, anxious to get away from the man's still-twitching hand and forearm, lying on the table top.

Sonofabitch! "Let's all be calm now," Ray said, putting his knife away and picking up the energy pistol.

Several of the stricken man's friends grabbed him, quickly tied off his arm with a belt, and led him away. They were especially careful not to do anything Ray might take for a provocative move.

The man whose throat Ray had slashed had not moved. "Hey, Otto, you okay?" someone called to him.

As if he was beginning to nod, the man's head tilted back and back . . . and back . . . and fell off. It hit the bar and bounced behind it, out of sight. The decapitated body finally got the message and slumped to the floor, bright blood pumping out rhythmically.

14

Ray looked at the quiver blade—aptly named, since his hand was shaking visibly. He hadn't meant to strike that hard and he stared at the almost frictionless blade as if it were to blame.

"Oops," he said. As soon as the word left his lips, he felt disgusted at himself for having uttered it. He didn't take the brutal ending of two men's lives as lightly as all that. A robot shrink once told him that his propensity for wisecracks was a common psychological defensive mechanism.

Whatever the reasons for it, his reflexive nonchalance had an instant and striking effect upon the bar's other patrons. They immediately acted the same way that small fishes and other sea animals did when a shark on the prowl swam through their area—they froze in place and pretended they weren't there.

All except for one grubby man drinking by himself. He came over, pointed at the dead man, and asked, "Ken I have his weapons if you don't want 'em?"

"I don't want them," Ray said, frankly astonished that he was able to keep his voice level.

"Louella?"

"You can take 'em . . . long as you take him, too," the bartender said. "I don't want anything here when the Blue Coats come by for their free drinks."

"Sure thing, Louella. Thanks. And thank you, mister."

"Ain't nuthin' so bad happen to a person that it don't mean

good fortune for someone else," the bartender said, shaking her head from side to side.

While Ray watched the man drag the headless corpse toward a rear exit, leaking blood all the way, the bartender pressed something underneath the bar and a little cleaning robot quickly appeared to begin mopping up the floor.

"What's keeping my order, Louella?" Ray decided to act as if nothing had happened.

"Right here, sir." The bartender put a tray with the drinks down in front of Ray and, smiling hard, moved away. "You still want those sandwiches?"

"Yeah. They're for my dogs, anyway."

"I'll bring 'em out right away, then." She wiped her hands on the bar towel more vigorously than was necessary.

"Terrific." Ray threw some of the five-credit notes on the bar, thought for a moment, then put them all down. He turned to stare at the little cleaning 'bot. A strangely familiar ditty was coming from it. Ray realized what the tune was with a sudden start: It was "Whistle While You Work."

★ ★ ★

"You all right, Ray?" asked Beowulf, who'd come over to provide backup for Ray if any of the dead man's friends attempted anything.

"Nothing getting this drink inside me can't cure."

Beowulf accompanied him back to the table.

"Wow, whutta fight!" said Sinbad. Beowulf shot him a "shut up" look.

"Ah, you feel like talking about what just happened?"

Ray took a big gulp of his drink and then answered his stunned partner. "No, not really, Ake. Not yet, anyway."

Ake just nodded and sipped his beer.

"Boy, this is some place," Tajil said.

"Ya see why we needs to rescue the dogs here," Beowulf rumbled.

★ ★ ★

The trip back to *The Spirit of St. Louis* did not take nearly as long as their trip uptown since they followed one of the major arteries.

They remembered to unload their weapons before they

reached the spaceport's front-gate. The two security guards who opened the back of the hover van stared intently at their pack and at the unconscious dogs, restrained by their original chains and by jerry-built muzzles Ray had fashioned out of large plastic pull-ties.

"You got an export license for those dogs?" an officious middle-aged bureaucrat asked them at the interplanetary commerce checkpoint.

"They belong to us, Mr."—Ake read his name tag—"Mr. Maxwell."

"Doesn't matter." He looked at a file cube. "I have you down here for nine dogs. You need an export license for those additional dogs."

"And where do we get this license?"

"Old Federation building, One Federation Square, Manhattan." He pursed his lips. "Haven't gotten around to changing the name yet. Deplorable."

"Sounds like a lot of red tape," Ray said. "What if we just paid you for the license here and now?"

"I don't think that would—"

"We'd really appreciate it," Ray continued, pulling out a roll of credit notes. "How much does it cost for eight scout dogs?"

Maxwell consulted his cube. "Each dog requires an eight-hundred-credit fee."

Ray pulled out eight one-thousand-credit notes. "Let's make that an even thousand—the extra two hundred a dog is for your trouble."

"Well, I suppose it would be possible. It *is* saving everyone time and money, isn't it?"

"Absolutely," Ray said, handing over the money. He waited patiently while Maxwell spoke into a cube. In a matter of seconds, a plaspaper printout was spit out of a nearby printer.

"Here you are, Mr. Larkin," Maxwell said. His eyes glinted and he added, "If you have any other such transactions you wish expedited, I work weekdays from ten a.m. to five p.m."

"We'll remember that," Ake said. Walking back to the hover van, Ake said, "I can't believe how much corruption there is now."

Ray clapped his partner on the back. "There isn't any more since the fall of the Federation, Ake. But it's out in the open now and available to everyone, not just big corporations and those with the right connections. Frankly, I prefer it this way."

They stayed aboard the ship for nearly twenty hours, putting the new dogs into secure holding pens until their physical conditions could be checked and nominalized. Ake and the computer were forced to activate a small service 'bot to take care of feeding and watering the dogs and cleaning up their wastes while they awaited cryogenic hibernation.

Ray performed a handful of tests and then, after making sure each dog had eaten and digested a big meal, pronounced them fit for hibernation.

"How are they doing?" Ake asked.

"About as well as could be expected—considering," Ray replied.

"Yeah, considering." Ake knew what Ray meant: considering their lack of training, considering their lack of strong human or canine role models, considering their diet, and considering their mean, brutish life.

"You think they live through sleeping?" a concerned Mama-san asked.

"I *believe* so," Ray told her. "They're all young." Left unsaid was the fact that while cryogenic hibernation was considered generally safe, three in two thousand "sleepers" never awoke. And that figure was based on people and dogs who were in excellent physical and mental health.

"Well, computer, you ready to do this?" Ray asked.

"Yes, Ray."

"What're we waiting for, then?"

Back on the expressway, heading north, Ake said, "Now what?"

"Where's that card the policeman gave you?"

II

Poppa Dalvi lived in and operated out of a residential tower surrounded by shorter, less intact structures. A twenty-second-century building, it bristled with urban self-defense mechanisms. The clearing away of many of its neighbors, through demolition and house-to-house fighting, allowed the built-in weaponry an increased effective range.

Though it was once home to four hundred families, the tower now housed only Dalvi and his band of renegades, thieves, and killers. It was unclear whether the former tenants left voluntarily, during the long years of conflict, or if they were forced to leave. Ray guessed it didn't much matter.

In addition to an assortment of floaters and surface vehicles, the team noticed that a half-dozen men stood guard outside the building's entrance—Dalvi clearly was not about to put all his trust in the computer-directed building defenses.

"Looks like Boppa Doll-vee gots lots of enemies," Beowulf observed.

After taking their time examining the card the policeman had given them, the guards grudgingly permitted Ray, Ake, and the dogs to enter. Not by themselves, of course: two of them tagged along to make sure the card wasn't a trick.

The building's interior was a mess. The clutter and dirt produced by the fighting—huge hunks of the ceiling had fallen and the walls had cracked and crumbled—was augmented by the accumulation of simple, everyday dust and litter. A slow-moving janitorial 'bot was listlessly pushing small piles of grit and debris around and then attempting to vacuum it into its base.

"Jeeze," said Frodo fondly. "This place jes' like home."

Ake kicked a golf-ball-sized piece of rubble out of the way. "No, our living quarters always had a higher class of garbage cluttering them up."

"Uh, Frick and Frack," Ray began. "About the lift tubes . . ."

"We know," the one Ray arbitrarily decided was Frick said. "Your mutts would prefer an elevator instead."

"How'd you know that?"

"Poppa Dalvi *does* have almost thirty dogs."

"So you guys aren't the only ones who hate using drop/lift tubes, after all," Ake said.

"Dogs is smart," said Mama-san proudly. "Even poor untrained dogs got brains."

They poured into a large freight elevator that beeped once in warning but nonetheless closed its doors and proceeded to the fourteenth floor.

"Fourteen," Ray noted when the elevator stopped and announced they'd reached their destination. "You know, because of our weird superstitious nature, buildings don't have thirteenth floors. I doubt that Poppa Dalvi realizes that calling it the fourteenth floor doesn't actually change the fact that this is really the thirteenth floor."

"Maybe he's perverse," Ake said. "Some people go out of their way to walk under a ladder or to allow a black cat to cross his or her path."

"I know a fellow who used to make a point of walking under ladders," Ray said.

"Yah?" asked Gawain. "Anythin' bad ever happen to him?"

"One day a black cat fell on him and killed him."

While the dogs hooted and barked in appreciation, the second goon—"Frack"—stared at Ray and said, "You know, you're a strange guy."

"I know. Thanks."

"Poppa Dalvi is pretty unusual himself. He has a Ph.D. in law enforcement and he is a high priest who serves Jogambé."

"You want I should tell him you're blabbin' his life story to strangers?" said "Frick."

The second goon paled and shut up.

When they reached a door that said "1421" on it, they stopped and "Frick" knocked once, sharply. "It's really 1321," Ray stage-whispered.

"Knock it off," Ake whispered back.

The door hissed open and two flunkies slowly moved out of their way, revealing the great man at last. Poppa Dalvi was a big man. His skin was pale, almost white,and his hair was jet black. It was hard to tell anything else about him; since his broad back was to the new arrivals as he sat before a bank of hol-vees, each one projecting a different program.

All of the hol-vees had the sound turned off. Dalvi was being bombarded by cartoons, pornos, soccer matches, old sinnys, game shows, and weird, poorly composed and focused images that his guests only gradually realized were home-holos of torture and rape. His eyes never leaving the compelling images, Dalvi scooped handfuls of food from various containers arrayed around him, stuffing it into his mouth like a railroad fireman shoveling coal into a steam engine's fiery maw, and washing it down by long pulls from a fat, three-liter bottle of wine.

Ah, a health food nut, Ray thought.

One of his entourage worked up the courage to interrupt his fearless leader with a gentle tug on the sleeve of his brightly colored shirt.

Dalvi belched and asked, "Yeah, what is it?"

"You have visitors, excellency."

Dalvi sighed and pressed a control beside him; the images disappeared as he swiveled around in the massive cuddle chair that supported his bulk. "Who is it this time?" he asked before he was completely turned.

"It's Karl," "Frick" said. "Sid and I just escorted a coupla new men in. They had a card from one of the Blue Suits in the Eighty-ninth."

Dalvi noticed the dogs for the first time. "Scout dogs!" He looked at Ray and Ake. "Where'd you get 'em? No, never mind that, how much are you asking for them?"

"Our dogs are not for sale, excellency," Ake said smoothly.

"Not for sale?"

"They are not dogs we happened to come by; they are our team."

Dalvi's eyes widened. "A team."

"Yes," Ray ventured. "We're a trained, fighting unit. Available for all sorts of work . . . including bodyguarding."

Dalvi wiped the back of his hand across his mouth and then wiped his greasy hand on a trouser leg. "Bodyguards? I don't need bodyguards! The magic of Jogambé protects me."

Ray lowered his head submissively. "Of course. But, as I said, we do all sorts of work."

"I must ask Jogambé's advice." Dalvi had a live chicken fetched. While a flunky held it over a bowl, Dalvi slit its throat and allowed the blood to rain into the bowl. The last few drops he spattered onto a plate holding a half-dozen bones. Dalvi picked up the bones and cast them down, peering closely at their configuration.

"It is good," he said finally. "Jogambé signals that the signs are good." He pursed his lips and looked up. "I can pay you five hundred credits a week."

Ake demurred, saying, "We can make that much free-lancing."

"Poachers don't last long in my territory."

Without warning, Dalvi released a tremendous fart, apparently involuntarily. "Ha!" chortled Gawain. "That guy—"

"—has made a reasonable offer in good faith," finished Ray quickly. "However, we hear that Jaijo Qi is paying more for a first-class, *trained*, scout dog team."

Ray later thought it was as if *he* had been the one to break wind in public. Dalvi looked at Karl and Sid. "You dare to bring me people who have the bad manners to mention that foul name!" he thundered. "And after I have called upon Jogambé's assistance!"

Both goons held their tongues. *I can see that sometimes his men wouldn't mind shoving a grenade down Dalvi's throat.*

"We're sorry to have offended you, excellency—or the powerful Jogambé," Ake said smoothly. "I submit, however, that we possess a unique blend of street smarts, skill, and resolve not easily come by these days."

Ray was impressed. If Ake got any more eloquent-sounding, he could easily make a living introducing stuffy British dramas on the Classics Channel.

Dalvi was impressed as well. "You speak well for yourself." His voice turned froggy and he twisted his head and spat into a napkin. "I will offer you a thousand credits a week—and expect you to pick up half again as much by helping yourselves to what the local merchants have in their stores."

Tight bastard! Ray thought.

"Yes, I'll be paying you a thousand credits each week . . . but what will I be getting for my generosity?"

Ray and Ake exchanged glances. "We offer you two things," Ake responded. "First, we will spend several hours each day training your dogs and—"

"You can do that? Train adult dogs, I mean?"

"To be a real scout dog team, no. It is too late," Ray lied. "But to follow orders and maintain discipline, to fight and die for their masters—that we can do."

Continuing as if neither Dalvi nor Ray had interrupted him, Ake said, "Second, when your dogs are ready, we will offer our services to Qi."

"What?!" roared Dalvi.

"And when we have won his confidence, we will help you to destroy him."

III

Karl and Sid (Ray had difficulty not thinking of them as Frick and Frack) took them to meet the warlord's dogs. The dogs were kept in the first underground level of the building, in an enormous plascrete-floored area which had once been a below-ground parking area. According to Sid, the ramps connecting the garage to the street entrances and exits and to the lower levels had been sealed up, making the huge, stark area one big holding pen.

"They keepin' dogs in there?" asked Littlejohn, shaking his shaggy head in disgust. "Dogs need fresh air and grass."

"Fresh air and grass!" laughed Sid. "There ain't much of that in the city."

"Fra . . . ah, Sid's right. And besides, these dogs aren't like you guys," Ray cautioned them. "They're not much more than savage brutes."

"How we do this?" Beowulf wanted to know.

"Good question." Ray looked at his team. In short order, he had pointed at Littlejohn, Tajil, Frodo, and Sinbad. "Okay, you four, with the addition of Beowulf, of course, are going in with me for the first contact."

"Hey," complained Ozma. "You choosed only males. Mama-san, Grendel, and me is tough, too, you know."

"I do know. But I want the four biggest dogs—and they happen to be males."

Ake coughed. "I have a sneaking suspicion that this is one male who doesn't get to go, Ozma."

"Of course you can if you want," Ray told him. "But I thought it best if you stayed with Ozma and the others and watched our backsides."

"I can live with that." Ake unslung one of the two energy rifles he carried and handed it to Ray.

"What's this? I don't want to show up with a gun."

"Just take it. With luck, you won't need it. If you do, well, there it is."

"We ain't got all day," Karl said impatiently. "You goin' in or what?"

"Let's go, guys," Ray said. "Sid and Karl want to get back to reading the scriptures."

When the door opened, it took a while for them to be noticed, so big was the garage. After some surprised yelps and canine shouts, more than a score of huge dogs rushed toward Ray and the others, barking and snarling. Ray's skin prickled and the hairs on the back of his neck rose, but he didn't flinch from the bellicose challenge. His senses tuned to laser sharpness, he felt Beowulf and the rest of his team's jumbled emotions: fear, anger, pity, and hope.

His fingers tightened around the stock of the energy rifle until his knuckles whitened. Then, without warning, he unleashed a medium-powered bolt into the floor. The spot he chose hissed and spat as the accumulated coating of grease and lubricants from hundreds of vehicles vaporized. The snarling, posturing dogs leapt back and fell silent. Ray knew that it was a silence that could not last, so he spoke his piece quickly.

"Good afternoon, dogs and bitches. My name is Ray Larkin and these handsome fellows are members of my team—my scout dog team." He enunciated the last four words clearly and firmly. "You are also scout dogs. You are not, however, a team. I am here to begin changing that."

A massive black-and-white dog, nearly equal to Beowulf in size and weight, stepped forward, stopping just centimeters away, and said, "Piss on you!" Ray noticed that he wore a chain collar pulled tight around his neck.

A low rumbling began in Beowulf's throat, but Ray simply said, "Biss on you? What does 'biss on you' mean?"

"Not biss . . . biss!" The dog showed his substantial teeth.

Ray pulled on his earlobe and said, "You're all tough guys and gals, are you? You tear out throats for your lord and master, Poppa Dalvi. Is that right, or do I have it wrong?"

"Yah, that right. One bite."

"One bite?"

"One bite all it take to fix you."

Ray smiled. Then his smile slowly faded as he made his face blank. He was pulling out everything he could remember from his canine psychology courses. The dogs grew restive at the change in his expression.

Good, he thought. *Next lesson*.

"Beowulf!" His big leader dog looked at him questioningly. Ray made a hand signal and Beowulf snarled and began barking furiously. Another signal and Beowulf ceased his hostile display. Ray crooked a finger at Littlejohn and Frodo and they took up defensive stances on either side of him. Another finger motion caused Tajil and Sinbad to do the same. Then he winked and they reassumed their "at ease" positions.

Addressing the black-and-white, Ray said, "My team doesn't need chain collars." Leaning forward a bit—the big black-and-white dog actually drew back in response—Ray stared at a patch of bare skin on the dog's side and said, "And they don't receive whippings, either."

"Bis . . . fuck you, mister!"

Ray smiled again, further infuriating the black-and-white. "What's your name, anyway?"

Again the big dog was caught off-guard. "Name?"

"Doan none o' you gots names?" asked Tajil. Then he looked guiltily at Ray. Ray shook his head almost imperceptibly, meaning, "Don't worry about it, Taddy."

"No," volunteered one of the other dogs, a yellow bitch. The black-and-white glared at her, but she simply glared back. Ray decided she deserved a strong name when the time came. She and the other females also seemed thinner than the male dogs; Ray guessed that in this "dog-eat-dog" atmosphere, the biggest got the lion's share of whatever food there was to be had. *One more thing that will have to change*, he vowed.

"A dog's not a real 'person' without a name." Ray turned to Beowulf. "Your name, please."

"Beowulf."

Ray looked at Littlejohn and nodded. "Littlejohn."

"Tajil."

"Sinbad."

"Frodo."

"So ya all gots names, so what?" said a cream-colored dog.

"So we gots a Man and we doan gots to live in a big cage," said Littlejohn. "We helps people."

"You gonna use us to 'help people' . . . or kill 'em?" asked the cream-colored dog.

Touché, Ray thought, admiring the big dog's smarts. "What do you do now?" he asked.

"We kill 'em."

Ray nodded. "And that's what you will continue to do for a while. But for just a while. Later—"

"Bullshit!" The black-and-white dog again. Clearly, he was the dominant male in this group.

Ray just smiled and regrouped his males near the door. He wanted a modicum of privacy to discuss what should come next.

"Lemme teach this whelp a thing or two, Ray," Beowulf pleaded.

"Tooth and nail, eh, Beowulf?" mused Ray. "I want to win them over through trust, not violence."

"We ain't got time for the slow way, not at first, anyway. Lemme fight 'im and the rest'll follow me . . . and you."

"Ah, shit!"

"Good."

15

Ray made a show of putting down his energy rifle. He didn't know if the dogs knew that he still wore his needle gun on his right wrist and his quiver blade on the left, but it didn't really matter. Thus "disarmed," he followed Beowulf and Littlejohn back to the new pack, the other three dogs bringing up the rear.

"So, nameless dog," said Beowulf. "I challenge you for your pack."

"Good, man-named cur. I show you how we fights here."

"They fights to the death?" another of Dalvi's dogs asked.

"No way," Ray said. No one argued the point.

The dogs crowded around while Beowulf and the big black-and-white circled warily, each looking for an advantage. Both dogs were in full aggressive display: teeth bared, mouth open, ears erect, pointing forward, trembling tails held high, legs stretched to their fullest, and the fur on their shoulders, back, and rumps standing on end. Each dog emitted a deep rumbling growl accompanied by an intense, unwavering stare.

Ray's mouth was dry. It wasn't that he didn't have faith in Beowulf's abilities. But the black-and-white dog's capabilities were a chance factor.

"You two gonna jes' dance around or what?" an impatient canine voice cried out.

Neither Beowulf nor his opponent acted as if he heard the remark. *Chalk one up for each side*, Ray thought. Both dogs were too savvy to be goaded into peer-pleasing acts that might prove to be their undoing.

Beowulf feinted an attack and watched the black-and-white's reaction. Realizing Beowulf's abbreviated charge was a tactic, the other dog duplicated it, evaluating Beowulf's response in turn. Since his mock attack was more monkey-see, monkey-do than an original maneuver, the black-and-white learned less from Beowulf's reaction that Beowulf did from his.

This period of feeling-out gave Ray more confidence in Beowulf's superiority. Beowulf was not only highly trained and disciplined, he was as much a professional as Ray. Just as Ray could probably handle any two of Dalvi's men, Beowulf could hold his own against the warlord's mistreated dogs. And, even if this dog's size meant he ate better than the others, Ray doubted that he ate as well as Beowulf and the other members of his team.

While all this was going through Ray's mind, the two dogs joined the battle in the blink of an eye. Ray had seen his own dogs fight among themselves, but those had been fairly low-key contests. Not so here: Both dogs ripped at each other with their teeth and attempted to use their great strength to gain the upper position. They butted, slashed with their fangs, pushed, and charged—all the while snarling and barking furiously.

As Ray had predicted—and fervently hoped for—Beowulf's intelligence and experience, combined with his superb physical conditioning, something denied the penned-up dog, allowed him to put his opponent on his back in less than a minute.

Beowulf seemed intent upon seizing his vanquished foe's throat in his jaws. Ray gulped. Whether Beowulf meant to kill the black-and-white or was simply going through the motions until the other dog could present an act of submission, Ray could not tell. He guessed the latter, but Beowulf's actions were so convincing that it was impossible to say that he would not have ripped out the beaten dog's jugular vein had not it resorted to whimpering, juvenile behavior.

"I yield."

"Beowulf beated him!" Littlejohn exulted.

★ ★ ★

Dalvi was not happy that Ray and Beowulf, Ake and Littlejohn, and the rest of the team decided that they needed two weeks to work with his dogs. After the first seven days, he came down to see what was taking so long.

"Hello, excellency," Ray heard one of Dalvi's men say respectfully when the bulky warlord showed up in the dogs' underground compound. Ray turned from his lecture to see Dalvi waddling toward them, his breath rasping in and out of his throat. Ever the fashion plate, Dalvi wore a blousy top that sported numerous grease stains.

"Good morning, excellency," Ray said, while thinking, *You fat pig!* He had problems dealing with "superiors."

Dalvi waved a hand in response and got right to the point of his visit. "I have bad ankles," he told Ray. "Despite that, I had to walk from the drop tube, into this smelly dog pen, and over to you. Since I dislike thinking that my effort was for nothing, I sincerely hope that you have good news for me."

"I do, your excellency. The dogs are much more responsive than Ake and I had dared to hope. With just a few more weeks of training, I believe—"

"Weeks of training!" Spittle flew from Dalvi's mouth. "Just a few more *weeks* of training, Larkin?" He shook his head and held up a finger. "One more week, Larkin. One more week and then you go over to Qi."

"But—"

"Seven days."

"Yes, excellency."

Suddenly, Ray became aware of a foul, acrid smell. "Boy, what stink?" asked Sinbad.

Dalvi stared at Ray, daring him to say anything. Ray decided that discretion was the better part of valor and remained tactfully silent.

Smiling at his ability to intimidate by virtue of his raw power—the power to have people tortured or killed on a whim—Dalvi turned and began walking away slowly. He had taken fewer than four steps before a flunky appeared with a null-grav floater capable of comfortably accommodating his vast bulk. He collapsed onto the floater, driving it toward the floor until its autocontrols adjusted for his weight.

The scene caused Ray to scratch his head. He felt a sense of *dèjá vu* at seeing Dalvi's corpulent form on the floater. Snapping his fingers, he muttered, "Jabba the Hut."

"What?" asked one of the new dogs.

"Ray jes' 'memberin' an old sinny," said Beowulf.

"What's a 'sinny'?"

"You guys have had a deprived existence, haven't you?" Ray said.

"Yah, guess so," said the big black-and-white dog Beowulf had bested.

"Uh, Ray," a tan-and-brown dog began. "We wuz wonderin' if you could 'splain somethin' to us."

"If I can."

"We heard some o' Beowulf's pack talkin' and we wants to know what 'the Law' is."

"The Law?" *Oh, boy!* "The Law is a compact between Man and dog, recognizing that we have depended upon each other for thousands of years. It is an unequal partnership. Men get so much more from it than do dogs, but both have prospered. Scout dogs say the Law to remind themselves of this special relationship, to affirm their commitment to serving beside Man." *Stop!* Ray rebuked himself. *You're blabbing on and on.*

"Ray wrong 'bout one thing: We gets as much from Men as they gets from us," said Beowulf, briefly lowering his head for having the temerity to contradict Ray about the Law.

"Why doan we say the Law?" suggested Grendel.

Beowulf agreed reluctantly. He had not wanted them to say the Law until after they were done with this assignment; it made him feel bad to lead the others in the saying of the Law knowing they would be killing more humans.

"What is the Law?" Beowulf intoned.

"*To place duty above self, honor above life.*" Dalvi's dogs were agape at the ritual.

"What is the Law?"

"*To allow harm to come to no Man, to protect Man and his possessions.*"

"What is the Law?"

"*To stand beside Man's side—as dogs will always stand. Together, Man and dog.*"

Beowulf and Ray both blinked rapidly and swallowed; neither wanted the other or anyone else to see the strong feelings the saying of the Law had evoked in them.

"That's it?" asked the big black-and-white dog. "Big deal!"

Ray went over to him and reached out with his hand. The dog started to pull away, then relaxed. Ray grabbed his ears, then rubbed and twisted them playfully, affectionately. "Tough guy, eh? Leader of the pack, huh?" He "knuckled" the dog's head. "Well, we're going to make a team player out of you yet. Someday the Law won't seem so stupid to you."

"Mebbe," the big dog conceded. "But mebbe not."

"We will say the Law?" asked the bright-eyed little female that Ray had grown to like more and more.

"Someday," Ray replied. "Not yet. You still have much to learn." Then, softer, he added, "And once we get you home, you will get more training, education, and help than Ake or I can give you."

"Home?"

"Slip of the tongue," Ray said. "Forget about that for now. We have a mission to accomplish and we may not survive it unless we are as ready as we can be . . . Athena."

It took the little female a moment to realize that Ray had given her a name. "Athena? I am to be Athena?"

"Yes." Ray pointed to the large male. "And since I am tired of thinking of you as 'the big black-and-white dog,' you are henceforth to be known as Socrates."

"Sock-rah-tease, hunh? Why that name?"

Ray smiled. "You prove my point. Socrates because you question everything, especially authority."

"Sock-rah-tease," the big dog said slowly, liking his new name more than he would admit.

"Now, let's get back to work," said Ray. "Suppose we're crossing a street and . . ."

"Why do *I* have to stay behind?" Ake asked.

"Because I'm only taking our team—*my* team," Ray told him. "The guys and I are like one. But we both worked hard with the new dogs, damn hard. Since someone has to stay with them, it makes sense that you're that someone."

"Yes, it does make sense," Ake admitted reluctantly. Then he looked at Ray and said, "Don't get yourself killed, partner."

"I'll try my damndest not to," Ray said, giving Ake a big hug.

"Hey," said the reserved Scandinavian.

II

The room in which Ray Larkin now stood was intended to intimidate and impress visitors, but the effect was lost on him. For a moment he ignored the man behind the overly large desk and took in his surroundings. On the high walls were holographic scenes of various Cadre triumphs: the landing field where the revolt on Alpha C was finally crushed, the attack against the strikers at Armstrong City on Luna, and a view of the death camp at Zelmka.

Besides these successes and horrors, the motif of power and wealth was further stressed by the sort of expensive and ostentatious trappings the *nouveau riche* and garden-variety megalomaniacs favored, objects whose main function was to impress. The Torgon wool carpet that covered the floor was itself meant to convey to a visitor the affluence and ruthlessness of its owner, most such remnants of the Cadre's subjugation of the Torgon humanoids having been destroyed long ago, to erase from the conscience of the Federation its occasional barbarism.

<If I were a ten-year-old boy, I would certainly be impressed,> Ray transmitted to Ake. *<As it is, I find it difficult not to laugh.>*

<If that's a real problem, Ray,> Ake replied, *<just envision yourself being sliced open from your crotch to your throat. Qi used to be a real General in the Cadre before they drummed him out for reasons no one seems to know—or want to know. Act your age for a change. This nutcase is dangerous.>*

<Yes, Pater.>

The man who looked down on Ray—in more ways than one—from behind his magnificently appointed desk, seated in a straight-backed chair (he believed cuddle chairs, which moved and purred beneath one, to be frivolous) was the only other warlord in the area with the men and material to challenge Poppa Dalvi for all the marbles. He was dressed in a gray suit tailored to resemble a uniform, and his skull was shaved.

"Please tell me why I should not simply have you killed and then take your team for my own. Why should I hire you at all?" Jaijo Qi asked Ray as he stood before the warlord.

"Good point. Because you have the makings of several

teams already. However, I am guessing that your dogs, while good berserkers and excellent weapons of intimidation, are not a trained, integrated team. They lack a real leader. My team is trained and professional. I can do the same for your dogs."

"I see. Tell me, why do you come to me with this great gift?"

"Gift? It is not a gift I am offering you, but a deal. You have money and power. I'd like some—money, that is."

"And how much did Dalvi offer you?"

"Oh, you heard about that? My congratulations to your spies. He offered one thousand a week."

"Why did you not accept his offer?"

"Because you will pay me fifteen hundred a week."

"What about your partner? Where is he?"

Ray nodded over his right shoulder. "The team is mine. I got tired of cutting him in for doing next to nothing. We split and he decided to stay with Poppa Dalvi and the other dogs."

"I see. You are a very brash young man," Qi said, bridging his fingers and staring thoughtfully at Ray.

<*You're not so young,*> Ake said.

<*Listen, J. Edgar,*> Ray told him. <*You're the one who warned me to be careful. I don't need your voice in my head at the same time I'm trying to keep Qi from standing me up against a wall, shooting me, and taking my dogs. So bug off for now!*>

<*Sorry.*>

"Do you feel all right, Mr. Larkin?"

"Ah, sure. Why?"

"You seem a little . . . preoccupied."

"I was just thinking what a nice place you got here," he said, his eyes once again taking in Jaijo Qi's "throne room."

"It is adequate for my purposes for the time being," Qi said.

"Did you know that Poppa Dalvi has a room like this one? Only it is twice as large, twice as richly appointed."

Although some of his men muttered at hearing this affront to their leader, Qi himself said mildly, "I happen to know that is not true." He raised his head and looked down his nose at Ray. "Now tell me, why would you say such an objectionable thing to your host?"

"How would you like to get rid of Poppa Dalvi, to take over his territory and to possess his things?"

"I would like it very much . . . after I had them disinfected."

Ray laughed. "Yes, he does have a thing for sacrificing chickens and goats, doesn't he?"

"What exactly is your point, Mr. Larkin?"

"Oh. Yeah, well, I thought that after I worked with your dogs awhile, I might then pretend to join Dalvi's band of merry men."

"Pretend, Mr. Larkin?" Qi was intrigued, but cautious.

"Sure. Once I was on the inside and trusted, I could throw open the gates, so to speak, and let your men in." He smiled as evil a smile as he could muster. "Such an act would, I'm sure, be amply rewarded."

"It would indeed, Mr. Larkin."

"Shall we shake on it?" Ray stuck out his hand.

Qi looked at the proffered appendage as if Ray were suggesting that he accept a dead rat. "My word is my bond."

"Mine, too." Ray grinned. *And you'll sit in Dalvi's chair when Velinov and Hitler come back as a dance team*!

★ ★ ★

The two weeks following Ray's acceptance into the Qi contingent were a blur and, for the most part, a replay of his first two weeks with Dalvi. He and Beowulf introduced themselves to Qi's dogs and had to overcome the same resistance, skepticism, and outright hostility they'd met from Dalvi's pack. Beowulf did his "thing" again and became their top dog. It was the beginning of the third week when things began to get interesting, however.

A weaselly-looking lieutenant of Qi's called Orlando Sepsi interrupted one of Ray's sessions with the new dogs. "Hey, new boy, stop playin' with them dogs and come over here. General Qi has a job for you."

Ray stopped what he was doing, said something to the dogs that caused several of them to chortle, and ambled over to Sepsi. "Yeah, and just what does his lordship have in mind?"

"You make fun of the General?"

"No more than Mother Nature," Ray said, smiling. "So, come on, tell me—what's up?"

Sepsi picked at his teeth. "The General wants us to carry a message to the Blades."

"What's a 'blade'?"

"They're a bunch of easties who think they can operate anywhere they damn please—in the General's territory or in Dalvi's. We got a message from 'em that they got their hands on some dogs. They want to trade 'em to the General in return for some territorial rights."

"Territorial rights to do what?"

Sepsi touched the gold ring around his neck that automatically delivered an injection of Ice on a predetermined basis. "To sell the big chill."

"I see." Ray had learned that easties were punks or whole gangs who tried to keep their independence, playing one warlord off against another. *Not unlike what Ake and I are trying to do, really*, he told himself. The "eastie" part came from an old sinny star named Eastwood, famous for playing loners. *Then why not "Woodies"?* he wondered, marveling at the mental processes that produced slang words.

"The General wants to know if the new dogs is ready to go with us."

"Not as a team," Ray said, rubbing his chin. "But a couple of them can tag along to pick up experience."

"Good. Be ready to go at midnight."

"Okay. Do I get my energy rifle back?"

"We'll see. That's up to the General."

Ray observed that the cliche was true: The city never slept. The streets were as alive at midnight as midday, crowded with Half-Heads, archies, winos, belters, street preachers, spacers, Cousteaueans and other genetically altered men and women. Just about anyone or anything.

The street vendors hawked diverse wares, from barbecued "Komodo Dragon" tail on a stick, to Eridani dancing stones, to Klassic Koke, to porno holopix from Hermaphrodite, to eighteen-centimeter-high replicas of the Statue of Liberty—not the revered ruins, but the way it looked before a smart bomb got dumb.

The dogs' heads swiveled around like they were on gimbals as they took in all the sights, sounds, and smells. Every once in a while brightly lighted commuter sleds shot through the transparent plasglas skyway tubes snaking from building to building high overhead, the motion invariably drawing the dogs' eyes upwards to center something seen out of the corners of their vision.

A hologram advertising "Rollie's Relaxers," a popular brand of happy sticks, floated by just above Ray's head. Its soft, appealing voice implored listeners to "Wrap your lips around a Rollie's and r-e-l-e-a-s-e your worries." Qi's dogs paid it no mind, but Ray's pack followed it with their eyes until it drifted away.

"Whew," said Ray as they walked past an alley that reeked of urine.

Sepsi laughed. "The official scent of New York."

"Boy, this sumpthin'," Tajil exclaimed.

"The Big Apple itself," Ray replied, wrinkling his nose in disgust.

"Huh?"

"The Big Apple—that's what they used to call Manhattan in the old days."

"What's that mean?" asked Balder, one of the five new dogs he'd brought along.

"I don't know," Ray confessed, dropping a one-credit coin into a Salvation Army 'bot's collection box.

"Thank you, brother," the uniformed 'bot said automatically as Ray kept walking.

"You mean there's somethin' that the super-genius admits he don't know?" said Sepsi. "I don't fuckin' believe it."

Ray concentrated on opening the connection to Ake. *<Ake, can you read me?>*

<Yeah, I "read" you. You're so melodramatic.>

<Excuse me. I wasn't once a spy like some people I could name.>

<Talk to me, Ray. Where are you?> Ray looked at the street sign floating over the nearest intersection and told Ake what it said.

<We're close, then.>

<Who's we?>

<You don't think I'd come out here alone, do you? I've got Socrates, Athena, Emo, Odin, and Asa with me.>

<When I call, don't be late.>

<Just how are you going to handle this?>

<You'll see,> Ray said enigmatically.

A passerby took his time getting out the dogs' way and Thor, another of Qi's dogs Ray had decided to bring along to observe how the team acted as a unit, growled menacingly at the man, causing him to blanch and half-walk, half-run away in fear. That was the wrong thing to do: Thor started after him.

"Thor! Stop that!" shouted Ray and Beowulf simultaneously. The big brown dog almost did a header in coming to a halt, suddenly aware that the rules had changed. "Get back here," Ray ordered.

Thor slinked back to take his place beside Balder, Leto, and Hester, the other new dogs. When Ray began, "Thor, I though you knew better than to—" the brown dog flinched and lowered his head.

"Easy, Thor. I'm not gonna hit you," Ray said, suddenly aware that the remorseful dog fully expected to be struck for his lapse. "C'mere, fella." Ray rubbed his head and thumped his side reassuringly. "You're no longer supposed to act that way toward civilians," Ray told him, "but then, you guys weren't properly trained. You were *expected* to treat strangers like the enemy. I don't like it, I want it to change, but I *do* understand if you forget yourselves once in awhile."

"Really?" asked a female he'd named Guinevere.

"Really," Ray confirmed.

"Ray leads a team," Beowulf told her. "He doan lead slaves."

"Shit, Larkin, people respect General Qi's mutts. What're you tryin' to do, turn 'em into goddamn lap dogs?"

Ray curled a finger and Littlejohn shoved his muzzle in Sepsi's face, growling and baring his teeth. "He remind you of a lap dog?"

"Get him away from me!" Sepsi shrieked. "*Please.*"

"Ah, the magic word." Ray gestured again and Littlejohn withdrew, a big canine grin replacing his fierce countenance.

Sepsi remained silent for the remainder of their journey to the Blades' hangout, so silent that Ray finally had to ask, "How far is it yet?"

"Not far," Sepsi replied. "As a matter of fact . . ."

Ray followed Sepsi's glance. "It's underground?"

"Yeah. In the old subway station."

<*The old subway station,*> Ray told Ake.

<*Gotcha. We're just a few blocks away.*>

Sepsi turned to stare at Ray, some of his vinegar returning.

"You *are* an outsider, ain'tcha? The subways, the old underground shopping plazas—they all belong to the people now." He laughed. "To the people that can take 'em and hold 'em, that is." He stiffened as a blast of Ice was automatically injected into his bloodstream. "They say that Thom MacAdoo in Manhattan has the biggest one—old Grand Central."

"Old Grand Central?"

"Yeah, abandoned in 2059."

They halted at the long-inoperative escalator leading down into the underground complex. The stairs descended about five meters, then made a ninety-degree turn to the left, denying a visitor the opportunity to see what was waiting for him farther down.

"I don't like this," Ray said.

"Oh, don't worry about it. Everything's gonna be okay."

Ray put out an arm, blocking Sepsi's way. "I said I don't like this," Ray repeated firmly.

"So whutta you wanna do about it?"

"Beowulf and Frodo. Come here." When the two dogs trotted over, Ray bent down and whispered something in Beowulf's ear. The big dog nodded. Ray continued giving instructions. Finally, he stood up and the two dogs started down the steps.

"Hey, what gives?" Sepsi demanded.

"Beowulf and Frodo are going to take a little look around. It's just a precaution."

"Shit, Larkin, someone sees a scout dog these days, he's liable to start shootin' without any warning."

"I realize. It's a calculated risk."

The dogs returned after a few minutes, bounding up the steps. "Ray, Ray!" Beowulf barked.

"What is it?"

"Theys dead. Theys all dead!"

16

"Huh?" Sepsi's mouth gaped open.

"What happened?"

"Dunno, but it looks like another dog team done it—their throats is torn out."

"I gotta report this," Sepsi said, reaching for his small cigarette pack-sized communicator. He fumbled around, patting each of his pockets, and growing more agitated.

"What's the matter?"

"My communicator—I musta lost it!"

"You get back to Qi's headquarters and bring help," Ray told him.

"What about you?"

"We'll go down and see if we can figure out what happened. There may still be someone there, hiding." Ray saw Sepsi's eyes widen as he considered that. With a flash of inspiration, Ray added, "You want to come with us?"

"No, you're right. Someone has to report to General Qi." He backed away. "Watch out."

"Oh, I will," Ray said softly, watching Sepsi depart. Then he pulled the communicator he'd lifted from Sepsi's back pocket, dropped it on the plascrete, and ground it to bits with the heel of his boot. He kicked the remains into the street.

"Let's go," he told the dogs. "Everyone—but especially you new guys—maintain silence until I say it's time to act."

"Okay," said Balder.

"Which way?" Ray asked Beowulf as they navigated the first turn.

"Bottom of steps, turn right, then left, then about"—Beowulf had to concentrate when figuring out distances—"a hunnert meters down a hall."

"All that way and no lookouts?" Ray asked before he saw the first body, its throat torn out. "Oh." They passed an arrow sign which said, TO TRAINS.

"There's 'nother body, past the left turn," Beowulf said in a low voice. They were getting closer.

"How come there's no blood on you?" Ray asked in a whisper.

"Frodo licked it off," Beowulf whispered back. Ray just nodded in admiration for Beowulf's quick thinking.

"Here," Frodo said. He, too, whispered.

His energy rifle held across his body and in a ready position, Ray took a deep breath and stepped around the corner and into what was once, a very long time ago, the entry plaza to a vast underground shopping and business center. "Hello, gentlemen," he said.

About fifteen gang members, their skulls shaved and adorned with vaguely obscene tattoos, were standing in a circle around two null-grav gurneys. Spread-eagled, their wrists and ankles tied down, were two naked girls. Five or six of the Blades were bare-assed, their pants around their ankles. There was a single Blade atop each girl, grunting and thrusting. The girls were moaning in protest, to no avail. Along the wall, a number of dogs were restrained by heavy chains.

Ray swallowed in disgust and gripped the stock of his energy rifle. "I take it you bags of pus are called the Blades?"

An onlooker to the rapes, a self-cooled can of brew in his hand, turned and stared in Ray's direction. "Yeah, and who the fuck are you?" he asked, ignoring Ray's calculated insult.

"Why, I'm Dirty Harry," Ray said, glancing at the twelve chained dogs in one corner.

"Dirty Harry? Who the fuck is Dirty Harry?"

"And you call yourselves easties," Ray said, shaking his head sadly.

One of the Blades started easing his hand into his pocket.

Ray couldn't resist. "Go ahead–make my day." The puzzled gang member stopped.

Another Blade went for a slug thrower. Ray swiveled, fired a bolt of energy that blew away his challenger, and, in the same motion, he smoothly swung the rifle back and burned a hole through the Blade who'd begun reaching into his pocket.

That galvanized everyone.

The dogs leapt into battle as the Blades grabbed for their weapons. Ray walked forward into the huge open space, firing as he went. Barking furiously, the dogs terrorized the outclassed gang members who quickly gave up any idea of fighting and began to turn and flee; the dogs ran them down and efficiently dispatched them.

The whole confrontation took less then thirty seconds.

Panting, blood dripping from their muzzles, the dogs vented their emotions by talking loudly and pointlessly. The idea was not to make conversation but to deal with the pounding of their hearts and the adrenaline flowing through their veins. The chained dogs were berserk with fear and anger, lunging toward Ray and his team, brought up short by their chains.

Ray touched the ruby around his own neck and said, "Wait a minute, everyone. Hold the noise down for just a moment."

The dogs quieted. "There's someone still alive," Ray said. "I can sense him."

Tajil's nose twitched as he sniffed the air. "Yah," he said, "smells like he's . . . he's back that way." He indicated the rear of the open space, much of it hidden by a jungle of empty packing cartons.

Suddenly, the cartons went tumbling. The Blade who was hiding pushed them toward Ray and the dogs and ran as fast as he could in the opposite direction.

"Taddy, you follow—"

"Let me. Please," begged Thor.

"Okay," Ray agreed. "But make it clean and fast. As painless as possible."

The big brown dog rushed after the fleeing survivor, maneuvering around the overturned boxes. Twenty seconds passed, and then there was a brief, high-pitched shriek that was abruptly cut off. Soon, Thor reappeared, his muzzle stained red.

"Someone find water somewhere—I can't let Qi's goons see you like this."

<*Talk to me, Ray.*>

<*The Eagle has landed.*>

<*Good.*> Then he added, <*Don't get cocky*!>

<*Don't worry: Now I gotta sell this to Qi.*>

"You talk to Ake?" Mama-san asked.

Ray tapped the side of his head. "Yeah. He and some of the new dogs aren't very far away."

Ray approached the two cowering girls. He didn't begrudge them their fear of him; for all they knew, they'd gone from the frying pan into the fire.

"It's all right now," he said soothingly. When he was certain that they were as calm as they could be under the circumstances, he cut them loose. He saw a pile of clothing lying on the floor and handed it to them. "How old are you two?" he asked them.

"I'm sixteen," said the girl with dirty-blonde hair.

"I'm fifteen," said the other girl, a redhead with a small crescent moon-shaped scar on her chin.

Well, you're both pushing fifty now, Ray thought sadly.

"What do you want with us, mister?" asked the blonde, pulling on her pants and buttoning her blouse.

Ray shook his head. "Nothing." He indicated the way he'd come. "Go on, get out of here."

They took his advice, looking over their shoulders the whole way out.

"Who was that I just passed?"

"Ake!" shouted Sinbad.

"Hi, everybody. Hi, short stuff. Well, isn't anyone going to answer my question?"

Ray explained the girls' presence.

Ake looked at the bloody results of the short, intense firefight. "You know, I was going to argue with you about the necessity of killing relatively 'innocent' bystanders, but now I just can't do it."

"They was bad Mens," Beowulf said.

"There doesn't seem to be too many innocent bystanders around here, does there?"

"I wouldn't say that," Ray told him.

"Huh?"

Ray pointed to the eight frightened, growling dogs chained in the corner.

"What you do now, Ray?" Mama-san asked after Ake had left with the latest dogs in his possession.

Ray bent over a fallen Blade, pulled the dead gang member's energy pistol out of his pocket, fired it into the wall, and returned it to his hand. "I've got to make it look like this nest of vipers really put up a fight, one against a huge party of attackers." He smiled grimly. "I can't let Qi know it was this easy."

II

General Qi picked up a bowl of fruit and threw it against the wall. Apples, bananas, and venusian oranges went flying as the crystal glass bowl shattered. "Goddamn that chicken-sacrificing sonofabitch!"

"So he had a bunch of easties killed before you could cut a deal; is that such a big thing?" Ray asked, feigning ignorance.

"It was an arranged truce, you moron!" Qi said angrily. Ray tried to look properly abashed. "Now all the easties we've been trying to win over are going to think *I* had them killed. Not only that, any Blades who survived by not being there will be convinced I killed their friends."

"So don't give anyone time to think," one of Qi's lieutenants said. "Let's hit Dalvi and hit him hard. Hit him before he can hit us." *Bless your heart!* Ray thought, staring at the man whose bright idea this was. *That saves me the trouble of suggesting the very same thing.*

"It looks like you hired me and my team just in time," Ray said. "You're going to need us."

"How good is your ex-partner?"

"Good, very good," Ray replied. "But not as good as me."

"That is reassuring to hear," Qi said. "Because you two may face each other sooner than you think. This ambush doesn't sound like the Dalvi I know. I'm guessing it was your old partner and Dalvi's dogs who did this."

Ray just nodded.

★ ★ ★

The next week or so was a very trying time for both Poppa Dalvi and Jaijo Qi. Qi did indeed hit Dalvi hard, raiding a number of Dalvi-owned or operated bars, drug dens, and gambling halls. Qi also set and sprang several daring ambushes, wiping out a substantial number of the besieged warlord's men.

Dalvi didn't simply lie back on the ropes and take it on the chin, however. He retaliated with raids and ambushes of his own. By day ten of the escalating warfare, each side had hemorrhaged men and territory so badly that Ray wondered how long they could keep up their conflict.

Ray also wondered how long it would take the new dogs—and even his own team, for that matter—to be psychologically rehabilitated after all this was over, assuming they got out of it alive. *We started all this because we wanted to "rescue" them from a life of vicious brutality*, he thought. *So what's the first thing I ask them to do? Kill humans by the score!*

It wasn't only their psyches that were at risk. Already, two of the new dogs, Isaac and Juno, had died in one of the raids. Ray knew it was only blind luck that none of his team had been killed. He had to do something and fast.

<Listen up, good buddy,> he transmitted.

<I'm all ears.>

<No, that's Ozma. You're all white,> Ray joked.

<I'd say that was Moby but that would be going along with you. So, partner, what's cooking?>

<I like the terminology. To stick with it, I want to turn the heat up.>

<How high?>

<Boiling.>

<Let's do it. What do you have in mind?>

<Well, here's what I think . . .>

Qi's men moved cautiously through the abandoned skyway tube behind Ray's dogs. In addition to his own team, he had a good baker's dozen of Qi's dogs with him. With kilometer after kilometer of this line's route destroyed and never repaired or replaced, the still-intact segments could be used for quick access between interconnected buildings.

"I think that's the Excelsior building just ahead," Ray told Beowulf and Sepsi.

"Yeah, you're right." Sepsi got out his new communicator. "We're almost to the Excelsior building," he told the twenty-five heavily armed men following them. "Load 'em."

"Let's go," Ray said. There were no lights in the skyway, but those from nearby buildings and the ambient glow from the pulsing, living street far below provided all the illumination they required. Some of the men had wanted to wear night goggles, but Sepsi had reminded them what could happen if they looked directly at an explosion or someone simply turned on bright lights. For a moment, perhaps a fatal moment, they'd be blinded.

Ray made a motion for everyone to get down. They'd crawl the last forty meters, the length of the tube linking their destination and the building they'd just passed through. Crawling on their stomachs, they'd be harder to see coming if anyone was standing guard or simply looking in their direction. At least, that was the theory.

The dogs wiggled forward, propelling themselves across the slick curved polyplas floor with their hind legs, their rumps sticking up in the air. "Boy, this fun!" said Sinbad.

"Yah," said one of the new dogs, a handsome male Ray called Robin. "Trainin' and learnin' be like this?"

"Shhh," said Beowulf.

"Ahhh," Robin said. "Beowulf no fun."

"Listen to your leader," Ray said firmly.

"Yes, Ray." Robin sounded properly contrite. Ray liked Robin a lot. Although not a young dog, he somehow had avoided becoming as savage and surly as many of the others.

<*We're almost to the Excelsior*,> transmitted Ray.

<*Then here we come*,> Ake beamed back.

Tajil and a Great Dane named Hamlet wiggled back from the point, their butts held high. Ray almost giggled at the comical sight. He recognized his desire to laugh out loud for what it was: a nervous response to the coming firefight.

"Can't go no further," Tajil announced to Ray.

"What's your mutt mean, we can't go no further?" squeaked Sepsi.

Ray knew the answer, of course, but he asked, "What's the problem, Taddy?"

"It's sealed off. Can't go no further," he repeated dutifully.

Someone back in the mass of men behind them shouted in alarm, "Hey, I think there's someone behind us!"

"Sonofabitch!" Sepsi swore.

"That's a real pisser, ain't it?" Ray said matter-of-factly.

The oddest look crossed Sepsi's face; it was the dawning of awareness. "You bastard! It's an ambush!" he shouted, reaching for his energy pistol.

"This what you're looking for?" asked Ray as he showed Sepsi the weapon he'd taken from him. "I have to confess that I took your communicator, too," he said as he pressed the firing stud at point-blank range. From that distance, the beam bored a pencil-sized hole through the astonished man's forehead. Sepsi collapsed onto the floor of the tube.

All hell broke loose behind them, and Ray told the dogs to wait for his word. Qi's men, realizing the threat was from their rear, turned and began returning the attackers' fire.

"Now." The dogs attacked Qi's men before they had a chance to realize they were being hammered from both ends of the tube. Firing Sepsi's pistol at targets of opportunity, Ray contributed to the one-sided nature of the conflict.

In addition to the sounds of energy rifles and automatic slug throwers, Ray could hear the battle cries of Dalvi's dogs, under Ake's leadership. *Music to my ears.*

Trapped between two huge teams of dogs, facing a deadly enfilade from either side of their position, Qi's outgunned men did the only things they could under the circumstances: They either died where they were or they raised their hands in surrender. After a great many of them did the former, most of the others chose to do the latter.

<I'm coming back. Tell everyone to stand easy,> Ake warned Ray.

"Ake's coming through," Ray told the dogs. "Settle yourselves down." Ray didn't say that lightly. Some of the new dogs had a touch of bloodlust. One of the men had tried to surrender, only to have his throat torn out anyway. *The sooner we can get these guys offplanet the better it'll be for everyone*, Ray told himself.

Even though he unconsciously reached up to his throat and touched the ruby that hung there, Ray didn't need its psi-amplifying powers to sense the closeness of his friend and partner. "Ake," he said, feeling a small lump in his throat that swallowing couldn't get rid of.

"Hi, short stuff," Ake said, beaming broadly. He embraced Ray and they patted each other on the back. "Damn, we're getting mushy in our old age, aren't we?" Ake said in a husky voice.

"Miss me, did ya?" Ray asked.

"The dogs did."

Ray smiled. Between Ake's Scandinavian origins and his own Swiss-German ancestry, the two of them openly displayed honest emotions about as often as the Pope took his wife out to dinner.

"How's Beowulf?" Ake asked.

"I fine," the big dog said in his gravel voice. "You good, Ake?"

Ake nodded. "I'm the son Dalvi never had." He looked back at Ray. "You're going to go to the head of the class, however, for setting up this little stunt."

"Just till we hand Dalvi *his* head."

III

"Why are you alive?" Qi asked Ray. "Why are you not dead like the rest of your party?"

Ray hunched his shoulders helplessly. "I don't know."

"You don't know? Everyone else is dead, but you alone survived and you don't know?"

Ray swallowed, hoping Qi wouldn't see his Adam's apple bob. "I can see the General wishes the absolute truth. And the truth is, I ran away when it became clear that it was a well-planned ambush. I even left my dogs behind."

Qi ran his hand over his shaved skull. "An ambush. Tell me, do you have any idea how they could have learned about our attack?"

Ray looked at Qi's subordinates in the room before saying, "It is not my place to speculate, General."

"Please do."

"In that case, General"—he glanced around the room again—"I would say that someone in your inner circle has betrayed you." *Well, I've played that card. Let's see what the response is.*

There were angry mutterings from Qi's lieutenants. He silenced them by raising his hand. "I must tell you, Larkin, that I concur with you." He dropped his hand. "Bring in the girl," he ordered.

Uh-oh.

The young woman with the dirty-blonde hair who Ray and the dogs had rescued from the Blades came into the room, trailed by one of Qi's goons. "Is this the man who . . . *interrupted* . . . the Blades' business with you?"

The girl looked at Ray, then dropped her gaze to the floor. "Yeah, that's him." She turned partly away.

"Look at him again," Qi ordered. "It is important that you are absolutely sure."

"Hell! Of course I'm sure! He blew those guys away like the shit they were!"

"And the other man and dogs you saw?"

"I dunno who they were. Me and Meg passed them on the way out."

"Thank you."

"Can I have my money and get out of here now?"

"Certainly. See that she is paid the amount we agreed upon," Qi said to the goon who'd ushered her in.

"Yes, sir." The girl and her escort left.

"What have you to say for yourself, Mr. Larkin?"

"How about I'm sorry," Ray said cheerfully. "I killed your men; it was wrong of me to do that when I was being paid by you, but I did it and I apologize."

"This guy's nuts," one of Qi's men said.

"That's it," Ray agreed. "Not guilty by reason of insanity."

"Very amusing," Qi told him. "You are a funny man."

You wouldn't know funny if it walked in here and bit you on the ass, Jack, Ray thought.

"It will be interesting to see if you are still so humorous after Daniel here is done with you."

<*Ray calling Ake. Ray calling Ake—code word "Help!"*> Nothing. <*No fooling, Ake, come in, please!*>

Qi seemed amused by Ray's look of concentration. "By the way, Mr. Larkin—we are jamming your signal. That is only a temporary measure, however." He glanced at one of his men and said, "Do it, Daniel."

Daniel, a man so angular his elbows could cut paper, found

the place on Ray's skull where the transmitter had been implanted. "You won't be needing this," he told Ray.

"Oh, I'll be *needing* it," Ray corrected him. "I'll just not be *having* it, will I?"

"Once again, Mr. Larkin, I look forward to seeing how you respond to Daniel's skillful ministrations."

"What do you expect me to tell you?" Ray asked him as several beefy goons seized his arms.

"Why, nothing, Mr. Larkin. I expect you to suffer . . . and then to die."

The thin man smiled and reached for the side of Ray's skull, something gleaming and nasty-looking held in his hand. "Please hold still; this will hurt."

Ray crouched on the floor of the small, featureless, white-walled room. Whether its normal function was to serve as a cell or not, it made a perfect one. He realized that he had only a few minutes until Daniel would have him dragged out and the torture begun.

So far, he had not been searched. Very likely, when they returned for him, that would happen. The large ruby he wore would be seen for the priceless gem it was and quickly taken from him. He had to act before it was discovered.

Ray fumbled open the bag he wore around his neck and dumped the ruby out into his hand. After holding it in his palm and feelings its intense psi power, he popped it into his mouth and swallowed it. To allay the suspicions of his captors, he slipped an old pre-Federation coin into the pouch. It was an odd thing he'd found in an antiques shop the day before. On one side was an eagle; the other side was inscribed "Liberty" and bore the profile of a stern-faced woman. Hopefully, they would think it a keepsake or his "lucky" coin.

Ray sat down on the cool tiles of the floor. He hugged his knees and listened for approaching footsteps. He didn't have long to wait.

"You not hear nuthin'?" Beowulf asked, his canine voice full of concern.

"Not a word." Ake smashed his fist into the palm of his hand. "Damn it! It was idiotic to allow him to return to Qi's headquarters. Particularly without you. Qi's not stupid; he can put two and two together as easily as the next person."

"There still dogs there," Beowulf reminded him. "Ray just wanted me and the team to help you with fat man."

"I know. That's the only reason Ray risked going back. Hindsight is twenty-twenty, but I never should have let him return!"

★ ★ ★

Ray had seen death often, and he had faced the prospect of his own death more than once. Knowing that death had come close to him, so very close, made Ray see the absurdity of it and left him with little fear of its finality.

Death was one thing; torture was another.

Ray strained against the plasteel restraints that bound him. He could see the gaunt Daniel crossing the space between them, holding a tangle of wires and electrodes in his hand.

"Tell me," asked Daniel, staring at the dried blood matting the hair on the left side of Ray's head, "is your wound feeling any better?"

"What's it to you, fuckface?"

Daniel smashed the injured area with the bristles side of a wire brush. A wave of nausea swept through Ray but he didn't make a sound. "Oh, a hero type, eh? That's good; heroes last longer."

Ray felt blood begin to flow again from the reopened wound where Daniel had used a sharp implement to dig out the small radio transmitter/receiver that had linked him to Ake. He also felt—and it chilled him to the bone—a pulse of energy directly from the thin man's *mind*.

"I would talk soon if I were you—chewers work fast," Daniel said. Ray looked away. "Good," he told Ray. "As I said, I hate people who give in too quickly and deny me an opportunity to do my job.

"Tell me," he asked as he attached the electrodes to Ray's forehead and skull, "have you ever seen a borer beetle?" When Ray didn't answer, he shrugged and continued chatting as if he was talking to an old friend.

"They're ugly things—squat, black little monsters with hideous mouth parts. They say an especially industrious one can chew through skin and bone and flesh in minutes. Then it bores into your brain. It is supposed to be very painful." He stopped and admired his handiwork. "But then I guess you will soon be able to give me first-hand information about that, won't you?"

The thin man walked to the door. "I'm leaving now. But never fear, I'll be keeping an eye on you. You may scream all you wish; they say it helps. Goodbye now."

"Daniel?"

"Yes?"

"I am going to kill you."

"Sure you are." He smiled. "Remember—it's all in your mind. Tell yourself that . . . if you are able."

Nothing happened for a long time. Ray felt a drop of perspiration roll from under the lattice of wires crisscrossing his head. Then he felt the first tentative touch of the nonexistent yet so very real insect's legs as it crawled onto his arm. Its feet tickling his skin, it made its way up his arm to his neck. Moving slowly yet surely, it moved up his neck onto his cheek. Then . . .

The sound of someone's screams filled Ray's ears until they blotted out everything else . . . except for the blinding pain and the realization that the screams were coming from his own throat. Ray thought he could hear Daniel and General Qi laughing as he felt the warm blood flowing down his cheek.

17

Ake had never seen any food that looked quite like what Dalvi was eating. Well, that wasn't true—the chunks of white meat in the stew that Dalvi was attacking with vigor could easily have been alligator, bascane, pork, bolla bolla, groundhog, or any of a dozen delicacies.

When he wasn't shoveling tablespoonfuls of stew meat and vegetables between his thick, ropey lips, he was squeezing the thigh of the young girl sitting cheek-to-cheek beside him. Ake saw an amber light on the warlord's neck ring briefly light up; Dalvi had just gotten his timed injection of Ice.

Ice. Ake stared at the mysterious white meat again. His eyes flicked up and met Dalvi's. Dalvi smiled, shoved a brimming spoonful of stew into his gaping maw, slowly worked it around the inside of his mouth, chewed, and swallowed it. That's when Ake knew for sure what the unknown meat was. Consuming large quantities of Ice gave one certain cravings. Unspeakable cravings. That's why the drug was banned in every known system, on every civilized planet.

"Are you not hungry?" Dalvi asked, having seen the look of recognition in Ake's eyes. The girl beside him made an odd feral sound and snugged in closer to his vast bulk.

"No thanks, I just ate."

"Tell me," Dalvi said. "Have I done enough to show you how much I appreciate what you have done for me?"

"Your excellency has been most generous."

"Not only have you and your dogs helped me pulverize parts of Qi's 'army' and take possession of the scout dogs that should rightfully have been mine from the beginning, but you also brought me new recruits." He smiled thinking about it. "Almost all of Qi's men who were captured have decided to join my forces after listening to my offer."

"I am delighted to hear that, excellency."

Dalvi nodded thoughtfully. He put down his spoon and pushed away his bowl; he was finished with his odious meal. He motioned to one of his flunkies to take away the remains of his food. "You may now speak to me of this problem you say you wish to discuss."

"Your excellency, one of the reasons we have been able to so decimate Qi's forces is because of Ray, my partner, and his secret communications with me. Well, for the past thirty-six hours, I have been unable to make contact with Ray."

"And you believe that Qi has learned he is really working for me?"

"I'm afraid so."

"I see." Dalvi stroked the girl's fine black hair. "I do not understand. What do you now expect of me?"

It took all of Ake's willpower to keep his jaw from dropping. "Your excellency, Ray's contributions were a major factor in your success—which you yourself have just outlined. We must do something to free him if he is a prisoner. We must do what we can to get him back."

"He has served his purpose," Poppa Dalvi said matter-of-factly. "To mount an offense to gain the release of one man is not worth it." The girl giggled.

"But—"

"Besides," said Dalvi darkly, "it is Jogambé who must be thanked. It is Jogambé's power that has defeated Qi." He leaned toward Ake. "Do you dispute this?"

Ake was trapped. He waved his hands helplessly. "Of course not, excellency. It is just—"

"You may go now."

"Please, your excellency . . ."

"I have many good thoughts and feelings about you," said Dalvi. "Do not darken my mood. You may go now."

Ake realized that further argument would not only be

useless, it would clearly be suicidal. "Yes, excellency." He made a modest bowing gesture, backed up a few steps, and then turned and walked toward the door. "This deal's getting shittier and shittier," he mumbled under his breath.

★ ★ ★

"Shane, don't go."

Ignoring the pain from the wound he'd suffered in the shootout in Grafton's Saloon, Ray reached out and tousled little Joey's hair. "I've got to go, Joey. There's no living with a killing. Right or wrong, the brand sticks and there's no going back."

"But, Shane—"

"You take care of your ma and pa, Joey. Grow strong and straight and take care of them. Both of them."

"Yes, Shane."

Ray wheeled his horse and rode off, heading for the mountains. He knew he was doing the right thing. When he'd told Ryker that his days were over, the old rancher had responded, "Mine? What about yours, gunfighter?"

"The difference is, I know," Ray had replied. And it was true; he had no place in the new West. The West was changing. It was no longer a land of hunters and trappers and unfenced prairie where cattle could roam free. It was becoming civilized—farms, families, churches, banks, and schools. Like Ryker, he was a remnant from another age, a dinosaur. He knew better than to delude himself that there was a place for him in the valley now that Ryker and Wilson were dead. No, leaving was for the best.

"Shane! Come back, Shane!" Joey's voice was growing more faint now as the mountains loomed ever closer.

The pain returned. Ryker's brother had wounded him before Ray was able to whirl and shoot him dead. If he could only reach the mountains, the pain—

"Come back, goddamn you! Come back!"

With the onrush of pain, Shane's/Ray's universe turned blacker than the prairie night.

"What is it?" asked Qi.

"It's happened again," Daniel said, regarding Ray's now-unconscious form.

"What has happened again?"

Daniel wet his thin lips. "I am not certain, but I believe he . . . he goes somewhere."

"Goes somewhere?" Qi said incredulously.

Looking for all the world like an atheist who is forced to consider the number of angels who might dance on the head of a pin, Daniel finally replied, "He is able to somehow withdraw into his mind, shutting out the pain I inflict. Not completely, but enough so he is able to resist."

"I see," said Qi. "Well, what about your supposed psi powers? Can't you go after him?"

"I've tried, General. I cannot . . . find him."

Qi narrowed his eyes in exasperation.

"Take him back to his cell and lock him in," he said. "You can return to your efforts tomorrow."

"Yes, General."

II

Ake, and seven of the new dogs—Thor, Athena, Loki, Cisco, Will, Bella, and Natasha—were cruising the streets, working out their frustrations over Ray's silence and presumed arrest. Ake almost hoped that some of Qi's followers would spot him and start something that he could finish. He was in a foul mood. "Ray has saved my bacon too many times for me to just stand around with my finger up my nose," Ake told the dogs.

"Wisht there was sumpthin' we could do," said Athena plaintively.

"Yah," agreed Cisco. Ake smiled and rubbed their ears. They were far from disciplined scout dogs, but they were trying their best to be "good," as they put it. They knew they needed to be retrained and shown the right way to do things.

"Thanks, guys, and I . . ." Ake stopped. He had the oddest feeling that someone was staring at the back of his neck. "Athena," he said in a low voice. "Is there anyone following us?"

Athena looked. "Yah. How you know that?"

They need so much work yet. Beowulf and the others would have spotted this guy long before I did. Ignoring the female's question, Ake asked. "What's he doing?"

"It's a she, and she ain't doin' nuthin' but lookin' at you funny."

Ake turned slowly, his hand on the butt of his energy pistol. He saw a young girl. She was red-haired with a small crescent-shaped scar on her chin. When she saw him staring at her, she lifted one hand in an almost imperceptible gesture of acknowledgment. Ake frowned; then he remembered her from the abandoned subway. He made a "come here" motion with his index finger. After only a second's hesitation, she took him up on his invitation.

"Hello," he said.

"Hello," she replied warily, her eyes darting around.

"You wish to talk to me?" She nodded yes. "You want to find somewhere a little more private?" She nodded even more vigorously. "Thor and Bella, would you two please check out that alley?" When the two dogs returned and said it was empty, Ake took the skinny girl's arm and said, "Shall we?"

In the alley, the girl continued glancing around nervously. She'd heard the dogs say it checked out, but Ake guessed that taking nothing for granted was a wise survival trait to possess in the city.

"Now then, what can I do for you?"

"I know who you are," she said.

"So does half the city by now. Who are you?"

"My name's Meg Cross." She tossed her long red hair. "But that's not important right now."

"What is?"

"General Qi has your friend, the one who rescued us. Qi knows he double-crossed him."

"How?"

"The other girl, Eva Kosler, told him."

"You mean that after Ray rescues her, maybe saves her life, she turns around and fingers him for Qi?"

The young red-haired girl shrugged. "Maybe Qi threatened to kill her family. Maybe she needed the money. It was a shitty thing to do, but Qi would have gotten the word from someone sooner or later. You guys don't exactly fade into the background, you know. Someone musta seen you comin' and goin' that night—just like they probably seen Eva and me." She cocked her head. "Yeah, that's probably what happened: Someone seen her leavin' and they grabbed her and squeezed her and she yapped." The girl swallowed. "It coulda happened to me."

"Would *you* have told him about Ray?"

"Probably." When Ake made a disgusted sound, she said, "Hey, when Qi's right-hand man gets you strapped in and starts playin' games with your head, starts torturin' you, you talk. Ain't no two ways about it."

"Sorry. You're right, of course," Ake said. Then he grimaced. "Torture."

"Yeah. How tough's your friend?"

"Very."

"That's too bad. Once Qi is done playin' with them, he has his victims killed. The longer this Ray guy holds out, the longer he has to suffer."

"Maybe," conceded Ake. "But it's also true that the longer he holds out, the more likely it is that I can get to him in time."

"Huh?"

"I'm going in and bringing him out."

"Not alone you're not."

"I have scout dogs."

"I don't mean that."

"You?" Taking in her insubstantial frame, Ake dismissed her offer immediately. "Don't be foolish; Qi—"

"Yeah, yeah. But I ain't talking about just me."

"Who, then?"

She smiled then, a sly grin that reemphasized her age.

Was I ever fifteen or sixteen? Ake wondered.

★ ★ ★

They met in an abandoned warehouse. Ake guessed there were possibly three hundred people in attendance. The turnout surprised and gratified him; he had to admit he was shocked at the number of ordinary citizens who professed to be willing to risk their lives to help destroy both Dalvi and Qi.

"I can't believe it. All these people are prepared to help you, me, and the dogs to overthrow Dalvi and the other warlords?"

"No," Meg Cross told him. "They're not doing it for you or me."

"Who then?"

"Themselves, of course."

"Why now?"

Meg Cross looked at him strangely. "You been in space too long, dog man." She sighed. "Take me. My dadder and mommer ran a clothing store just down the avenue. It was a shitty little place and they barely made enough to keep going what with all the looting and the gangs. Then one day Dalvi showed up and demanded a cut of their profits. He told dadder he'd protect him and mommer from the easties. He never said who would protect them from him. One day, one of Dalvi's collection agents thought my dadder was holding out on him." She paused for a moment, swallowed, and continued. "He beat him to death. When mommer tried to come to dadder's defense, Dalvi's goons put a slug in her head."

Ake stared at her. "And you?"

"I've been livin' on the street. I do all right."

"I'll bet you do," Ake said. *And Ray and I think we're tough hombres*.

"You still haven't told me why all of a sudden they've decided to fight back," Ake pressed.

"They didn't want to lose what little they had, I guess," Meg Cross replied. "They didn't want to lose their lives."

"And now they're willing to?"

"They don't want to go on any longer like they been going. They're tired of eatin' the scraps bastards like Qi and Dalvi leave for them. This is their home. They got nowhere else to go." She made a face. "They ain't got space yachts like *some* people. They're sick of sharing their home with killers and rapists—with scum. I told them about you and your friend. And—well—it's like maybe we've got a chance now."

Ake nodded. "Then it's time for some housecleaning."

"You are the man with the dogs?" asked a scrawny man with a Santa Claus beard. *Christ, is everyone around here skin and bones?* Ake asked himself. Ake saw that Santa Claus was half carrying, half dragging an ancient slug-throwing rifle nearly as big as he was.

"I'm the man with the dogs," Ake confirmed.

"Come with me, then. The meeting is about to start."

III

"Your excellency wished to see me?" Ake asked.

"Yes." Dalvi belched and broke wind simultaneously. *How* does *he do that?* Ake wondered. "I have good news for you."

"Yes?" Ake said flatly.

Dalvi frowned. "Oh, come now, Ringgren. Surely you can muster more enthusiasm for my news than that . . . especially when it concerns your friend."

"Ray?"

"Yes. We are going to mount a final assault against my longtime enemy. Tonight, we will attack Qi's headquarters and crush his men and their fearless leader once and for all." He stretched out his arms as if bestowing a blessing. "As a consequence, your friend may be freed. If he's still alive, that is."

"Oh, he's alive."

Dalvi frowned. "How do you know that?"

Ake smiled wickedly. "Why, Jogambé told me. In a vision."

"Jogambé . . . ?" Dalvi's frown deepened. "You make fun of Jogambé? You mock Jogambé?"

Ake shrugged. "Yes, I guess so." He reached inside his jacket and withdrew a carved piece of ebony teakwood. It was a thirty-centimeter-high figurine that was half head and half upper torso.

A gasp of recognition escaped from Dalvi's lips. "Jogambé!"

"Yeah, it's the teeny termites' delight himself. I thought he might be tired of being cooped up all the time in that little shrine you built for him in your quarters, so I liberated him. He seems to enjoy the fresh air, but he's gotten a bit dirty. I think he could use a shower."

Ake threw the wooden figurine on the floor and said, "Do it, Thor."

The big brown dog lifted his leg and directed a stream of urine onto the figurine. Dalvi gasped in horrified disbelief.

"Now he's all clean," Ake said.

Struggling to lift his immense mass to a standing position, Dalvi shouted, "Kill him!" But before the words were out of his mouth, Ake shot two of his bodyguards dead and the dogs happily made quick, bloody work of the others.

Dalvi raged. Picking up plates, glasses, utensils, and anything else within reach, he hurled them at Ake—who calmly ducked while keying a remote charge. A huge explosion rocked the building to its foundations. Speaking into a button-sized communications device on his jacket, Ake said, "I've 'opened the doors.' It's time for you to do your thing."

Dalvi brought his fist down on a table and smashed it. Bending over with great difficulty, he extracted one of the table's thick plaswood legs and advanced upon Ake. "I'll kill you myself!" he shouted.

Bella and Will growled and moved forward but Ake waved them back. "No thanks, dogs, but he's all mine." Thor came over and dropped the chain he'd once been forced to wear at Ake's feet. Ake picked it up, test-whirled it a few times, and said, "Allright, fat boy. Come and get it."

Had Dalvi been able to grab hold of Ake, it would have been all over in a matter of seconds. Keenly aware of this danger, Ake kept his distance. He was content to allow Dalvi to waddle clumsily after him, swinging the table leg futilely at a target he could never quite catch up to.

"Stand still, you coward," Dalvi snarled, his arm cocked.

"Fine." Ake waited until Dalvi was committed to his swing and then stepped back. The impetus of his vicious roundhouse arc carried Dalvi forward and he stumbled and fell on his bulging stomach. He looked for all the world like a fleshy beach ball with stubby arms and legs.

The dogs never forgot the expression on Ake's face as he coolly climbed on Dalvi's back and wrapped the chain around his thick neck. It was a look of hatred and resolve that they never saw again and never wished to.

"This is for Meg and her parents and for everyone you've ever hurt, you fat pig bastard!" Ake braced his feet on Dalvi's back and, holding the two ends of the chain in his hands, pulled with all his strength and with the weight of his body behind it.

Athena closed her eyes until the gurgling sounds ceased. Then she opened them, looked once at Dalvi's swollen face with his tongue protruding from his mouth, and said, "He dead, Ake."

"That's one down," Ake said.

IV

Ray gradually sensed that he was at the bottom of a black well and began swimming for the surface, toward the light. It was just above him now; his chest aching for oxygen, he reached for the light . . . and awoke.

Looking around, he saw that he was back in the small white room. *Home sweet home*, he thought.

He put his hand on his stomach as if by doing so he could somehow touch the ruby that was inside him. Well, why not? Maybe he could touch it—with his mind.

"Oh, Leonardo, if you could see me now," he whispered hoarsely. He wondered if the K'a-niian native who'd given him the pouch of rubies had undergone the transformation to the next level yet. Then, without knowing *how* he knew, he knew that his reptilian friend had crossed over. *Don't get all mystic, Ray,* he chided himself. *It doesn't take a genius to figure that, if twelve years have passed, Leonardo's turn to undergo the transformation ritual must have come a long time ago.*

"What's it like, Leonardo? Where do you go? Where *are* you?"

The door opened. "Talking to yourself, Larkin?" said Daniel. "That's not a good sign. I think I'll break you this time. Break you and kill you."

"Maybe you'll shit a golden egg, too," Ray spat back at him. *I know I will a ruby one!* he added to himself. "Ha . . . ha . . . ha!" he laughed. *A ruby one, that's rich!*

Daniel misunderstood his laughter. "So, you still think this is funny, eh? Well, I'll wipe that smile off your face soon enough." He stepped back out of the tiny room to allow two of Qi's goons to enter and haul Ray to his feet.

They carried him down the hall and into the room where Daniel administered the torture. "Strap him in extra tightly this time," Daniel ordered them. "This trip is to the end of the line."

Feeling the electrodes being fitted to his forehead and skull, Ray thought simply, *Leonardo—help me.*

Had he been able to peer inside himself—literally physically, not psychologically—Ray would have seen the ruby begin to glow. First dully, then more brightly. Suddenly, a wave of psi energy radiated out invisibly, washing over everything within a radius of one thousand meters.

Standing patiently in the observation area and watching Daniel attach the electrodes for this final assault, Qi received an urgent message.

"Yes, what is it?"

"General, we are being attacked! What shall we do?"

"Resist them, you fool!" Turning off his receiver, he said to the mercenary beside him, "Let's get out of here."

The mercenary looked at Daniel and the human fly in his *VR* web. "What about Daniel?"

"Leave him. He's happy. One should die when one is happy." He turned and strode away. The mercenary shrugged and followed.

"Now, my friend, it is time for you to . . ." Daniel's voice trailed away. Ray was staring over his shoulder. Angry, Daniel turned to see what was engaging Ray's attention when it should be on him, the grand inquisitor.

Daniel's mouth worked silently. Across the room the shimmering, ephemeral outline of a creature of light had coalesced. When it beckoned to the two of them, Daniel shrieked and collapsed in a heap. The being of light gestured again and Ray felt his restraints loosening. He got out of the chair.

"Hello, Leonardo . . . or whatever you call yourself now," he said smiling. Although he was all but certain that it was not literally possible, he thought that the apparition was smiling, too.

18

After overwhelming Dalvi's headquarters and killing or capturing most of his men, Ake and the dogs, Meg Cross, and the people who rose up against Dalvi's iron-fisted rule were on their way to administer the same rough justice to Qi and his followers.

"This won't be so easy," Meg Cross said.

"Easy?" Beowulf said. "You thought that was easy?"

"She's right, Beowulf," Ake agreed. "Remember, you and I were on the inside and helped open the doors. As for Qi, I can't imagine that they won't know we're on our way after what just happened to Dalvi."

"I thinked—" Thor began.

"Thought," corrected Mama-san.

Thor shot her a look but otherwise did nothing. Although "only" a female in the canine hierarchy, Mama-san was respected for her warmth and wisdom. And she *was* a member of Ray and Ake's number one team. "Okay, I *thought* Ray seen to it that this Key guy was jes' 'bout done for. I *thought* that he dint have too many mens left."

"He's clearly lost a lot of men," agreed Ake. "But like all petty tyrants, he's afraid of his own people and feels he needs to be protected from them. So, we're facing a loyal core group of followers."

"Qi's place is just ahead," one of the leaders of the new

coalition reported. "We've formulated a plan of attack. It's a simple one: We blow down the front door and come in shooting."

"Good," said Meg Cross, pulling out a huge slug thrower and checking to make sure it was loaded. It looked immense in her hands.

"Yeah, good," echoed Ake. Then he added, "Listen, ah . . ."

"Veitch. Gunther Veitch."

"My partner is in there, Veitch. I don't want him or any dogs to get hurt in the attack."

"I can't make any promises, especially about the dogs," Veitch said. "But we have a description of your friend; we'll do what we can." He glanced at Meg Cross and then looked back at Ake. "Remember, it might be best for all concerned—him especially—if your friend is already dead." He licked his lips. "I'm sorry, but you must consider that."

"I understand," Ake said wearily. "It's just that—"

There was shouting and consternation from the front of the mass of people. "Something's going on up there," said Veitch. "Come on!"

The advance scouts had returned to report that it was impossible to get closer to Qi's headquarters than a hundred meters. "Are they shooting at you to keep you back?" someone asked.

"No, it's not that at all," one of the scouts said. "It's the damnedest thing, but there's a force field around the place."

"A force field?" Veitch asked.

One of the other scouts shook her head. "Kind of. But not exactly. It's more like you get a really bad feeling when you get close."

The dogs began to circle restlessly. Several of them howled uneasily. "What is it?" Ake asked.

"Somethin' weird goin' on," said Beowulf. "Somethin' really weird. My head hurts."

"Yah," echoed several of the dogs.

"This is bullshit!" said Veitch. "Who's coming with me?" Several "I can-eat-broken-glass-and-laugh" tough types joined him. They began walking toward the headquarters. "See, there's nothing here and . . ." He put a hand to his head and stopped. Suddenly, he and the others doubled over and vomited.

"Jeez, lookit that!" said Frodo.

"I give that guy on the end a ten for distance," Ake said. *That smartass remark was for you, Ray.*

Still gagging, spitting, and wiping their mouths, Veitch and the others backed away as quickly as they could.

Meg Cross touched his arm. "What was it like?"

Veitch shook his head. "My God!" was all he would say.

★ ★ ★

"There, that should be comfortable," Ray said, stepping back to admire his handiwork. Before him, in the chair he had until recently occupied himself, sat a tightly bound Daniel.

Ray gently slapped Daniel's face. "Wake up and smell the coffee, Daniel," he said.

Daniel opened his eyes and saw Ray standing before him. "What happened?"

"You took a gander at my friend Leonardo and turned out the lights in response," Ray told him. Daniel saw the ghostly apparition in the corner of the room and then became aware of his bonds.

"What is this? What's going on?" he demanded, his voice quivering.

"I'll give you three guesses, and the first two don't count," Ray said.

"You can't do this!" Daniel shouted.

"'Course I can," said Ray as he went into the small "control" room and stared at the console that manipulated the images and sensations through the electrodes. He shook his head at humankind's ability to create and operate such devices.

"Please don't," came Daniel's voice faintly.

"I'm starting it now," Ray said. In reality, he did nothing. Giving the equipment one final look and noting that it was German-made—*That figures*, he told himself—he returned to confront Daniel one last time.

"Well, I've turned everything on," he lied. "It should be reaching peak power in about five minutes. I really don't have any idea what it'll do to you, but if you have half as much fun as I did, it should be interesting."

"Please—I'll do anything you want. Anything!"

"Sorry, I'm not Qi or Dalvi. Have fun with your new head."

Ray turned and saw that the apparition was gone, replaced by a glowing globe of white light. Ray followed the ball of light down the hall toward the lift/drop tubes. "In there?" he asked. The ball didn't respond in any way. Since the globe didn't warn him not to enter, Ray hopped into the tube . . . and immediately dropped like a rock. "Jesus and Mohammed!"

He "fell" fifteen floors to one of the sub-basements, coming to a gentle and apparently gravity-free halt. Normally, a body drifted gently down a drop tube. His too-rapid journey left Ray breathless. "I guess this is my destination," he said, happy to scramble out. The ball was outside the tube, waiting for him. "Took a shortcut, eh?"

He came to a molecular steel door at the end of the hall. "Allo, allo," he said. "Whot 'ave we got here, now, matey? I'm to go in, I take it?" Ray asked the pulsating globe. It seemed to glow more brightly for a moment. "I thought so." He found an energy pistol lying on the floor outside the door, apparently dropped by someone in a great hurry to get away. Picking it up, he contemplated it and then the door. With a shrug, he tapped on the door with the butt of the pistol. Immediately, there was an answering burst of frenzied barking.

"Dogs," he said to the floating ball of light. "But you knew that, didn't you?"

Ray stared at the coded entry patch beside the door and scratched his head. "Now if I only knew the combination . . ." Suddenly, without knowing *how* he knew, Ray knew that he *did* know the combination. *Well, I guess I do know how I know*, Ray considered as he punched in the correct number and color combinations. When blood trickled from his nostrils and leaked from the corners of his eyes, he was positive.

The door swung open and twenty hysterically happy dogs exploded out to surround him. "Hi, guys," he said weakly.

Seeing the blood on his pale face, one of the dogs said, "Ray, you looks like shit." Ray recognized the gray-and-white dog he'd named Icarus.

"It's good to see you, too, Icarus," he said.

"Male dogs! Always thinkin' with your tools!" scolded a female named Mamie. "Ray comes to rescue us, you insult him."

"Sorry, I dint mean to be rude," apologized Icarus.

"No offense taken," Ray said. He rubbed Mamie's ears. "I like being defended, though."

"We gettin' out of here?" asked another dog.

"Unless you want to stay for the dog-skinning contest."

"Uh . . . yah. We gettin' out."

Ray took one look at the lift/drop tubes, laughed, and said, "Let's find some stairs."

They encountered a chilling scene on the ground floor. "Wow, lookit them!"

The dogs crowded around several bodies, their faces frozen in a horrible rictus of death. They appeared to have torn their hair out and ripped at their skin with their own nails. One of them had gouged his eyes out.

"What coulda—" began Mamie. "Oh!" she said then. "Ohhhh!" Ray and the dogs could both feel the strange psychic energy flowing down from high above them.

As they made their way toward the building's entrance, they encountered more and more bodies. Qi's men. It looked like no one had made it to the door, not even Qi. Ray found his body closest to the exit. It must have taken great inner resolve to get as far as he had.

"The General," Ray said softly.

"What killed 'em?" wondered Icarus.

Ray felt a sharp twinge, a strange painful "tickling" sensation. "Daniel," Ray said. "It must be!" He glanced at the glowing ball, which didn't respond in any way.

"What you mean, Ray?"

"The man who tortured me is hooked up to the same machine he used on me," Ray explained. "Except it's not really turned on. A monster who would do anything to you if he could, he now imagines the worst is being done to him. Except it's not. He only thinks that it is. In turn, his fear-crazed mind is broadcasting its psychic venom. He's torturing himself and everyone else like him inside this building."

"I kin feel it," said Icarus. "But it ain't bad."

Ray looked at the globe. "I think we're being protected by an old friend of mine. Either that, or there's not enough sickness within us to cause us to react like Qi and his men."

The ball glowed more brightly and once again became the

ethereal being that Ray had dimly glimpsed before. It raised an appendage as if in benediction and farewell.

"Goodbye, Leonardo—or whatever you call yourself now. Goodbye . . . and thanks."

II

Beowulf was the first to notice the difference. "Hey, that tickling feeling gone."

"Yah," agreed Mama-san. "Beowulf right."

"And look—someone's coming out!" a voice shouted.

Ake looked. Ray, surrounded by Qi's dogs, made his way out of the building. "I hope he's okay," he said to Beowulf.

Ray looked at Ake and his team. "Hi, guys."

Beowulf grinned a canine grin. "Ray okay!" As if that was a signal, Beowulf's team surrounded Ray, laughing and leaning against him in happiness. "It so good to see you, Ray!" said Grendel.

"Yah," agreed Frodo—and all the others.

"This is gettin' to be a regular routine," said Ake gruffly as he shook Ray's hand.

Ray laughed and wrapped Ake up in a bear hug. "I knew you wouldn't forget me, partner."

Ray's team waited as long as they could and then they were all over him, barking and shoving close.

"Hate to interrupt your celebration, son," said the old man with the Santa Claus beard, "but is it okay to go in there or what?"

"Sure, it's safe to go in, Gabby," Ray replied.

"Yeah, but how? And why?" pressed Meg Cross.

"You!" Ray said. "So we meet under different circumstances."

"Forget about that—what's the story?"

"General Qi is dead. Everyone in the building, all his men, everyone's dead."

"How?" Ake asked.

"It was Daniel. He's dead now, too. Probably scared himself to death."

"Daniel? Who's Daniel?"

"Come on," Ray said, throwing an arm around his friend's

shoulder. "Buy me a nice heavy meal and I'll tell you all about it."

Ake looked at him quizzically. "A meal? Normally you'd ask me for a drink before food any day."

Ray made a face. "You see, there's this ruby I need to get my hands on again and it would help enormously if I had a big meal to move things along."

"You mean . . . ?"

"Please, let's not be crude, shall we?"

The dogs hadn't heard Ake laugh so hard in a long, long time.

★ ★ ★

They decided to take off a week or so to recover. First, they took a number of dogs back to the ship and put them into hibernation. Meanwhile, Ray continued with the rest of the new dogs' basic training lessons while Ake planned their move against the Manhattan warlord, Thom MacAdoo.

"I thought you said the peoples was revoltin'," Gawain said to Ray when they learned from Meg Cross and the others that they would be on their own once they crossed the East River.

"Some of them *are* pretty revolting," Ray replied. "Did you see the bits of food trapped in that old character's beard? Disgusting."

"Gawain dint mean that kinda revoltin'," Frodo said impatiently.

"Oh, I get you," Ray said.

"The people rose up against Dalvi and Qi because they were running their lives here in Queens," Ake explained. "They see no reason to go into the city to confront someone else's problem."

"The peoples in Manhattan gonna help us 'tack this MacAdoo guy?" asked Gawain.

"I don't know," Ake admitted.

"The way I understand it," Ake said, spreading out the old-fashioned paper blueprint, "this MacAdoo has sealed off most of the old subway entrances in Manhattan. Those that are still accessible are guarded day and night and wired out the whazoo with explosives so that they can be destroyed if it looks like someone has even a remote possibility of getting through his defenses."

"Golly!" said Beowulf.

"Golly, indeed," agreed Ray. "I guess that's it. We can't get in; we're going to have to call the whole rescue plan off."

"Ray!" said Beowulf sternly.

"Oh, okay." Ray looked at Ake. "I suppose you just happen to know a way in?"

"I thought you'd never ask." Ake jabbed at the map with his finger. "Right there. If we can find a way to enter this train tunnel, we can follow it as far as Lexington Avenue, connect with the old Lexington Avenue line."

"Then what?"

"Then we follow the tracks up to Grand Central. At least, I hope that's what we can do."

"Hope? Why shouldn't we be able to?"

"Supposedly no one remembers this old train tunnel. At least, that's what Meg says," Ake explained. "But the abandoned subway lines into Grand Central—and that includes the Lexington Avenue line—are under MacAdoo's control. We're fine until we transfer from the train tunnel into the subway line—assuming that's even possible. Unfortunately, this map can't tell us that."

"How many city blocks is it from where we link up with the subway line to Grand Central?" Ray asked.

"Nine or ten."

"If MacAdoo guards access to the tunnels from the street, we shouldn't encounter many obstacles underground. I mean, we're already down there, right? If all his defenses are geared to stopping people from gaining admission to his underground fiefdom, it should be a cakewalk."

"And if it isn't?" asked Ake.

"It doan matter," said Beowulf. "We gots to try."

"Yeah," agreed Ray. "We gots to try."

Meg Cross half slid, half ran down the embankment. Her knees buckled when she reached the bottom but she maintained her balance and did little more than stumble. Turning around, she shaded her eyes against the bright morning glare, and stared up at where she'd come. "Well, come on down! What're you waiting for—an invitation?"

"Let's go!" shouted Beowulf gleefully and the dogs scrambled over the edge. Most made it on their feet, but a few lost their footing and slid down in a cloud of dust and loose stones.

Coughing melodramatically and waving his hands in front of his face to blow away the dust, Ray turned to Ake and said, "I guess it's our turn."

"Let's show them how it's done," Ake said. Ray made a thumbs-up sign. They showed everyone how it was done until they got about halfway down and their feet flew out from under them. They landed on their butts and slid the rest of the way to the bottom.

Brushing the dirt from his seat, Ray said, "I'd say these trousers are ready for the laundry."

"Come on, willya?" Meg Cross said to them. "I want to show you where the hole is." She led them along the floor of the gully, stopping in front of an opening no more than a meter high. "Here it is."

"That's it?" asked Ray. "It doesn't seem like much."

Meg Cross put her hands on her hips. "They tore down the big floating arrow that pointed at it and said, 'Entrance to secret tunnel'!"

"When they tear it down?" wondered Gawain.

Staring into the hole's yawning emptiness, Ake intoned gravely, "'Abandon all hope . . .' and like that."

"Boy, it sure look dark an' creepy," Sinbad said.

"I'll say," seconded Grendel.

"Is it time to say goodbye?" asked Meg Cross. "If it is, I have a going-away present for you."

"What kind of going-away present?" asked Ake, suddenly suspicious.

"Good news."

"Thom MacAdoo has seen the light, is joining the Neo-Christian Brotherhood, and is setting free all his dogs?"

"Almost as good as that," Meg Cross said. "Because of what we did here in Queens, a citizens' group has gotten together in Manhattan."

"Are you kidding?" said Ray.

She shook her head. "Veitch and some others set up secret meetings and told them it could be done."

"When did all this happen?"

"We've been busy the last couple weeks." She smiled.

"What does this mean?" Ake wondered.

"It means that three days ago the citizens' group began knocking off MacAdoo patrols, closing down MacAdoo Ice palaces, and generally starting to put the boot up *his* ass for a change."

"That's terrific!"

"It gets better. MacAdoo's been warned to evacuate his underground headquarters before it's blown up." She looked at her watch. "If you get there by early afternoon, he should be moving out and leaving behind stuff that's too much trouble to take with him."

"Like scout dogs?" asked Beowulf hopefully.

"That's the idea," Meg Cross said.

★ ★ ★

The fastidious Grendel lifted one paw out of the cold, brackish puddle of water she was wading through and sniffed it. "Yecch!" she said, wrinkling her nose in disgust. "This is yucky."

"Yah," agreed Athena.

"It's not that bad," Ray said.

"Easy for you to say," shot back Littlejohn. "You gots boots on."

"Hey," Ray told him. "Clothing is one of humankind's greatest inventions. We need it—we don't have fur like some people."

Several dogs gave him the canine version of the raspberry.

"Besides," Ray continued. "This is an old, abandoned railroad tunnel. What did you expect? Fusion lighting and moving beltways?"

"Doan know," replied Sinbad seriously. "Jes' dint know it was gonna be crummy . . . and dark."

"That's why Ake and I have our electric torches—so it can be crummy and light." Ray held his electric torch out in front of himself and, waving it around in the dusty air, said, "Check this out, Beowulf—I'm Darth Vader and this is my light saber. 'You have learned to use the Force well, young Jedi.'" Beowulf laughed, and Ray considered the effort worthwhile.

In addition to Beowulf's team, Ray had molded some of Dalvi's dogs into an eight-dog pack headed by Socrates and some of Qi's dogs into a seven-dog pack headed by Robin. Ray shook his head at the numbers.

"Why you shake your head?" Socrates asked him.

"Instead of just nine dogs to worry about now," Ray told him, "I've got twenty-four."

"You gots it wrong, Ray," Socrates replied.

Beowulf bristled a bit at that, but reconsidered when Socrates explained, "You gots twenty-four dogs worryin' 'bout *you*."

"And Ake," added Robin.

"Thanks," said Ake dryly. "Always glad to be included—even as an afterthought."

Ray coughed into his hand, touched by their loyalty. "Ah, maybe we should be better organized than this. Spread out a little."

"Spread out?" questioned Tajil. "How? We in a train tunnel, Ray."

"Well, yeah, but it's a two-tracker." Ray clapped his hands. "C'mon, let's do it. Let's spread out."

"Okay," said Tajil with a sigh.

"Socrates, Will, Cisco, and Natasha—you four take the point."

"Right." Off they trotted.

"Robin, Jerry, Festus, and Mamie—you four bring up the rear." They dropped back to take their positions.

"Bella, Athena, Loki, and Thor—take the left side. Sinbad, Ozma, Frodo and Mama-san, you take the right side."

"What about us?" asked Hamlet.

"You stay here with Ake, Beowulf, and the rest of us."

"Hey, what's that?" asked Bella.

Ray pointed his torch at the side of the tunnel. Dozens of little red eyes reflected the cone of light. "Ah, rats," Ray said.

"Ugly suckers, ain't they?" asked Hamlet rhetorically.

"And big," Ake said. "I didn't know rats got that big."

"Wonder what they eat?" Ray mused. He felt Ake's stare. "Sorry. It was a logical question."

"Well, it's one I'd rather not contemplate. Dogs, stay close."

"Doan worry 'bout *that*!" said Mama-san nervously.

"Shit!" exclaimed Ake. "Shit/piss/F-word!" He'd stepped

in an unexpectedly deep puddle and the cold water had flowed over the top of his boot.

"You could always walk the rails, Ake," Ray said.

"No thanks. That would take forever, wouldn't it, trying to balance on top of that narrow strip of plasteel?"

"Just plain old steel, I should think," Ray said. "That is, if this tunnel is as old as you say it is."

"It's old, all right," Ake replied. "For instance"—he aimed the beam of light from his torch at a junction box—"I have no idea what 'AMTRAK' means."

"It means smelly, dirty, wet hole in the ground," said Hamlet.

That made many of the dogs laugh. "Yeah, maybe it does, Hamlet," Ray agreed with a laugh of his own.

19

"I know this is a crazy city, and must have been just as crazy over a hundred years ago," Ray said to Ake. "But why would they call a junction 'mad'?"

"What the hell are you talking about?"

Ray walked over to an old sign and wiped its surface. "This must have once helped the rail workers know where they were," Ray said, showing it to Ake. It read MAD and pointed down the tunnel.

"That must mean Madison Avenue," Ake said. He put his hand to his head, a picture of concentration. "We've gone past the Lexington subway line; it must be either above or below us." Then Ake's eyes widened. "Why didn't I see this before? It's not just the subway tunnels—the old railroad lines come down from Grand Central. We can take that tunnel up to Grand Central instead of using the old Lex Avenue subway tunnel!"

"How?"

"There must be a junction nearby."

"Let's keep going, then."

Socrates returned from the point with news. "Hey, there's big cave up ahead." The "cave" proved to be the railroad north-south, east-west switching junction Ake had mentioned.

"Would you look at this place," said Ray, eying the surprisingly large volume of space carved out of the soil and rock beneath the city centuries ago. "They did all this without fusion borers or other modern equipment, too."

"We goin' north?" asked Beowulf.

Ray looked at Ake, who nodded. "Yes, Beowulf."

Ray noticed several of the dogs sniffing the ground. Not expecting a real answer, he asked, "What is it, more rats?"

Mama-san looked up. "No. Something came through here today. Something weird." She put her nose to the damp ground again and then shot Ray a strange look. She turned to Littlejohn. "You smell what else I smell, too, Littlejohn?"

"Yah."

"So tell me already," Ray said. "I don't smell so good."

"Try bathing more than once a week," Ake said.

"Dogs."

"Dogs?"

Mama-san nodded. "They bin through here today."

"*Dogs?*" Ray repeated. "How and why would dogs—"

"Hey, what was that?" asked a scrawny dog named Festus. He was the smallest male and the second smallest scout dog after Athena.

"What was what?" said Ray. *What the hell's going on?*

"Yah, I thought I hearded somethin', too," volunteered Thor. "Up that-a-way," he said gesturing at the inky blackness of the tunnel heading north toward Grand Central.

"Since you two heard it, take a couple more dogs and go find out what's up there," Ray told Festus and Thor.

"Jerry, Loki, an' Ozma, come with us," said Thor. The others joined them and they trotted briskly off.

"You know," Ake said slowly. "There's no reason why this tunnel can't continue west. I mean all the way west—toward the west side of the city, under the Hudson River, and, finally, to Jersey."

"And if it does?"

"Well, what if MacAdoo, the lord of this underworld, knows about all these lost tunnels? Couldn't he—"

They heard the outbreak of frenzied barking. Then, as if demons from Hell were behind them, the dogs came scrambling back.

"Whoa, whoa," Ray said. "Settle down. What did you see?"

"Monsters!"

★ ★ ★

A ferocious roar echoed down the tunnel. "What the hell was that?" Ray asked.

"I don't think I want to know," Ake replied.

The two men backed together. "Dogs, stay close," Ray ordered. "Something wicked this way comes."

Ray dug into his pack and pulled out a soft, malleable mass of plastic, pushed in the activator, and then hurled it against the tunnel wall. The mass stuck to the wall like a blob of bread dough and began to emit a diffuse light. As a temporary source of illumination, the glo-globe wasn't meant to provide more than ten to fifteen minutes of low-level light. Right now, ten to fifteen minutes was an eternity.

"Mother of pearl!" Ray whispered as several enormous products of Svoboda's mad genetic manipulations shuffled into the light provided by the glo-globe.

"Those look like a thousand kilos of bear each to me," Ake said. "Half Kodiak, half grizzly."

"And both halves madder than hell!"

Beowulf barked orders and the dogs, looking like toy terriers in comparison to the bear creatures, darted around the huge carnivores. The bears swiped at them but weren't fast enough to catch the agile dogs.

When one of the bears stood on its hind legs, Ray saw that its head almost brushed the roof of the tunnel. Making an odd keening sound, the bear walked forward, intent on reaching Ray and Ake. The dogs would have none of that and leapt to the attack. Beowulf, Littlejohn, Bella, and Natasha took turns rushing in to slash at the bear's belly and legs, forcing it to drop down on all fours again.

While Littlejohn slashed at its left side, Beowulf worried it from its right. Between them, the two big males had the bear twisting its head from one side to the other, trying to catch its tormentors in its teeth. Suddenly the bear whirled and rushed at Littlejohn. The charge knocked the big dog off his feet and the bear, sensing an opportunity to inflict serious harm, swiped at Littlejohn with a paw the size of a manhole cover. Littlejohn yelped in pain as the bear's claws raked his side, drawing blood.

"Beowulf!" Ray shouted. Already in action, Beowulf leapt

squarely on the huge ursine creature's back and tore savagely at the tight neck muscles bunched atop its shoulders. It was more than enough to make the bear forget about Littlejohn and whirl, attempting to throw off Beowulf.

The second of the three berserkers now charged Ray and Ake. Both men brought up their weapons and fired into the midsection of the furry mass looming over them. The bear took several direct hits but kept coming. Ake fired twice more as Ray shoved the barrel of his rifle against the bear's chest and held his finger down. The mortally wounded bear finally toppled and fell—directly onto Ray.

"Shit!" Ray shouted, his voice muffled by the mass of the bear on top of him. Blood from its wounds poured over him and he could smell the dead animal's rank odor.

As several dogs rushed in to help pull the slain creature off Ray, the third bear counterattacked. It was gang-tackled by Cisco, Loki, Frodo, Gawain, Tajil, and Hamlet.

Beowulf ripped and tore at the neck of the bear he was riding until it managed to throw him off. The big dog hit the dirt and rolled, absorbing the energy of the fall and regaining his feet.

Enraged beyond making use of whatever brainpower it may have possessed, the bear attempted to ravage anything in reach. As it came to the aid of the bear beset by Frodo and the other dogs, Ake calmly drew a bead on its skull and fired a pencil-thin bolt of energy through its left eye. The bear slumped to the floor of the tunnel like a rag doll.

The surviving bear batted Gawain and Frodo aside only to have their places taken by Mama-san and Cisco. Ray, meanwhile, managed to pull himself clear of the carcass and pump bolt after bolt into the besieged bear. Finally, the combined man-dog assault proved too much and the bear joined the others in death.

"Anyone killed?" Ray asked a bruised and battered Beowulf.

"Doan think so," Beowulf answered. "I better count noses."

While no one had been killed, more than one of them had taken a pounding. Both Gawain and Frodo were also battered and bruised; there was a possibility either or both had suffered cracked ribs. Littlejohn, his right side a bloody mess from the clawing he'd absorbed from one bear, was the most severely injured and Ake quickly attended to him.

"How are you doing, Littlejohn?" Ake asked, washing his wounds with an astringent.

"Okay, Ake," the big dog said through clenched teeth.

"That's good," Ake told him, appalled by the sight of Littlejohn's exposed ribs showing through his fur. He worked quickly to clean and cover the wounds, shooting Littlejohn full of painkillers.

Ray was unaware of the extent of Littlejohn's injuries. "Could have been worse," he said, wiping blood off himself. "It could have been a lot worse."

The sound of something . . . or some *things* . . . splashing through the tunnel's murky pools of water reached them.

"I think it just got worser," Tajil moaned.

II

"Watch out!" Ray shouted as he brought his energy rifle up to his shoulder and got off several bolts at one of the impossibly huge crocodiles rushing down the tunnel at them, mouth agape. One of the hastily fired bolts hit a croc, but it quickly became apparent to Ray that one wasn't going to be enough to stop such a monster. He fired again and again, one bolt finally burning a hole through the creature's tiny brain and sending it spinning violently in a paroxysmic display of mindless rage and pain.

"There's another one!" Ray shouted at Ake. Ake pivoted toward Ray's voice, saw the great reptile rushing toward him, hissing and growling, and brought his rifle up in time to pump several bolts down its throat. It also flipped and rolled in a spectacular spasm of death.

One of the crocs lunged at a pack of dogs. The dogs scrambled backwards, but not all did so quickly enough. The creature's jaw closed on Mamie's right rear leg and it began dragging her toward a shallow puddle of water between the two sets of tracks. The water was only centimeters deep, not nearly enough to drown a victim, but the crocodile was responding to an ancient imperative.

"Mamie!" shouted Robin. Robin, Icarus, Frodo, and Will dashed around the retreating croc and began slashing and ripping at its thick tail.

"No!" shouted Ray. "Stay away from its tail!"

Too late. The creature's thick tail lashed right and left,

sending the dogs tumbling. Both Ray and Ake rushed over and blasted the crocodile with a volley of high-energy bolts at point-blank range. When it loosened its grip on Mamie's leg, Beowulf and Socrates closed their mouths on Mamie's thick fur and pulled her from the beast's jaws.

"Stay with her, Socrates," Ake said, seeing Mamie's dangling leg and correctly assuming that she was in no condition to be moved. Then he looked more closely at her injury. Her leg was still attached, but it was hanging by a thread. And the blood she was losing would mean her death in minutes if he didn't do something.

"I have to do a fast and dirty patch-up job on Mamie," Ake told Ray.

"Do it. I'll try to give the time you need," Ray said, finding and slapping another energy cell into in his rifle.

Ake sprayed Mamie's injured leg, gave her an injection, wrapped the wound, and applied a fast-drying quik-splint.

"Anybody ever tell you that you're a great doc?" asked Ray.

"Only the patients who lived."

"Thanks, Ake," Mamie said through her pain.

"How many more monsters you think we run into?" Beowulf asked, the concern in his voice obvious.

"I don't know, Beowulf," Ake admitted. "Its a good six or seven city blocks yet to grand Central."

Ray pulled a flask from his pocket, unscrewed the top, and took a long drink. "You know," he said, offering the flask to Ake, who shook his head no, "something's been bothering me since we left the other tunnel."

"Yeah, what?"

"Well, didn't the guys say they could smell the other dogs? I mean, they smelled that they had been through there?"

"Again, yeah."

Ray took another drink. "Well, why? How?"

"I'm sorry, partner, but you're losing me."

"If this tunnel we're now in goes *up to* Grand Central and MacAdoo, then it also comes *down from* there, too." He put the flask down and straightened up. "Hell, have we been blind!"

"Ohmygod!" Ake said, seeing what Ray was getting at. "MacAdoo knows about the east-west tunnel! He hauled ass out of Grand Central, made his way down here—leaving his mutated playthings behind to skunk up any pursuit—and now he's headed west to Jersey. He's headed out of the city and away from the people who want to cut off his balls and feed them to the fishes!"

"What that mean?" asked Beowulf.

"We're going the wrong way," Ray lamented.

★ ★ ★

Ray chose Natasha and Loki, both fast dogs, to go after MacAdoo and his people as fast as they could. "Remember," he told them, "just find MacAdoo's rear guard and report back. Turn back immediately if you run into any more nasty surprises like the crocs or the bears. You got that?"

"Okay," said Natasha.

"Loki?"

"Yah."

"Good. Now take off." Ray watched them disappear into the darkness. "And be careful!" he yelled after them.

"No sense wasting any time waiting for them to report back," Ake said. "Let's start heading in that direction."

"Let me check on Littlejohn and Mamie," Ray said. He walked back to two rude travois he'd jerry-built to carry the injured dogs. "How are you, Mamie?"

"I be okay," the little female said. "But you better check out Littlejohn—he breathin' funny."

"Littlejohn?" Ray said, his voice full of concern. "How are you, Littlejohn?" Beowulf and Ozma joined Ray at Littlejohn's side—Beowulf in his role as leader, Ozma as Littlejohn's favorite.

"'Lo, Ray," the big dog said, his voice weak.

"You're scaring us, Littlejohn. You've got to fight this thing."

Littlejohn stared at them, his brown eyes dulled by pain. "You is my team. You is Ray, my Man. And Beowulf, my leader. And Ozma, who keeps me warm." He glanced down the tunnel. "You is my pack and my family and I love you."

The rest of the team came over, Ake with them.

"Now, Littlejohn, you'll be—"

Littlejohn smiled a doggy smile and looked past them. "Anson . . . Pandora?" he said, wonder in his voice. Then he put his head down.

It was ten or fifteen seconds before they realized he was gone. After Ray gently closed Littlejohn's eyes, each member of the team came over and touched their friend with his or her nose and then walked stiffly away.

Ozma, her sides heaving, raised her muzzle and unleashed a mournful howl of rage and loss.

While Ray buried his face in his hands. Beowulf, his gruff voice cracking, said, "What is the Law?"

III

After awhile, the realization that they had to continue their mission compelled them to put aside their grief and to follow Natasha and Loki. Just five minutes later they heard the sound of distant weapons fire. "C'mon," said Ray. "Let's move it!"

As they got close to the origin of the sounds, they slowed down a bit but still maintained a brisk pace. Soon Ray and Ake's torches picked out something in the center of the tracks. It was a small pile of bodies.

"Is it . . . ?" began Ake.

"Yeah," Ray answered tonelessly. "It's Loki and Natasha."

The two dogs lay crumpled in death.

"Lookit," said Mama-san, her voice husky. "They dint die by themselves."

Beside the two slain dogs were three other bodies: a scout dog and two humans.

"MacAdoo?" asked Ake.

"Yeah, they're his people, I'm sure."

"They not be far ahead, I'm thinkin'," said Beowulf.

A tinny voice said something garbled from the tunnel floor. Ray bent over and picked up a small communications device. "This must have belonged to these two guys," he said.

"Can you work it?" Ake asked.

"I don't know why not." Ray keyed the transmit button and said, "This is Ray Larkin, General. Ake Ringgren and a very large contingent of scout dogs are with me. We're right behind you, General MacAdoo. Can you read me?"

After a long pause, the communicator came to life. "This is General MacAdoo. I read you. What do you want?"

"General, I'm looking at the bodies of two of your men and one of your scout dogs—and the bodies of two dogs who came with us. I'm getting pretty damned sick and tired of bodies. Just a few minutes ago we lost a . . . a—" Ray swallowed and went on. "We lost a member of our team."

"What do you propose?"

"That you leave your scout dogs behind and keep going west. We have no quarrel with you. The citizens of New York whom you brutalized may want to string your guts on a wire, but we'll settle for the dogs. That's all we're after."

"And if I refuse?"

"Then we keep coming until everyone on your side or ours is dead. That's the way it's going to be, General."

"You would do this for . . . for dogs?"

"Yes."

"You are willing to die for them?"

"Yes. Are you?"

"If I leave them for you, you promise not to continue your pursuit?"

"Leave them behind, healthy and alive, and we're quits."

"You have a deal."

Ray put the communications device down and leaned against the tunnel wall. Beowulf and several of the others came up to him and said, "Thank you, Ray." They licked his hand with their big pink tongues.

"Think it's really over?" Ake asked him.

Ray nodded soberly, staring at something. Ake followed his gaze to the sheet-covered form on the travois and felt a lump rise in his throat.

"Ray . . . ?" began Mama-san tentatively.

"Yeah, Mama-san?" asked Ray tonelessly.

"We love you."

Ake turned and walked discreetly away, not wanting to burden his best friend by standing by helplessly and watching Ray cry uncontrollably for the first time in their long association.

20

The team returned to Gandhi with the dogs they had freed from their Terran masters. If one added the dogs they had found and liberated in Svoboda's lair to the one hundred and thirty-five dogs they brought back with them, the number of dogs they had rescued rose to over one hundred and fifty.

"This is fantastic," Kenneth Kamala exclaimed. "So many dogs to train."

"We're counting on you five to do a good job," Ray told Kamala and the others. "These dogs have been through a lot. After receiving counseling, they not only have to learn how to be proper scout dogs, they have to *unlearn* a lot of bad habits."

"I think we're up to it," Monique Vanel said dryly.

"We are the best," Ludmilla Cherkassov agreed.

Ray was impressed by their confidence. "Yeah, maybe you are."

"No maybes," said Sinead McGarry with a smile.

"I guess there's no need to ask how your work with the dogs we found with you went, is there?" said Ake.

"We learnded a lot," volunteered Bunter, stepping forward, his tail wagging.

"I can see that," Ray said. Then he turned to Sinead McGarry and asked, "Can you do me a favor?"

"Sure, Ray. What is it?"

"I want you to work with one of the dogs I brought back with us this trip."

"We're going to work with them all."

"I realize that," Ray said patiently. "I mean I want you to put him at the top of the list. I want you to get him ready as quickly as you can."

"Sure, what's his name?"

"Robin."

"Robin?"

"Yeah." Ray turned to Beowulf. "Beowulf, go fetch Robin now."

When Beowulf returned with the handsome red dog, Ray said, "Sinead, everyone: I'd like you meet Robin."

"Hi, Robin," they chorused.

" 'Lo," Robin said shyly.

"And why is Robin to be given the red-carpet treatment?" asked Ludmilla Cherkassov.

"He's joining my team."

★ ★ ★

"You know," Ray said, "this is a damn fine planet, John."

John Skerchock, walking with Ray, Ake, and their two teams, wasn't about to argue Ray's point. "I do know," he replied. "It kinda grows on you." He reached over and scratched Maximilian behind one huge ear.

Smoking one of John's cigars, Ray trailed acrid smoke like a steam engine of old. "I did a little research and confirmed that the new owners have the right to give their property whatever name they wish to."

"Yeah? So, what're you gonna rename Gandhi?"

Ray looked at Ake, who nodded. "We thought 'Anson' was a good choice."

"Anson? He was one of your original nine dogs, wasn't he?"

Ray puffed extra hard and extra long on his cigar before replying. "Yeah."

★ ★ ★

The gravesite was atop a grassy knoll that overlooked a lush, green valley. In the distance were white-peaked mountains. Ray sat down on the still dewy grass, plucked a long blade, and stuck it in his mouth.

"What do you think, Littlejohn?" he said to the mound beside him. He nodded as if hearing a response to his question. "Yeah, I think it's a fine place, too. I know we could have called this planet 'Littlejohn' instead of 'Anson,' but your legacy is all those dogs we brought back here with us. It's all the good they're going to do for the rest of their lives—and the lives of their offspring."

Fingering the ruby around his neck, Ray stood up, brushed himself off, and found a stick. He threw it as far as he could. For a moment he imagined he could see a big, eager-to-please dog chasing after it. Maybe he could.

Ray sat by Littlejohn until it was too dark to see.

With leaders Bill Kelley and Kyle Sterling and trainers Sinead McGarry, Kenneth Kamala, Monique Vanel, Ahmad al-Robayan, and Lumilla Cherkassov looking on, the team was making its farewells to the new dogs.

"Why you gots to go?" asked Athena.

"It's who we are," Ray replied. "We're a scout dog team. We're not happy unless we have something worthwhile to do."

"And stayin' here with us not worthwhile, huh?" said Socrates.

"You know that's not what I mean," Ray told the big black-and-white dog.

" 'Course he does," remonstrated Athena. "He jes' being a prick."

Socrates briefly showed his teeth but otherwise did nothing. Ray smiled. Already they were fulfilling their destiny—they were on their way to becoming scout dogs.

"Goodbye, Athena. Goodbye, Socrates."

There were goodbyes for the others: for Bunter and Nell, for Jack and Mamie, for Festus and Will, for Thor and Morgana, for all the dogs who didn't have names yet.

There were farewells for John's team, too.

"It be a long time 'fore we sees you again?" asked Maximilian.

"Mebbe. Doan know for sure," replied Beowulf.

"Maximilian, you take care of yourself and watch out for Emma, Telzey, and Clementine," Mama-san told him. She could still visualize the handsome, burly puppy he once was.

"I will." Maximilian and his sisters licked their mother.

Ake and Ray rubbed a lot of ears and thumped a lot of sides. Then they gruffly hugged John and said goodbye to him.

"Don't lose another twelve years on me," Skerchock said. "I'll look like Father Time if you do."

"John, how can we ever thank you for everything you've done? You're the best friend two slippery adventurers could have."

"Thanks, Ray."

Ake wrapped his long arms around both Ray and Skerchock. "As usual, Ray got there first with the mostest," he said. "But I still have to tell you that you're the best."

The two packs rubbed noses and everyone was especially solicitous of Ozma. Then it was time for the Ray Larkin/Ake Ringgren team to be on its way. *The Spirit of St. Louis* was waiting patiently for them.

"Come on guys," Ray said. "Come on Beowulf, Littlej—" For just a moment a look crossed Ray's face. "Come on Mama-san, Frodo, Ozma, Grendel, Sinbad, Gawain, Tajil . . . and Robin."